Where Destiny Plays

Harwell Heirs Book 3

Regina Kammer

Viridium Press

Copyright © 2015, 2017 by Regina Kammer
This title was previously published. It has been reedited with minor revisions.
Story originally conceived as *Miss Danby's Condition* © 2013 by Regina Kammer.
Cover: Dar Albert, Wicked Smart Designs

Published by: Viridium Press, Friday Harbor, Washington
ISBN-13: 978-0-9910166-7-9 (paperback)
ISBN-10: 0-9910166-7-X (paperback)
ISBN-13: 978-0-9910166-8-6 (ebook)
ISBN-10: 0-9910166-8-8 (ebook)

The Harwell Heirs

Victorian aristocracy has very strict rules concerning marital connections and familial obligations. But the Harwell heirs—Helena, Sophia, and Arthur—discover love doesn't always follow the rules. Scandalous affairs force these scions of society to choose between duty and desire, deference and destiny.

Book 1: *The Pleasure Device*
Book 2: *Disobedience By Design*
Book 3: *Where Destiny Plays*

Acknowledgments

Thank you to my family—especially my parents and my husband—and friends for their enthusiastic and continued encouragement, and to my colleagues for their advice, knowledge, and support.

Dedication

Memories can be powerful, their emotions overwhelming. This book is dedicated to the following who helped me purge the bad and forge ahead with the new: Adriana, Amy, Burcu, Calia, Cindy, Claudine, Daphne, Dave, Dawn, Deborah, Gail, George, Janell, Jason, Jessica, Jimmie, Joshua, Kaari, Lindsey, Marika, Marnie, MaryBeth, Matt, Megan, Minda, Miranda, Monique, Nensi, Nika, Orkan, Paula, Sheila, Steve, Susan, Tara, Tavia, Todd.

Thank you all.

PROLOGUE

London, July 1869

Lavinia Ainsleigh, the Viscountess Foxley-Graham, stared at the naked eighteen-year-old dozing in bed at her side, his face softened with satiation in London's fading sunlight. Nicholas Atherley was impossibly handsome, virile and vibrant. His university career stretched before him, and after that, who knew? His life was full of possibilities.

He did not yet know heartache, crushed hopes and dreams, or a lover's betrayal.

But Lavinia knew and she would never let it happen again, never rely on someone for her security, never allow the ambitions of another to rule her life.

And never *ever* fall in love again.

Nicholas stirred, turning over with a throaty rumble, offering her a view of his muscled back. She resisted the urge to lick his spine, to trace the ridges and hollows with her tongue, tasting his potent masculinity. She wanted him to sleep a little longer. She needed the respite. She was still astonished by what had transpired that afternoon.

Earlier that day, she had been visiting her dear friend Louisa Atherley, the Countess of St. Albans, at the family's Mayfair residence, a property still retained despite the infamous gambling debts accrued by the earl and his eldest son. Louisa preferred listening to the problems of others, a diversion which took her away from the stress of her abusive husband. Her advice was often very astute.

Over tea in a cozy corner of the elegant drawing room, the two women sitting across from each other on gold damask sofas, Louisa had offered guidance. A married woman had few options for a happy life; a widow had far more. Yet happiness eluded Lavinia despite having been widowed for seven years. The affair with the man she truly loved—a man not her husband—was over. The loneliness, the anger, the regret was smothering her.

"Vinny, forget him. Forget your Dr. Christopher."

"I've tried!" Lavinia stared blankly at the contents of her teacup. Julius Christopher had proven far too fascinating a man to forget.

"Darling, you need distractions."

The gilded porcelain cup and saucer quaked in Lavinia's hand as she placed them on the tea table before her. "Julius *was* my distraction." She squeezed her eyes shut to dam the tears.

Louisa slid her handkerchief across the polished table. Emblazoning a corner of the fine linen square was a flamboyant *R*, the full, rounded bowl of the top of the letter balanced by exuberantly curling stems. The emblem represented the initial of Louisa's maiden name "Ramsay," and was a reminder of the loving family she had left behind to marry the cruel Robert Atherley, Earl of St. Albans.

Louisa stared into the fireplace, as if gathering solace from the glowing embers. "An unhappy woman must find a distraction outside the home. I suggest you find several."

"Such as?" Lavinia dabbed her eyes.

"Charity work. Surely there are relief efforts you admire?"

"And be with a gaggle of old women?" Lavinia laughed. "I want to be with a man, Louisa. I crave such companionship."

"We're not all old, dear. You forget I'm only forty. I quite enjoy my work with the poor."

"Humph." Lavinia turned her gaze to the depths of the carved stone hearth.

"You've always had an interest in politics. Are there not causes for which you could muster enthusiasm?"

"We still need men to effect any sort of change."

"Well, what about a hobby? Starting a collection of something?"

"What about a collection of men?" *That* sounded like a great distraction. Perhaps she could collect them through political work. She giggled grimly.

Louisa sighed and returned to her tea. "Just be discreet about it, dear."

The door to the drawing room swung open and Nicholas Atherley strolled in, immediately charging the air with his energetic vitality.

He went to Louisa, bending his height to take her hands and kiss each cheek. "Mother, I see you have company so I won't keep you."

"Nonsense." Louisa's eyes misted at the sight of him, her youngest, her favorite son. "You're always welcome no matter what I am doing." She turned to Lavinia. "Nicky is just home from Cambridge. He's reading medicine."

Nicholas approached, his hair as dark a brown as the mahogany tea table, his coffee-colored eyes sparked with an enchanting gleam. He had changed for the better since he had left for university, the angles of manhood now sculpting his once-boyish features, a provocative charisma pulsating under the refined façade. Lavinia held out her hand and he took it, his hold firm. With a lift of a brow and an appreciative smirk, he raised her hand to his lips.

"Always a pleasure, my lady."

Lavinia smiled. Apparently he had learned a thing or two about charming the female sex from his year at Cambridge.

"And what are your plans, Nicholas?" She patted the couch next to her.

He took his place in the corner, lounging his athletic frame against the delicate rosewood arm. "London for a few weeks, then I really don't know. I might go abroad when Mother and Father return to St. Albans." He picked at the upholstery a moment before surveying the paintings along the mantel wall.

"Nicky, darling, Lavinia was just lamenting how she lacked an escort for the ballet this Friday. Would you mind accompanying her?"

Lavinia's scalp prickled. Nicholas was practically half her age. Surely his mother was not suggesting—

"I would be delighted, Lady Foxley-Graham." His attentive smirk was tinged with recklessness.

"Thank you, Nicholas," Lavinia said smoothly. "It's very generous of you to take time away from your friends."

Louisa turned her attention to her tea.

"I think my friends would be impressed," Nicholas said with a wink.

Good Lord, he was flirting with her.

The rattle of Louisa's teacup in its saucer was overly loud. "Then it's settled," she said cheerily.

The mantel clock chimed.

"Oh, my word. Louisa, I've overstayed my welcome, I'm sure." Lavinia stood.

Nicholas immediately stood, as well. Once side-by-side, they seemed too close.

Lavinia's heart thudded. Nicky had always been Louisa's baby boy. Suddenly he was a red-blooded man, oozing sensuality.

Of course. Some time between when she saw him last and now, he had *become* a man, had had a taste of what a woman could offer. And clearly he wanted more.

"Vinny, didn't you say you walked?" Louisa asked.

"I did." She had been frustrated and the two-mile walk through Kensington Gardens had eased her mind. She'd need the exercise of the return trip to rid herself of the effects of Nicholas' magnetic charms.

"Well, it's much too far, dear. We'll order you a cab. Nicky, will you see Lavinia home please?"

The implication was too obvious. Louisa could not possibly be so daft as to not know how attractive her son was. She definitely knew full well how vulnerable Lavinia was. Yet, the idea of being left alone with the beguiling son of one's best friend was both loathsome and thrilling all at once.

Nicholas did not attempt seduction in the cab, at least. He waited until he had seen her through her front door, her butler Sims registering no reaction to her gallant companion. Once inside, Nicholas placed a hand at the small of her back and guided her to what he probably hoped was a room devoid of any other servants.

After he closed the door to the morning room, he gave her that reckless look again. Carelessly, she caressed his cheek, deliciously roughened with maturity. She raised herself on her toes and touched her lips lightly to his.

He took her in his arms and kissed her back with the enthusiasm of youth.

She melted against him, desperate for any man's touch, and when he deepened the kiss, his tongue breaching her mouth, her qualms scattered. She was desperate for *his* touch.

He broke free, his hands still holding her fast at her waist. "My lady," he panted. "Lavinia, I've wanted you, well, it seems for forever. I've dreamed of you since I—" He stopped short.

"Since you learned what it was like to be with a woman?"

He blushed and glanced away before turning his pleading gaze back to her. "Yes."

She should have been merely flattered that such a handsome young man thought of her in his erotic musings. Instead, she'd become aroused, the fullness between her thighs commanding her thoughts. She needed a man and a splendid specimen stood right in front of her.

"Let's go to my bedroom, Nicky."

It had been too long. She trembled with need and he with nerves, but somehow she ended up naked and splayed across her bed, staring up at his gorgeous body, not wanting preliminaries, needing to feel his hardness inside her. The shock of his invasion was glorious but he came too soon. The second time, he was abashed and a bit flustered. She was only his second lover, he had confessed. He was a practiced flirt, but despite his valiant efforts had garnered very little actual experience. Girls his age were jealous of their virtue, he complained. She reminded him they had to be.

"I know. But it's damn frustrating."

By their third tumble, he had found his courage and with it came cocky confidence. He was a quick learner, taking over when she had reached between their bodies with her hand, gaining mastery of her desires as well as his, waiting for her climax before he came inside her.

One lasting perk of her failed affair with Julius was the knowledge he had imparted regarding methods to prevent pregnancy. Nicholas had been very appreciative.

And she was appreciative of his ardent attentions.

Afterward, awkward words became comfortable chitchat, melting into satisfied slumber, until Nicholas stretched with a loud groan, jolting her from a sensual dream.

"God, I feel wonderful!" He reached for her, pulling her to him. He took a nipple in his mouth and sucked.

A pleasurable heat shot straight to her cunt.

He moved to the other breast. Then lifted his head. "I have an incredible urge to—"

She raised her eyebrows.

"Take a piss."

She shoved him off. "Down the hall or under the bed, Nicky."

She got up and went to her wardrobe to find a dressing gown. Behind her, he slid the commode box out from under the bed.

The sound of evacuation never ensued. She turned around. He stood naked before her, his half-hard prick in his hand.

"How about right here?" He shook his sex at her. "I should mark you as my own."

The cocky overconfidence had not been subdued by an hour's nap.

"Don't you dare, you dog."

He laughed. She would have to teach him a lesson.

She lunged and grabbed his cock. He yelped in surprise, before trying to push her off. When she grabbed his stones with her other hand, he froze, his face pale.

Maintaining the unusual restraint, she led him to the commode and flipped the lid open with her foot. She let go of his balls then pulled down on his slack cock, aiming it at the bowl.

"Piddle, Master Atherley."

He flushed. "I don't think I can, Lavinia," he said softly, thoroughly subdued. "I think I need a moment." He cleared his throat. "Without any help."

She gripped harder. "I'll let go after an apology. A sincere apology."

He looked at her, helpless. "Vinny, I'm sorry, believe me. I didn't—I'm sorry."

She let go.

She leaned her back against his and waited, arms crossed. It took a few minutes, but he finally pissed his long-awaited stream, giving his cock a jounce at the end.

"Damn," he murmured. "That was arousing." He turned to her.

They watched together as his cock twitched to erection.

A smile spread on his lips. A very wicked smile.

He grabbed her and threw her onto the bed. Lavinia let out her surprise in laughter, excitement welling within as he tore open her robe.

And then he was on top of her, inside her, laughing with her, until the culmination of desire raged and she let him take his pleasure. He held her eyes as he let loose inside her, lost in his moment of bliss.

He sagged on top of her, his puffing breaths hot on her neck. "My God, Vinny, you've tamed me."

"That is the only way I'll allow you to mark me, Nicky. Remember that." She stroked his hair. "Never *ever* do anything to hurt or humiliate a lover."

He raised his head to meet her gaze. "Yes, Vinny."

He rolled to her side then pulled her close, holding her, kissing her hair. "This has been the most incredible afternoon. I don't want to go home." He propped himself on an elbow. "I can't stand it there. Father is horrible to Mother." He drew a finger between her breasts. "Can I stay with you?"

She cupped his cheek. He looked like a lost puppy. "We can't be obvious about it, Nicky. You should sleep at the Mayfair house most nights."

"Yeah."

"But I would love to have an escort to finish out the Season."

He smiled a genuine smile. *That* he had not learned in Cambridge. The affable grin was Nicky through and through. She kissed his cheek then smoothed down his riotous curls. She said nothing as she nuzzled against him once again.

An hour later, she woke up, amazed to find him still there. Amazed that an eighteen-year-old paragon of vigorous manhood snored naked and slaked at the side of a thirty-five-year-old widow who had been discarded one too many times.

He rolled onto his back with a yawn. "Vinny?"

"Yes, Nicky?"

He wrapped his arm around her shoulder. "I love you."

Of course he had only a vague understanding of what that meant. She burrowed against him. Transitory affairs with youthful lovers was a life she could get used to. As long as she never fell in love with any of them and they never betrayed her.

CHAPTER ONE

London, November 1879

Devoid of her cloak, Lavinia shivered, her skin prickling to gooseflesh. November's chilly air only heightened the overt seductiveness of her chiffon *odalisque* costume. The sheer panels of her baggy pantaloons and overdress barely obscured her feminine charms. Her nipples peaked against her tight bodice, her flesh tingling without the benefit of arousal.

Yet.

She stood on the landing of Countess Winthrop's dramatic entryway overlooking the grand lobby and surveyed the guests at the masquerade. Most of the other women had the forethought to wear something in fur or velvet. The men, of course, were generally fully dressed, their attire perhaps a bit more form-fitting than usual. A few hid their overdeveloped girths with capes. Her costume, or lack thereof, was already drawing flirtatious attention from men *and* women, the latter of which she barely acknowledged, as Sapphic affairs had not tempted her for decades. Besides, she was there to forget men—two in particular—and only another man could make her forget.

Or maybe she was there to remember what it felt like to have a man between her legs.

She danced a few dances to warm her blood with men whose stature matched her height and whose honed physiques matched her own vanity in maintaining her slender figure. She was not there to fuck just any man—certainly not a man who had decided middle age was an excuse to let charisma and his bank account be his only attractions. She wanted a man with as much experience as she, plus the willingness to maintain his health and improve his temperament to perpetuate the fiction of youth. She wasn't old yet. Her last lover had been seventeen years her junior.

After dancing, she wandered through the sprawling mansion. Every room was accessible to all guests—no doors were to be locked. Such openness was the reason masks were not a perfunctory afterthought but a necessity, and remained secured to heads and faces. Her own of molded leather covered her eyes and nose, a head scarf concealed her hair—dyed a darker shade for the occasion—and wrapped around the lower part of her face. In the dark, she'd want use of her mouth, for lips and cocks were meant to be savored.

All around her, party-goers flirted and joined, gender unimportant given the anonymity of the ball, men free to embrace men, women to grasp women. Some guests preferred the spectacle, their masks purposefully askew, challenging observers to make accusations, and by doing so revealing their own sexual proclivities.

Lavinia smirked as she passed through the smaller drawing room, for there in the corner, unabashedly unmasked, was Sophia Phillips dressed as Marie Antoinette, and her husband Joseph dressed as…George Washington? Or some other American revolutionary war hero. The couple had given up their lifestyle of extramarital affairs but still savored the lascivious pursuits the sexual underground had to offer. They fornicated publicly against a piano to the delight of appreciative onlookers and passing voyeurs, the joining of their bodies obscured by Sophia's voluminous skirts.

Sophia had suggested Lavinia attend Countess Winthrop's affair, had suggested the odalisque costume, and had marveled it was "exquisitely sublime" when Lavinia modeled it for her. Sophia had said if any man was overly assertive with unwanted attentions, to tell her and she would have Joseph dispatch the brute without question.

Lavinia's friendship with Sophia was one of the few pleasant aftereffects of an otherwise wrenchingly emotional Season. She had finally ended her affair with Nicholas Atherley. Her vulnerability had allowed her old flame Julius Christopher to swoop in and seduce her cruelly. He'd been driven by his animosity toward Nicholas—his estranged protégé. In the space of a few months, she had been stripped of the attentions of two extraordinarily skilled lovers. Their absence was weighty.

She had to stop thinking about both of them. Nicholas was desperately in love now. And Julius, well Julius was simply dangerous. Their on-again off-again affair had proven so, time after time.

She stared at Sophia and Joseph, each engaged in post-coital chatting with other guests. A sultan, his costume a richly decorated Venetian-red robe, complete with jeweled turban, conversed with Joseph. But it wasn't mere conversation. Their familiarity went beyond typical male rapport, their touches lingering, sensual, the sultan shooting furtive glances toward Sophia. When Sophia took her husband's arm with a smile, the sultan stepped back.

A charge remained between the two men, seemingly arcing over Sophia standing between them. The sultan matched Joseph in height but not in brawn. His casual confidence suggested he was not a young man, although his face was obscured by a mask and a dark beard of the imperial style, shaved and trimmed around his mouth. The same manner in which Julius wore his beard.

Lavinia shook her head. She had to stop seeing Julius everywhere, especially in the countenance of a masked and costumed stranger. A stranger who suddenly caught her staring at him, his gaze spearing her core, enlivening her sex, his sensual magnetism bridging the span of the drawing room to ensnare her. Lavinia's face grew hot under her mask.

She pulled away from the intensity. She did not want to meet anyone she knew or might know. She'd eventually find a lover, for tonight was a night to indulge, to give her the impetus to move out of the past and into the future.

A night at Countess Winthrop's was a first step in reminding Arthur Harwell, the Earl of Petersham, that there was a wondrous assortment of women in England. A gorgeous banquet of sensuality set before him for the taking, including the harem girl he had just locked gazes with in the most carnally intense connection of his life, before she turned away.

He had been trying to distract himself from the scene he had happened upon quite by accident. The last thing he had wanted was to watch his sister Sophia fucking her husband. So he had removed himself while she and Joseph finished their spectacle against the piano in the countess's lesser drawing room, wishing Joseph was fornicating with any other woman so he could watch. Afterward, a relaxed—and pleasantly drunk—Joseph had pawed at him, a dangerous intimation of their affair begun almost twenty years prior. Had Sophia not been present, Arthur would have dragged Joseph into the butler's pantry to tear off his colonial garb and appreciate the robust athleticism that never ceased to stir his senses.

Then Sophia had joined them, and Joseph had turned his tipsy attention to his wife's low-cut neckline barely covering her areolas. As Sophia basked in her husband's ogling, she had gently scolded Arthur that he needed to keep his distance if he was to engage a lover. No woman would ever approach a man while he was with his own sister. It was "too terribly Byronesque".

He had smiled at that. As if a guest would draw the conclusion that Marie Antoinette was the sister of a masked sultan.

She was right, though. He needed to intermix and socialize. Sophia and Joseph's ardent fervency only reminded Arthur he lacked such intimacy. After his niece Helena's wedding, he had lamented to Sophia and Joseph that he wanted to fall in love again, wanted to find that rare woman with an independent attitude who would thrive on conversation, a woman of experience who would crave his touch, a woman of means who might buy him the occasional gift. He was tired of vapid mistresses who gossiped rather than read, who climaxed in rote fashion, who cared only for his money and not his heart.

He wanted a woman of like mind. A woman who had thought to dress as an *odalisque* at a masquerade, the perfect accompaniment to his sultan attire. A woman whose fabulous proportions stretched her costume in all the right places, who did not balk at wearing fabric so filmy it might reveal her feminine attributes not just to her lover, but to everyone.

Of course, he'd have to get a closer look.

He followed her to the conservatory, the sounds of fornication and vapid conversation wafting from behind potted plants up to the slender iron girders spanning the space. The odalisque seemed to skim along the floor, her embroidered slippers sounding softly, her chiffon costume billowing and fluttering as she walked. Her costume was profoundly provocative. Sheer green pantaloons tightly cinched at the waist and ankles, the gathered fabric only slightly concealing her buttocks and the hair of her mons. Over this she wore a dress of the same fabric but blue, the skirt sliced to flare and ripple as she walked, the bodice perfectly fitted to her abundant bosom and secured by a row of buttons up the front.

To unfasten those buttons suddenly became his goal.

She walked with confidence, no stranger to such scenes of overt sexuality, no shy miss to bold advances. She deflected a pirate, a musketeer, a priest…each with a nod and a wave, probably knowing full well their leers followed her backside as she continued unfailingly in her path.

And then she walked into the library. Arthur smiled. He knew about the alcove where the countess shelved her special collection of erotic books. One couldn't readily discern it upon first entering the room, one had to know about it. For a woman of almost sixty, Countess Winthrop had a very open mind when it came to matters sexual and, he had to admit, great skill in bed. They had been lovers briefly—all her affairs were brief—about ten or so years before, and she had shown him the alcove then.

He followed his odalisque into the library and closed the door quietly. Anyone who knew the rules of the masquerade would know they could simply open the door, but he wanted to keep the novices out. The countess, knowing a library was the most sensual of rooms, had lit it with the soft glow of candles shrouded in cut-glass shades, the dim atmosphere lending itself to seduction both physical and intellectual.

The odalisque moved to the bay window, the shadow of trees outside visible with the dull light inside. She gazed for a moment beyond the glass then moved to the bookshelf to the right.

Perfect.

Lavinia tried to ignore the presence behind her in the library as she reached for a book, its leather spine intricately gilded with a design of flowering vines spiraling and interlocking. The cover would be engaging even if the text was not. She needed a respite before she dived back into the fray of the masquerade.

"My Lady Odalisque, I see we enjoy similar diversions."

His slightly accented, husky baritone resonated to a spot deep within. She turned to find the sultan standing behind her, his voluminous, embroidered red robe utterly obscuring what lay beneath, his mask, beard, and turban shielding his face. Yet somehow, despite the encumbrances, his very presence attracted, enshrouding her in a cocoon of sensuality. She had sworn she would not be done in by charisma and charm yet suddenly she could not resist.

"My Lord Sultan, is a thirst for knowledge such an amusement that you forgo carnal pursuits?" She too effected an accent that was not her own and addressed the man according to Countess Winthrop's rules.

"Ah, but Lady Odalisque, I have just begun my carnal pursuit."

He stepped forward. His warmth penetrated through the sheer fabric of her costume. His spicy scent imbued her senses with the mysteries of exotic lands. She did not flinch as he took the book from her hand and glanced at the cover. "*The Rubaiyat of Omar Khayyam.*" He smiled. "'Ah, Moon of my Delight who know'st no wane'."

He leaned over her and slid the book back into its space on the shelf.

She stifled a gasp. She was trapped between him and the bookcase. She looked up, meeting his gaze, his brown eyes boring into her, sweeping from her face to her bosom, a smile playing on his lips as soon as he spied the latter. His ragged breaths matched the rhythm of her thudding heart. The world slipped away, the space between them suddenly too distant. He leaned forward even more; she flexed in invitation. He pulled the scarf from her face and hair then traced a finger around her lips as he licked his own.

And then his mouth covered hers.

They melded perfectly, as if it were not their first kiss but their hundredth. He dared dip his tongue and she opened for him, sucking and tangling, humming her delight, wrapping her arms around his neck. He was good, so very good. Her thoughts were consumed by what thrills lay ahead.

His arms draped in loose sleeves enveloped her. His hands traced the curves of her back, holding her steady as she undulated against him. One hand cupped her buttocks, lifting her until her toes just barely reached the ground. He walked them behind the bookcase, she dancing on air, then set her down, releasing her from his embrace and his kiss.

"I think you may find this intimate space more conducive for indulging your darkest desires," said the sultan as he opened a folding screen to cut them off from the rest of the library.

They were in an alcove made up of bookcases completely filled with books. In the center of the nook was a red velvet divan, upon which a reader might relax—or a lover might seduce.

He strolled along the shelves, running his finger over the spines. "In these volumes you will find a description of every lewd act known to man." He flashed a smile her way. "And woman." He walked around the divan, unfastening the robe's corded frog closure at his shoulder. "But I'm not in the mood for reading at the moment." The robe hung undone yet stubbornly continued to conceal that which was underneath.

Lavinia wanted to rip the garment off him.

He took hold of the edges of his robe. Lavinia sucked in her lower lip, watching his slender, masculine fingers stroke the fabric up and down. He chuckled.

"Your costume leaves almost nothing to the imagination, my Lady Odalisque, whereas mine shields all. What lies beneath my robe, you wonder? Will it please you?"

"It will have to, my Lord Sultan, or I am at liberty to leave."

He grabbed her wrist and yanked her to him. She fell against his chest. Their mouths poised a hair's breadth apart, her free hand sliding under the opening to discover hair-covered flesh hot under her palm. Her hand trailed lower. She bit her lip as she smiled.

He was utterly nude beneath his costume.

He released his hold, allowing her to slip the robe over his shoulders, down his arms, until it crumpled to the floor. She gasped at the sight of him, his body perfect in its athleticism, muscles sculpted and honed, and on a man her own age, his years betrayed by a gray hair or two amidst the brown at his chest and groin.

Every inch of her flesh tingled with anticipation. It had been months since she had been with a man and here was a glorious exemplar of maleness before her for the taking. She trailed her fingers down his rippled abdomen, following the tantalizing path of hair—

He pulled her against him and took her in a violent kiss, preventing her hand from finding its aim. Did he not want her to give him pleasure? She struggled but he held firm, putting his strength to its intended use. One hand wrapped around both her wrists, holding them behind her back, depriving her of the feel of his body. He pulled down, forcing her to bend into him, his face dipping to her neck, his teeth and tongue nipping and licking until he reached her breasts, a growl escaping his throat. His free hand quickly loosed the buttons of her bodice and parted the diaphanous dress, freeing her to his gaze.

The growl became a sigh. "The beauty of my harem is revealed to me."

He pulled her wrists harder, intensifying her arch. His hot breath fanned excitedly over a nipple for only a moment before he drew it into his mouth.

She melted, his singular attention to her sensitive tip shooting tingling chills to curl her toes. He knew how to please a woman. How to please *her*. God, she wanted more, so much more, but she could be happy with just this. She moaned with an encouraging nudge. His chuckle reverberated in her chest to mingle with the thrumming of her heart. He ground his hips against her, his rock-hard cock digging into her thigh. His free hand cupped and caressed and pinched, his beard tickled and scratched, his tongue swirled and teased, keeping her on the edge, somehow knowing if he sucked harder, she would come.

She wanted to come. She needed to come.

"Please," she begged, flushing in shame.

He stopped his torment and drew his tongue from her chest to her chin, pausing at her mouth. "Ah, my desert rose, do you crave release?" His palm hovered over her breast, cruelly not touching, the heat taunting her piqued nipple. "Have I inflamed you?" He left her breast bereft as he skated his hand over her waist to cup her buttocks and squeeze the flesh. "So delicious." He skimmed over her hip, pausing to stroke her thigh before cupping her mons.

The breath hitched in her throat. She tucked her hips to better fit the curve of his palm.

One corner of his mouth lifted smugly. He reached between her legs and discovered the slit of her pantaloons, inserting a finger through the opening, then slowly through the swollen folds of her sex.

She sighed an oath.

His smug smile widened to a lascivious grin. "So deliciously wet, so utterly ready." He explored her depths, dipping a finger in and out, while another dallied near her clit, toying with her, taking her only so far before retreating, then starting the torment again.

She tried to capture the pleasure, to hold on to it, to bring herself to climax. She was desperate for the release he refused to allow.

Two could play that game.

She shoved against him, startling him, breaking free of his hold. She fell to her knees, gripping his hips with her nails, his cock jutting before her, potent and erect. She drew the tip into her mouth, circling her tongue around the cowled prepuce, and sucked.

He grunted a curse and rolled his hips.

She pushed back, preventing his length from entering farther. He would know what it was like to be held captive to another's wicked desires. She sucked mercilessly on the smooth glans, lauding herself when she tasted a droplet of his emission, salty and sour.

He grabbed her head, impelling her forward as he rammed his hips. She grabbed his shaft and tore her mouth from him, laughing. "My sultan, do *you* desire release?"

He lifted her from the floor and tossed her on the divan, extending over her a moment before crushing her. He cradled her cheek, his gaze falling to her mouth. And then a grin spread over his lips.

"We shall see who is the true master of our mutual desire."

He urged her legs open with his thighs, spread the slit of her pantaloons, and positioned himself at her entrance, playing in her wetness. He paused, searching her eyes, his own holding a glimmer of a memory.

She would help him forget his past, as he was there to banish hers.

"Please, my lord, I ache for you. Take me."

He slammed inside, swallowing her yelp of surprise with a kiss. He moved gently at first, his slow rolls punctuated by moans of approbation hot on her neck. He bent over and took a nipple in his mouth, sucking ruthlessly, determined to complete the act he had earlier cut short. She encouraged him with sighs, basking in the glorious seduction of a roguish and skilled lover.

She came in his arms, the physical release threatening to break the dam holding back the emotional. She trembled as she kept back her tears. He lifted her up, his palms spreading across her back in support, until she straddled him, he on his knees. He rocked into her tenderly, seeking her mouth again, kissing her softly, the bristle of his beard recalling Julius' kiss and their last embrace full of anger and betrayal.

The sobs she'd fought to contain burst forth.

He stopped and clutched her to him. "Shh, shh."

"My lord, I apologize," she sniffled. "I…please believe me, this is wonderful."

He chuckled. "I know it is." He kissed the mask covering her cheek. "But his memory persists. Let me try to erase it."

She smiled. "Please."

He handily lifted her and turned her onto her stomach, grabbed her hips, and pulled up. He drove into her from behind, the shock of his force spiraling her to ecstasy. He continued his assault as he reached around, finding her clitoris through the slit, barely grazing it. She came, her moan joined by his howl of delight. He rubbed relentlessly, the thrusts of his cock matching the frenzied strokes of his finger.

She let go, allowing him, a stranger, to take her on the journey to orgiastic oblivion. The familiar warmth coiled in her belly above his hand, unraveling with his continued ministrations, tendrils of lust coursing through her limbs until all at once her center imploded.

She screamed into the divan. He pounded into her, grunts and curses filling the air, then with one final plunge he held himself aloft and jerked against her, filling her with his hot emission.

He slumped over, pulling her to him as he slid back to the divan, then threw his robe over them. He held her and kissed her hair.

She wanted to ask his name, wanted to ask if they could remain lovers. But such conversation would be against the rules. He could be married, could be a priest, could be a politician who eschewed scandal. He could be anything besides an unmarried, attractive, intelligent, affable man.

She fell asleep satisfied with the creation of a new memory.

Arthur fastened his robe, trying to be as quiet as possible as his beautiful odalisque slept on the divan, still stunned by what had transpired moments ago. It was, without a doubt, the best sex he had had in his life. Better—he hated to even think it—than with his precious Henrietta. But the lovemaking of youth was often made imperfect by inexperience, and the memory of that lovemaking had dimmed over the course of nigh on twenty years and a dozen lovers.

His odalisque, too, had been plagued by a memory, one he hoped he was able to quash with his kisses and caresses. For only a moment, he was tempted to lift her mask while she slept, to see if serenity or regret cast her expression. But, she might awaken and despise him for it. And if it turned out she was the wife of one of his business associates, he would never be able to look the man in the eye again.

He chuckled to himself. Or he'd have a newfound respect for the man's hidden talents.

She shifted on the divan then moaned a quiet sigh, a luscious, sensual sound. He smiled to himself. He would know her if he ever kissed her again for she had breathed the very same moaning sighs when he had kissed her. He would kiss every woman of a certain age and certain endowments to find her again.

He retrieved a blanket from the window seat and covered her, shielding her from the chill apparent on her luscious body under her thin costume. There was no reason to stay at the masquerade. He had experienced the pinnacle of the event.

When she awoke he would be gone.

CHAPTER TWO

"Dr. Christopher?"

Julius looked up from reading to see his assistant standing in the doorway of his study, her woolen dress somehow provocative despite the high collar and drab gray. "Yes, Grace?"

"Your next appointment is here." Grace moved to the window and closed the drapes against the clouds of November clustering darkly outside. "I've let her into the examination room and told her to remove what clothes she needs to remove."

"Thank you, Grace." Julius smiled as he laid his science pamphlet aside. Every once in a while, Grace's East End manner of speaking came to the fore. She'd only been with him for six months, but in that time, sheer determination on her part had softened her accent and uplifted her vocabulary. She'd also learned a great deal about the medical profession by mere observation and was quickly learning how to read beyond street signs and shop placards.

"I'll give you a few moments to get ready before I begin." She smiled sweetly. "But don't be too long. I don't want the patient to catch cold." Her skirts swished as she exited.

Julius stood and stretched before heading downstairs, slipping quietly into the little room under the stairway. There he sat in an easy chair positioned before a small observation window, looking into the examination room. The "peephole"—as Grace called it—was cleverly disguised on the other side of the wall so as not to be detected by a patient.

In the examination room, Grace chatted with his patient, a wondrously voluptuous nineteen-year-old who had been most unequivocal about her virginal status. Which probably meant she had let a young man or two have a bit of fun—but only so far. Real virgins simply blushed and stammered when he queried them about such matters.

He unbuttoned the fly of his trousers and the fly of his drawers. He was only semi-hard, which wasn't at all unusual as he had been reading Dr. Drysdale's paper on germ theory, and, while the work had been most enlightening, it had not been arousing in the slightest. Seeing Grace stirred him. She had been sashaying around of late, swaying her hips invitingly. She had even begun to dress for dinner, the low-cut necklines of her gowns quite distracting. At night, in their bedroom, her desire for lascivious delights and her creativity in their exploration led to memories that refused to dissipate during the day.

Grace instructed the girl to lie down on the medical table and slide her heels in the metal stirrups. She had to spread her legs to do so, providing Julius a view of her glorious cunt, fringed in the same ginger-red curls as were on her head. Grace knew his letches all too well, and girls with coppery-red hair were one of them. Grace began her ministrations, all the while explaining what would be happening. First she would lubricate a sensitive area between the girl's legs then massage the area in preparation for the real treatment—"Dr. Christopher's special electro-mechanical vibrating device for the alleviation of symptoms of hysteria". Grace always said that part with pride. Then she advised, if at any time the girl wanted to vocalize, she should feel very free to do so.

Julius liked it when the girls moaned and screamed. They had even set up a system of tubes and horns to capture the sounds so he could hear all when sequestered in the little room under the stairs.

He grabbed his cock, now rock-hard, mesmerized by Grace's stroking of the girl, her fingers nimble and well-practiced. The girl flinched then calmed, the signal for Grace to begin the real treatment.

Julius stroked his shaft slowly.

Grace moved the cart housing the device closer to the table then grabbed the brass baton fitted with the phallic wooden peg. The baton concealed a small vibrating machine, she explained, which was the secret to the cure.

Grace bent over, knowing full well that Julius would be delighted by a view of her backside, and turned on the motor. The familiar and arousing whirring sound began.

He quickened his pace.

She pressed the phallus to the girl's clit. The girl jerked and yelped then, after a calming word from Grace, merely writhed under the stimulation of the machine.

Grace bit her lower lip, sucking on it a moment before she flicked her tongue out to the side of her mouth, drawing it along her upper lip, wetting it. She kept a watchful gaze on the device under half-lidded eyes, her expression soft, the only emotion an eagerness for the girl's success.

The girl screamed her climax.

Julius blinked. He missed it. He hadn't been watching the girl. He had been watching Grace.

He still gripped his cock, suddenly waning in the shock of anti-climax. He chilled. He should still be hard. Was it age? He had never before felt the effects of age. Other men nearing fifty had such problems, but never he.

The girl must have come too quickly. It was a testament to Grace's skill with his patients that the girl was relaxed enough to achieve her culmination in a matter of minutes.

He blinked again and the girl was dressing, Grace clearing away the equipment. The two chatted for a moment before Grace showed the girl out.

Julius stared through the peephole, disbelieving, dismayed by what had just transpired.

"Jules?" Grace's voice at the door sparked a little thrill inside him. He squeezed his cock as it grew hard again.

She approached. "You're still here."

"I am."

"She had her climax too quickly."

"She did," he sighed.

"Let me help you."

Her words were a balm to his unrequited resolution. She knelt before him, ran her hands up his thighs. She uncurled his fingers still holding fast and pushed them aside.

And then her mouth was around him, hot and wet. He closed his eyes to block out the view of the examination room, letting the moment contain just him and Grace, lovely Grace, whose magical mouth was sucking, whose hot tongue was stroking. He leaned back into the chair.

He lay his hands on either side of her head, threading his fingers through her silky brown hair, letting her bobbing motions move his arms, letting her take him to a place he could not take himself.

Did he rely on her too much? A man shouldn't rely on a woman. They were as inconstant in their hearts as they were capricious with their fashions, yet they somehow remained jealous of a man's affections.

Grace's attentions grew urgent, dragging him away from his thoughts to focus on his cock. He was almost there, he needed to stop thinking, stop thinking about her, about her mouth, her heat, let her take him there, let her take control—

He bucked up, spewing his seed in her swallowing throat. She continued sucking as he softened. She sat back on her heels and smiled up at him.

"Thank you, Grace." With a gentle touch of a finger, he lifted her chin and kissed her, tasting himself on her tongue.

What would I do without you?

* * * * *

Grace lay in Julius' bed, staring into the night, the spatter of rain against the windows badgering her thoughts. She turned onto her side and pulled the covers over her head.

The full effect of what had happened earlier that day was only now sinking in. Had Julius finally lost interest in his sexual experiments? Was he putting aside family practice altogether? And if so, did that mean he no longer needed her?

He had been, of late, reading about some new medical procedure, something about germs, had even recently purchased a shiny brass microscope. He spent quite a bit of time in his study with his new toy, offering gentle smiles when she joined him to enrich her reading skills with one of his scientific journals. She had interpreted these quiet moments as comfortable, domestic silence. But what if, instead, it was polite disregard for her presence?

Over the last six months, she had hoped Julius would not tire of her, yet deep down she had expected it. Like all men, he would eventually feel the relationship no longer exciting. And, for the first time with a man, Grace felt the sting of abandonment. Julius was so different from her other lovers. He had helped her so much with her education, been so patient with her presence in his house, had been so generous with his purse, lifting her from the oppression of abysmal poverty. He had truly been her savior.

She needed something to remember him by.

They had been sharing his bed at night for months now but it had never held any emotional meaning for them. The bedroom was only one of the rooms where they fucked. If Julius was in the mood for something unusual, he would poke her in the little room under the stairs where the strange erotic equipment was stored. Often he would shag her in the examination room after his final patient had left. Julius was simply insatiable and when the mood struck he would take her. She really only slept in his bed so he could wake up and satisfy his morning erection. The bedframe was huge, the mattress comfortable, the quilt warm, so there was never the need to spoon and cuddle like couples did on bleak cots under thin blankets in frigid East End hovels.

But she wouldn't go back there again.

She had saved every penny from the wages Julius insisted on paying her, had taken care of the dresses he had purchased for her, had taken every opportunity to further her knowledge about the world around her. She would request he help her find a respectable position in another medical office, and, Julius being kind and generous as he was, would oblige.

And she would never tell him about his child.

He regularly supplied her with appliances of birth control and a calendar to chart her courses. He claimed it was out of mere medical curiosity, that he wanted to know what items inserted inside her body felt like—for both him and her—during intercourse. But surely a man of his age with legions of past lovers and a tendency toward medical experimentation would already know what it felt like to engage in sexual congress with a pessary inside his lover?

That evening, she had decided she would stop using birth control.

He wouldn't know. Julius no longer watched her preparations, no longer inquired about her courses and had often remarked how imperceptible the various barriers were. From her work in his office, Grace learned how some women concealed their pregnancies, learned how the female body—and disposition—changed over nine months and beyond, learned the names of highly regarded midwives. Many of the patients complained about their husbands' disinterest in their children. Grace could handle a baby on her own. She would gaze into her child's blue eyes and remember what she and Julius had once shared.

The bedroom door opened, the dim light of an oil lamp illuminated Julius' slender form. He set the lamp on the bedside table and removed his clothes, fastidiously placing each garment on his wooden valet stand. And then he was naked, the glow of the lamp gold against his pale skin. Grace would never tire of the sight of his nude body, sleek and muscular. It would be something she would surely miss.

He turned off the light and crawled under the covers, the mattress dipping slightly under his weight, sliding Grace toward him. She righted herself but as she shifted he pulled her against him, enveloping her in his arms. He hiked up her nightgown, his cock slack at first in the furrow of her buttocks but quickly growing hard. He didn't take her immediately. They lay quietly, breathing to the same rhythm, his naked heat suffusing her with drowsy warmth, lulling her to doze off. When he wanted her, he would make the first move.

The heat of his palm cupping her mons startled her awake. He slid his finger through her slit, arousing her from her sleepy state, finding her clit and stroking gently. He rarely massaged her in such a way. He spent most of his working day inciting women to orgasm and Grace accepted that Julius would not perform such acts on her. She was capable of achieving her own climax. If a man touched her in such a way, it was because he held some romantic notion about her.

And Julius was not the type of man to give in to romantic notions.

Except right now, he was insisting quite adamantly that she climax.

He rubbed relentlessly as she flailed against him, trying desperately not to moan his name, instead murmuring approbations. It was too easy to fall under his sensual spell. His expert touch was unflinching, so she simply gave in. Desire pooled in her belly as he pressed harder, goading her forward with whispered encouragements, knowing every twitch of her body meant she was closer to the brink.

With a final jerk and a cry, she came against his hand. She closed her eyes and drew in a long breath, relaxing with each exhale. But suddenly Julius tugged off her nightgown, pushed her legs apart and slid inside her, thrusting with resolve until the queerest look came over his face and he slowed.

He gazed down at her, his expression soft, his lips parted. And then he bent over and kissed her.

She came at the touch of his mouth, came again when he deepened the union, tangling their tongues, his whiskers tickling her face. He rarely kissed her and this kiss was like nothing he had ever bestowed, a kiss full of the passion she felt, the passion she was certain he did not feel for her.

He broke free to quicken his pace, moments later slamming inside her with a growl, holding himself aloft as he came inside her. His chest heaved from exertion as he lay beside her, coiling an arm around her shoulder.

Grace stared at the ceiling, stunned. Their lovemaking had never been so profound.

She shouldn't read too much into what had just happened. Surely Julius was simply expressing his gratitude for that afternoon's release. She smiled as she burrowed into the crook of his arm. Rumor among some in her old neighborhood held that a child conceived amidst a woman's pleasure would most certainly be a boy.

A boy with black hair and blue eyes to remember her Julius by.

CHAPTER THREE

"So good to see you, Lavinia." Sophia kissed both Lavinia's cheeks in greeting as they stood in the foyer of the Phillipses' Belgravia home.

"You're looking well, Sophia." Indeed her friend had a healthy color in her face that spoke of excitement or, knowing the Phillipses, recent sexual activity.

Sophia took her arm and led her to the morning room. "I wanted to have a private visit before Joseph and I leave for Lincolnshire." She opened the door and waved toward the hand-crafted couch with tapestry cushions. "Sit. I have news."

"Helena's pregnant?" Lavinia blurted. She covered her mouth. "Oh, that was most unladylike." She sat primly as if that would make up for the blunder.

Sophia giggled, gazing coyly from under thick lashes as a servant brought in a tray laden with a most unusual tea service of hammered silver adorned with copper twigs and flowers. She took her seat next to Lavinia as the servant left.

"I don't know about Helena." Sophia poured from the squat, bulbous teapot. "Well, at least I haven't heard. My daughter and her new husband may very well have news. No, I wasn't referring to Helena." She broke out in a wide smile. "But me."

Lavinia gaped.

Sophia took both Lavinia's hands. "Oh, Lavinia! I'm pregnant!"

Lavinia's stomach dropped. She was excited for Sophia, really she was. But something pained her, something she was loath to admit. She would never have children, probably could not have children, and had resigned herself to not wanting children. Yet, for one moment last summer, one man had made her question all of that.

She had foolishly fallen in love with Nicholas. Their new affair was supposed to have been merely a continuance of their old one and she certainly hadn't been in love with him ten years ago. Yet, Nicholas was no longer a curious youth of eighteen but a kind and caring man of twenty-eight. And a fabulous lover. She had recklessly entertained the fantasy that he wouldn't achieve the goal of finding a wife and they would end up together. She hadn't counted on his falling deliriously head over heels for Helena Phillips.

"Oh, Lavinia, don't cry."

"Tears of joy, dear." Lavinia kissed Sophia's cheek. "I'm so happy for you." She squeezed her friend's hands. "When are you due?"

"April." Sophia giggled. "You know Helena was born in March. Looks as if the summer is a good time for me to conceive."

"What does Joseph think?"

"He's ecstatic of course. And we'll stay in England for a while. That's why we're going to Lincolnshire." Sophia let go of Lavinia and resumed pouring tea. "We're going to live at Harwell Hall. Mama is looking forward to taking care of me and imparting all the advice she didn't get a chance to offer when I was pregnant with Helena." She handed a cup to Lavinia. "Papa and Joseph have promised to be civil to each other. But the best part is that Arthur will be there."

"Arthur?"

"My brother. The Earl of Petersham."

"Oh, yes. I met him at the wedding in September. Handsome chap, isn't he?"

Sophia smiled. "Excessively so. And unmarried." She winked.

Lavinia furrowed her brow. "Oh? Because he's a boorish arse? Or because women don't attract?"

Sophia laughed so hard she had to put down her cup. She wiped a tear. "Oh my. Nicholas speaks highly of your sense of humor and now I see why."

Lavinia sipped her tea, still perplexed.

Sophia patted Lavinia's knee. "Arthur likes women a great deal and he's quite the gentleman. Perhaps a little protective of his heart." She took a sip of tea. "So he remains unattached."

Lavinia eyed her. "You're trying to play matchmaker, aren't you?"

"We're all adults, Lavinia. And sometimes I wonder if you are a bit lonely now that Nicholas is married."

"You mean take a lover? Take *your brother* as my lover?"

"Well, you and my brother will have to work that out for yourselves, really. But you were not averse to attending the masquerade so I know you're ready for a new adventure, as it were."

Lavinia turned her attention to her teacup. Sophia had chatted with the man in the sultan costume and probably knew who he was. But it would be indiscreet for her to reveal his name. If she were going to start a love affair with anyone though, she'd want it to be with him.

"Arthur will be joining us at Harwell Hall and won't be settled back in London until the Season. So you're safe from my romantic plots until then." She smiled a mischievous smile. "But I'm warning you, I will make sure the two of you have a few waltzes together."

Sophia was simply looking out for her. She was in love. Her daughter was in love. She just wanted a little happiness for her brother and her friend.

"I will not say no to a few waltzes. Thank you, Sophie, for thinking of me."

The boisterous guffaws of men drifted in from down the corridor, getting closer until a forceful knock sounded on the morning room door.

"Sophie! I'm coming in!"

And in walked Joseph Phillips with the Earl of Petersham and Geoffrey Peel, their masculine energy instantly filling the room, rousing Lavinia's senses. Each oozed a confidence only found in men of a certain age and each man clearly had a right to such confidence. Together they were successful business partners and singularly each was devastatingly attractive. Joseph's brawn was softened by his shock of close-cropped gray hair. Mr. Peel's almost boyish features restrained the impact of his impressive height and exuberant mustache.

And Lord Petersham was somehow far more dashing and appealing—and taller—than what Lavinia had remembered. His thick brown hair glinted with strands of auburn and gray, the lines around his eyes crinkled with good humor, his clean-shaven face drew attention to his full, luscious mouth.

Perhaps a few waltzes would be enjoyable.

"Darling." Joseph went to Sophia just as she moved to stand.

"Don't get up, Sophie!" Mr. Peel ran to her and sat her back down, shooing Joseph away. He folded his lanky form next to her.

Lord Petersham laughed out loud and kissed Sophia's hand. "Congratulations, dear sister, for making me an uncle once again."

Sophia blushed. "Joseph, I see you divulged our news."

"Damn right I did!"

"And you've been drinking brandy." She leaned toward Mr. Peel and sniffed. "The lot of you."

"We were celebrating," Mr. Peel said softly, stroking her hand. "Everyone at the club knows now, darling."

Sophie brushed a lock of Mr. Peel's thick brown hair behind his ear. "Geoffrey, I'm pregnant, not dying. You don't need to handle me with such care."

Joseph strutted, grinning. "How do you do, Lavinia? Sorry to burst in on your *tête-à-tête*. I suppose Sophie's told you?"

"Luckily for you, Joseph, she just did."

"Darling," Sophia cooed, "where are your manners? You should introduce your guests."

Joseph stretched out his arms. "You all met at Helena's wedding, didn't you?"

Lord Petersham shook his head with a grunt of exasperation. He approached Lavinia and gave a slight bow. "Lady Foxley-Graham, if I remember correctly? I am the brother-in-law of this overly familiar and half-drunk American fellow." A twinkle flashed in his hazel-brown eyes, highlighting the flecks of green in their depths.

"Yes, Lord Petersham, I do remember." She offered her hand with a smile. His firm touch sparked an unexpected frisson of excitement. "And Mr. Peel." She nodded in his direction, slipping her hand from Lord Petersham's dangerous hold. "The solicitor."

"My lady." Mr. Peel nodded.

"And what keeps you all here in London in November, gentlemen?"

"Business," Joseph grumbled. "Always business. It's just easier down here."

"*Up here*," Lord Petersham corrected, taking a seat in a blocky armchair opposite Lavinia. "London is *up*."

"It looks *down* on a map, Arthur."

Mr. Peel chuckled. "We were all just at Harwell Hall last month for the Richmonds' revived hunting ball. And now we're all going back for Sophie's confinement."

"You too, Mr. Peel?"

"My family home is not far from this lot." He gestured at his friends. "Anna—you met my wife at the wedding," he said to Lavinia, "will be thrilled at your news, Sophie. Unless you've already told her."

"She keeps my secrets very well, doesn't she?"

Mr. Peel chuckled. "I should have known."

"You have children, do you not, Mr. Peel?" Lavinia asked.

"Yes. Three. I'm glad we started just after we were married. I don't think Anna would want any more now."

Sophia smiled sweetly in Mr. Peel's direction. "Geoffrey's daughters were Helena's attendants at her wedding."

"Oh yes! Pretty little things, aren't they?"

Mr. Peel flushed and grinned. "They take after their mother."

Sophia patted Mr. Peel's thigh. "And William takes after his father. He's very handsome and tall."

Lavinia studied the two on the sofa. Sophia was far too intimate with Mr. Peel. An old lover? A new one? Perhaps Mrs. Peel was a modern woman who did not mind so much.

Lord Petersham turned his attention to her, his courteous expression exuding sensuality. "I understand you're widowed, my lady. Any children?"

There was that clenching pain in her stomach again. "No. My husband and I never had children." She smiled politely. If Sophia had a mind to match-make then she should find out how the unmarried earl handled shocking questions from an independent woman. "And you, my lord?"

He colored. "No—"

Joseph let out a sharp laugh. "None that we know of, eh, Arthur?"

"Joseph! Don't tease." Sophia fussed with her skirt. "Now, gentlemen, if you would please excuse the two of us Society matrons, we would like to get back to our tea and gossiping."

Joseph leaned over and kissed his wife's cheek. "I'll see you tonight, my beautiful bride."

Sophia blushed.

"Gentlemen." Joseph indicated the door.

Mr. Peel kissed Sophia on the cheek and followed Joseph. Lord Petersham did the same but offered Lavinia a devastatingly beguiling smile before he left.

Something about his mouth was so familiar…

Still reeling from the excitement of impending fatherhood, Joseph ushered Arthur and Geoffrey into the library for further celebratory drinking.

Geoffrey placed a hand on Arthur's shoulder. "Did you see the way Lady Foxley-Graham looked at you?" he teased. "Anna gives me that look sometimes when the girls have gone to bed."

Arthur flashed him a perturbed scowl. "I hardly think so, Geoff."

Joseph poured out three sherries from a crystal decanter. "Don't try to tempt Arthur, Geoff," he said. "He's still nursing Cupid's deadly aim from Countess Winthrop's masquerade ball."

"Oh? Do tell." Geoffrey stretched out on the leather couch, letting his head fall back against the tufted armrest.

"I can't." Joseph handed him a sherry. "The rules of the ball are that guests refrain from divulging anything about anybody."

Arthur grabbed his glass from the liquor cabinet. "Except now Geoff knows we were both there."

"I never said *I* was." Joseph smirked.

"Oh, Christ." Arthur rolled his eyes.

Geoffrey turned his resting head to face him. "I'm your best friend, Arthur. Surely you can tell me."

"I thought I was your best friend," Joseph said, feigning insult.

Arthur sighed from the depths of an overstuffed club chair. "I'll let you two draw pistols for that dubious honor. Still, I'm not telling anyone anything."

Joseph chuckled. Arthur had been in a funk since the day after the masquerade, lamenting he had lost the woman of his dreams. That her odalisque costume had complemented his to perfection only added to the romance of star-crossed lovers. Yet despite the intimacy between Joseph and Arthur, Arthur had refused to divulge any of the details of his amorous encounter.

"Okay." Joseph lifted his glass. "Let's discuss Lavinia then. Sophie's got a mind to get you two attached next Season."

"Well, thank God Sophie will be busy with a baby." Arthur nursed his drink.

"I'm sure Anna will help out." Geoffrey yawned. "She loves babies. And Sophie loves the Season. I'd say you were outnumbered, Petersham." He grinned and winked at Joseph.

Arthur glared at them. "All right," he said, waving a hand in defeat. He narrowed his eyes at Joseph. "What do you know about her?"

Joseph sipped his sherry. He'd have to be diplomatic. "She was widowed about twenty years ago and never remarried. She has a penchant for seeing young men get established in careers and young women get married well."

"How generous." Arthur looked thoughtful. "I suppose that might have something to do with not having had children herself?"

"Possibly. But rumor has it she's simply incredibly well-connected in Society."

"Ah." He took a sip of liquor. "Lovers?"

"She's discreet but as far as I know she's had a string of them."

Arthur quirked a brow. "You?"

Joseph's jaw dropped. "Oh, God no."

Arthur guffawed.

Geoffrey chuckled. "Methinks Phillips protests too much."

His friends knew him too well. "Okay, yeah, she's beautiful. But we had some squabbles over Helena and Nicholas last summer that sort of dulled any ardor I may have felt had I met her under other circumstances." Not to mention it would have been impolitic to pursue the ex-lover of one's future son-in-law. "Besides I've given up all that."

"I hear she's close to Nicholas," Arthur said. "Sort of like a mother?"

Joseph chuckled at the thought. "I wouldn't say that. There is a lot of history between them. Lavinia was good friends with Nicholas' mother." He took a seat opposite Arthur. "Look, to be serious for a moment, it's not for me to say too much about her. One man's conversation is another man's slander. She's forthright and honorable and of independent means." He sighed. "There'd be no deception, no expectation of economic support. You can't say that about all your past lovers, Arthur."

"Unfortunately not," he said glumly.

Geoffrey stroked his mustache. "Anna says Lady Richmond wants you married off now you've settled your family differences," he said. "You have to admit Lady Foxley-Graham is quite a stunner."

"Agreed," Joseph said. "You could do a lot worse and possibly not much better at the moment." He flashed Arthur a look of mild reproach. He'd have to forget his odalisque. "But you're old enough and experienced enough to make your own decisions."

"Thank you, Joseph."

"Of course there will probably be neighboring daughters invited to Harwell Hall this Christmas." Joseph smiled slyly. "You'll have your pick of those."

Arthur mumbled an oath and sank deeper into his chair.

Geoffrey sipped his sherry. "Thank God my girls are too young to be in the running."

"You underestimate my mother, Geoff. I'm sure she's keeping them in mind for when I'm fifty." Arthur drained his glass.

That got a rise out of Geoffrey. "Don't you dare, Petersham."

"He might be the Marquess of Richmond by then, Geoff. Rumor has it he's also pretty good in bed." Joseph winked at Arthur. "You only want the best for your daughters."

"Oh, Christ! We are not having this conversation!" Geoffrey place his empty glass on the carpet. "Why I'm still friends with a couple of corrupt libertines, I hardly know."

"I thought I was your best friend," quipped Arthur.

Joseph laughed. A baby on the way and finding a wife for Arthur. After twenty years, being back in the family fold was going to be interesting.

Arthur lay on his side in bed, staring at the window where clouded moonlight played in the shadows of the curtain, the movement keeping him awake rather than lulling him to sleep. He was overly occupied by the day's events. Sophia's pregnancy reminded him he had been delinquent in providing an heir to the marquessate, and Geoff and Joseph reminded him Mother intended to do something about that.

And then there was the allure of a certain viscountess. Helena's wedding breakfast had been something of a blur as the event had been the stage to reconcile the estranged members of the Harwell family, so he had not had a chance to get to know Lady Foxley-Graham as he ought to have. But there she was earlier that day in Sophia and Joseph's ridiculously fashionable morning room, wearing a stunning dress of lapis lazuli blue that set off her dark amber eyes quite exquisitely. Of course, when he hadn't been admiring her eyes, he was admiring her bosom, its generous proportions accentuated by two rows of buttons running over her breasts, down her waist and ending at the point of a V at her crotch, where a tuft of fringe implied what lay underneath…

But even the promise of such charms could not stop him from dreaming of the spread legs of a willing odalisque. Although Lady Foxley-Graham's tightly corseted bosom did seem to be as abundant as the unbound breasts of his odalisque.

His odalisque.

He untied the waist of his pajama bottoms and fondled his half-aroused cock, awakening it.

She danced on the edge of his thoughts, a constant reminder of their encounter. While she had slept in the library, he'd tarried, smiling a satiated smile at seductive women and provocative men. But he played no more games that night. He would not mar an incomparable memory.

And an hour later, he had watched her leave. Alone. Her provocative costume and entrancing endowments hidden beneath the folds of a too generous cloak.

She had left having been satisfied by him and needing no other.

He gripped his erection.

She was the best kind of woman, a woman of true experience, a woman who knew what she wanted and how to tease a man into giving it to her. Not some coquettish miss who only wanted to flirt and toy yet when it came to actual sex, had no skill, no creativity, and many reservations.

A woman who was at the masquerade not to find a lover but to forget a lover. Was he the lover she thought of now?

He stroked the length of his cock, rubbed his thumb over the head. She had put him in her mouth and, more amazingly, had enjoyed it. How rare to find a woman who enjoyed fellatio. He had been tempted several times to seek out a man in the catamite clubs but he hated whorehouses. Why would one catering to homosexuals be any less devoid of soul and emotion?

He squeezed his glans then languidly continued his strokes. She had let him take control, let him use her roughly, not seeking any rewards or promises for indulging him his letches because she shared the same desires.

The remembered thrill of slamming into her from behind stirred him into action, propelling him to pump harder. Her uninhibited moans, her freedom in reveling in her body's sexuality, her frank expression of a deeply held emotion all spoke of a highly sensual woman, a woman he had been longing for, a woman he needed, a woman he was going to find.

He arced his back above the pillow, coming on his hand, remaining poised in the air a moment before collapsing onto the mattress. He stared at the ceiling, exhaling the last of his release.

He would find her. That coming Season he would attend every damn ball, soiree, luncheon, and tea to flirt with every unattached woman over thirty-five like a man possessed. Of course, there was no guarantee his odalisque was unattached, but the fact she was trying to forget a lover was a strong indication she was.

And once he kissed her, he would know exactly if it was she or not.

He sighed. That would be a lot of women. And what if he didn't find her?

Well, there was one other woman who did attract. So be it. If he couldn't find his odalisque, perhaps he'd pursue the lovely Lady Foxley-Graham. At least she wasn't one of the adolescents his mother had been recommending to him of late. As a woman of experience, well, that meant she would know a little about what to expect in his bed.

And the shape of her mouth reminded him of another, recently wrapped around his prick.

CHAPTER FOUR

London, February 1880

Lavinia paced the Persian carpet in her morning room. Nicholas was in town and had sent a message he wanted to see her, to visit her at her house. She had thought to suggest they meet at a restaurant or café. But how would he have responded to such an unusual suggestion from an intimate friend? She was the one who had qualms, who worried that they hadn't been alone since the wedding and wasn't sure she would have complete control of her emotions.

Nicholas probably thought a visit nothing more than a visit.

And when he entered, he immediately went to her and kissed her on both cheeks. She had nothing to worry about.

Sims brought the tea tray and left it on the table before the sofa.

Nicholas strolled around the room. "I'm staying with the Phillipses. Helena and I have our own suite there." He brushed his fingers across a fruitwood side table then picked up and examined a blue-and-white porcelain box. "Everything there is so modern. Everything in your house is so…*familiar.*"

"Will you try to acquire the former Atherley property in town?"

"No." He looked out the window briefly then continued his pacing. "I thought about it, but I'm not sure it's worth the expense. I hear the new owners have done a fine job with renovations. I'm glad of that. When Helena and I feel we need a London house of our own, we'll find something."

"And how is married life treating you?"

He sat on the other end of the sofa. "Vinny, I cannot express the utter joy I feel with Helena. It is pure heaven."

"But surely you expected it to be, darling." She handed him his teacup.

"No…no I didn't think it would be like this. Not from watching my parents, not from what you said about how things were with your husband." He took a sip. "It's like being with my best mate from university days and a lover all at once."

She and Nicholas had been just that a year ago. Or perhaps she had mothered him too much for him to think of her as a *mate*. "And to think it's only been a few months."

"I know! I can only imagine what a lifetime will be like." He sipped his tea then placed the cup on the table. "And we have news."

Lavinia gasped. "So soon?"

He colored. "We didn't want to wait."

She held out her hand. "Congratulations, Nicky."

He squeezed her hand. "Oh, Vinny, it's absolutely marvelous. I mean how many wives take such an interest in their own bodies when they are with child? We both find it utterly fascinating the changes day to day. We write everything down in a journal—how she feels, what she eats, even how big she's getting. We measure her belly and well, other places. She's more plump all over." He grinned against a blush. "It's quite amazing really. And to have a wife who is as fascinated as I—I'm still astounded."

She laughed. "I see you've never stopped being a doctor." It was wonderful to see him so excited, so joyful. "Darling, I'm so very happy for you. Helena's parents must be thrilled."

"They are. Mr. Phillips is crowing like a rooster in a hen house." He eyed her. "You must know about Sophia by now?"

"I do. Mother and daughter pregnant at the same time is an unlikely occurrence. Is this why you came all the way to London?"

"It was important to me to tell you in person." He turned a gentle smile to her. "You mean a great deal to me."

She gulped down tea to quash the lump of emotion in her throat. "Nicky, you could have sent a letter. I would have understood."

"Well," he sighed, leaning back against the sofa, "there is the opening of Parliament on Thursday and I am the Earl of St. Albans now. I was advised by the Marquess of Richmond that as a new peer I should make an appearance."

"Of course. Richmond is very astute. Although I gather he's decided to stay in Lincolnshire?"

Nicholas chuckled. "He says old peers aren't expected to show their faces in the middle of winter. Something about the chill in his bones." A smirk twisted on his lips. "Although the marquess does not seem to be the kind of man to let a chill in his bones get in his way."

"Politically, he lets nothing get in his way and he hates defeat."

"I presume you've been on the other side of one of his battles."

She smiled at the memories. "A few times."

Nicholas reached for his teacup and stirred the contents absentmindedly. "Vinny," he began with a hint of bashfulness, "there is something else."

"Oh?"

"Since I left you last summer, I know there hasn't been another."

She flushed. "That's really none of your concern."

"Yes it is. You are my dear friend and I don't want you to be lonely."

"Are you going to play matchmaker this Season like Sophia?"

"I hadn't thought of that. Would you like me to?"

"No! I'm fine. I have plenty of friends."

"But you lack a lover." His gaze held an earnest intensity.

"I—" She stared at him, realization sending a stabbing chill up her spine. "Nicky, you have a wife and a baby on the way."

"I have a most unusual wife. It was she who brought it up."

Lavinia stood and walked to the window, turning her back on him so he wouldn't see the tears dampening her lashes.

"Helena's like her parents in that regard. Besides, I was yours before she met me so she feels you have some sort of right."

"I no longer have a right, if I even had one to begin with."

He came up behind her and placed his hands on her shoulders.

"Besides, you were never mine," she said. "Our affairs have always been brief."

He turned her to face him. "I will always be yours, Vinny."

With his fingers under her chin, he tilted up her face as he lowered his. He pressed his lips to hers, tenderly yet persistently.

She wanted him, oh, how she wanted him. But it was wrong. He held her steady at her waist, continued his kisses down her neck, running his finger under the high collar of her dress to flick his tongue against her pulse point.

"Nicky, stop." She tried to make it sound as if she didn't want him but her words came out breathy.

"Tell me you don't want me."

He would know she'd be lying. Her cunt throbbed in anticipation. "I don't sleep with married men."

"Now you do."

He pulled her close to ravage her mouth. She relented, letting him plunder her depths with his tongue, crushing her needful body against his, circling her arms around his neck.

"Let's go upstairs, Vinny."

"The servants will talk." Well, that was a lie. She prided her staff on their unfailing loyalty and discretion.

"I very much doubt that. Besides, the scandal is mine to have. I'm a married man, remember?"

She led him up the stairs to her bedroom, closing and locking the door behind them. He wasted no time in tearing off his clothes, a distracting sight while she removed her own. In a few months, his body had changed, had bulked and thickened, his muscles more defined. She stared, slack-jawed at the wondrous sight.

"Vinny?" He stepped forward. "Don't tell me you're having second thoughts."

She ran her hand down his torso, along the ripples of his abdomen, stopping at the dark hair at his groin. A sensual thrill coursed through her. That he was already hard added decoration to the sculpted beauty. "Married life has been good to you."

He chuckled. "More like being the earl of a dilapidated estate has been good to me." He tugged open the fastenings of her corset. "Although I will admit a regular regimen of calisthenics in the bedroom has helped." He pulled off her chemise. "Let me demonstrate."

He scooped her up in his wonderfully thick arms and carried her to the bed, tossing her on the mattress before jumping on himself. He straddled her, propped on his arms and legs, a perfect position for her to continue her inspection of his glorious body. He smirked as his cock twitched playfully between them.

"I'm ready. What about you?"

She had been ready the moment he had kissed her, probably before. He slid a finger through her wetness, chuckling in satisfaction and victory.

He put his glistening finger in his mouth and sucked provocatively. "I see we can forgo preliminaries."

He poised himself at her entrance and arched a brow, his expression one of challenge—which one of them would capitulate to the forbidden desire first? He jabbed the head of his cock against her, not bothering to direct his aim, a game to get her to do it for him.

She quirked a brow in response then tilted her hips.

He slipped in easily with a groan of approval.

Her last encounter had been months ago, with the sultan at the masquerade. Anonymous sex had its pleasures, but joining with Nicholas had so much more. His cock filled her like any man's but the joy that accompanied it remained unmatched. He knew her body, knew to suck her nipple during his first few strokes, knew to massage her clit as he increased his speed.

And now the familiar joining was accompanied by a new visual treat.

"I want to see you, Nicky."

He pulled back onto his knees and grabbed her ankles, spreading her legs wide. She held the position and reveled in the view of masculine perfection.

He released an ankle to move her hand to her sex. "I want to see you, too."

She touched herself, her flicks and strokes quickly devolving to an unfocused frenzy as Nicholas' lust overtook them both. He bent over her, his hair tickling her cheek, his breath loud in her ear, keeping her mired in the present as her orgasm built to transport her to ecstasy. She clenched around him with a cry. He raised his head to meet her gaze, his eyes glazed in hunger, his brow furrowed in uncontrolled surrender. She touched a finger to his cheek.

He jerked backward, tearing himself from her, spasming amidst growls as he came on the counterpane.

He curled at her side, his pounding heart music to her ears.

"Thank you for having the presence of mind to pull out, Nicky. Although I should have known a doctor would do such a thing."

"You taught me how to do that." He was still slightly breathless.

She laughed softly. "I suppose I did."

He shifted onto his back, wrapping a strong arm around her and pulling her close. "And I seem to recall we had fun reviewing the lesson."

She threaded her fingers through his chest hair then followed the new contours with her palm. Their affair of over a decade ago had been quite a bit of fun. Unwittingly he also helped her pick up the pieces of her broken heart, giving her confidence to pursue others.

"There's one day in particular I remember about that summer, Nicky."

"Oh God," he groaned. "Not the pissing story again!"

She laughed. "No, dear. Afterward. When you told me you loved me."

He smoothed her hair before kissing her head. "Yes, I do remember."

There was a beat of silence, Lavinia expecting Nicholas to qualify his answer with a denial of current emotions. But he did not.

"Last year," she continued, "I think I fell in love with you a little."

His breath lay hot on her scalp. "I was a different man then. Nicholas Ramsay, ambitious doctor of independent means, distancing himself from his past."

"Ah yes, but when you became earl and embraced that past, my heart did not change."

He pulled her close. "I guess our emotions just weren't synchronized." He kissed her hair. "I'm a very lucky man to be loved by two wonderful women."

Synchronized. That was an interesting way to put it. Her emotions had never been synchronized with a lover. She sighed and nuzzled against him. Perhaps one day her heart would match the beat of another.

Julius skimmed his hand over Grace's nude body as she lay next to him in their bed. As they had been doing far too often recently, they had simply made love. No devices, no equipment, no creative positions. He had lain on top of her, between her legs. She moaned beneath him. They came moments apart. Then he had rolled off and they dozed. There was an unexpected satisfaction in the simple act.

A dream had woken him, a dream of her laughing, smiling. She did that so infrequently—there was not really cause for it in their lives—but when she did, it stirred his heart, a relaxing warmth overtook him, a feeling that matched one Grace had described as a cat stretching in a sliver of sunlight.

And then he had looked over at her, her brown hair spread over the pillow, and she really was smiling, lost in her own pleasant dream.

He cupped a breast, weighing it, then the other. They were heavier and fuller than a few months ago. Her belly, no longer flat, curved with a healthy plumpness. Of course living with him meant she ate regularly and healthily. She was no longer the skinny waif who had walked through his door, willing to participate in his sexual experiment for bed and board.

Perhaps another man wouldn't have noticed the changes in a lover's body. But he was a doctor and women's bodies were his specialty. Missed menses, morning nausea, erratic emotions, increased appetite, the sudden craving for meat. The last was what had startled him to realization. She had not balked at his vegetarian diet when she had first joined his household. He had, at first, refused. An hour later he was instructing his housekeeper Mrs. Jennings to purchase a portion of meat for Grace. The old woman had done so without question. It was Julius' diet that was unusual, not Grace's request for a typical English dinner.

He rested his palm on her belly, letting his warmth penetrate her skin, a slight thrill teasing his loins at the knowledge that her body was changing because of him. She shifted, curling away from him, forcing his hand to slide over her hip and fall to his side, leaving him bereft of comforting contact…

Releasing a long buried memory.

A chill crept across his flesh. There had been only one other time in his life when a lover had carried his child. And that had gone badly. Very badly indeed.

This time, with Grace, he swore it would be very different.

Lavinia crumpled the *Morning Post* and threw it on the floor then stood and paced before the couch, trying to make sense of the restlessness that plagued her. Was it because most of her friends were still holed up in their country estates for the winter, leaving her alone?

No…it was because making love to Nicholas during the past week had left her with a vague sense of irritableness.

She stopped and stared at the clock on the mantel. It was already almost three in the afternoon. She needed to get out of the house despite the chill in the air and the late hour. But where to go?

Perhaps the milliner's. A new bonnet often cheered her. Or the dressmaker's to discuss ideas for the Season. She hadn't purchased herself any new jewelry recently…

Nothing moved her from her spot. Her gaze wandered to the *Post* on the floor, the paper perfectly creased at the column for the Imperial Parliament.

She exhaled. What she needed was politics.

Before Nicholas, she had been a frequent visitor to the ladies' galleries of both houses of Parliament. Years ago, the Earl of Thuxton, whose talent with his tongue went beyond his abilities as an orator, had made sure the porters knew exactly who she was and to treat her with the utmost respect. It might be hot and stuffy in the Ladies' Gallery at the House of Commons but it afforded a change of venue with a bit of privacy.

Besides, it was always a fine thing to see dozens of men peacocking about, their displays of bald power having less to do with running the country than conceit and arrogance, their hubris of a type reserved only for other men. Behind the grille of the gallery—her presence obscured and forgotten—a woman could observe what a man would be like in the bedroom. Observing Parliament was not just politically enlightening…it was sexually arousing.

Plus, watching laws being discussed vociferously while making snide comments with other women would dispel the loneliness that had filled her otherwise busy days of late.

She quickly changed then took a cab to Westminster.

It was a dreary day with a bit of rain, which cleared by the time they reached the edge of Hyde Park. When stopped in traffic, she asked the driver to take a detour to Westminster Abbey. She would walk the short distance to the Palace of Westminster from there.

Alighting on the pavement near Broad Sanctuary, she breathed in the foul air then took the path along the side of the abbey. Her pulse quickened. She hadn't realized how much she missed politics. She had been too preoccupied with Nicholas last year—a most satisfying diversion to be sure, but politics was like spending time with an old flame.

As she approached the Neo-Gothic Houses of Parliament she spied a figure coming toward her. A tall man, with an elegant bearing, his beaver hat brushed to a sheen, his coat of the finest tailoring, his confidant gait punctuated by the swing of his umbrella. His features, from a slight distance, were somewhat classical. A beard in the imperial style covered his mouth and chin.

Her pulse quickened. Could it possibly be her sultan? And did he just smile as if he recognized her?

She chuckled at her foolish whim. *Old flame indeed.*

"Julius," she greeted when he stopped before her.

"Lavinia." He smiled a warm smile, a smile she hadn't seen for years, his blue eyes brilliant against the stark gray of February.

"You're looking well." He really was. There was almost a glow to his complexion.

"Thank you," he said.

Was that a blush?

"As are you," he added.

His gaze grazed over her body as if she were naked before him. Unwittingly her nipples hardened under her corset.

"How have you been?" he asked.

"A little restless." She glanced at the clock tower behind him.

He followed her gaze. "Ah, hence a visit to Parliament."

"You know me too well." She longed for a companion who knew her like Julius did. But the last time they had been together had been dreadful, she too yielding to his brutal carnality. Even now his force of presence subdued her into civility. "What are you doing in Westminster?"

He colored again.

"I beg your pardon. That was merely conversational. I have no right to ask."

"You have more right than you think." There was a twinkle in his eye, reflecting memories. "I too have been a tad restless of late. I've been out walking."

"All the way from Chelsea?"

"It's really not that far when one is absorbed in one's thoughts."

"No." She understood completely.

He opened his mouth as if to say something, as if he wanted to say something. Instead he looked down at the ground then away before offering her a weak smile.

Something affected him greatly.

Perhaps a change of subject. "How is your practice, by the way?"

"Going very well." He cleared the frog in his throat. "Grace has been invaluable since Nicholas Ramsay, or Lord St. Albans rather, left."

"I didn't mean to bring up a sore subject."

"I've moved on, Lavinia," he said gently. "How is the Countess St. Albans? Or should I not ask?"

Lavinia smiled. "Helena is pregnant."

Julius chuckled. "Of course she is. I should have known. She's in good hands. The earl is a fine doctor."

There was that look again, this time with a hint of glaze to his eyes.

He sucked in air. "Lavinia…Vinny… The last time we…I…" He trailed off then straightened his shoulders and met her gaze. "I apologize."

She stared at him, amazed. Their last encounter had been brutal. But a vague notion of pleading in his expression implied something darker. Something from their past.

He took hold of her hand and raised it to his lips to graze a featherlight kiss on her gloved fingers.

"Enjoy observing government, Lady Foxley-Graham."

She could have sworn she saw a tear in his eye as he walked away.

CHAPTER FIVE

Lincolnshire, February 1880

Arthur stared into the library fireplace, the flames dancing cheerily as if welcoming him back to his old apartment in Harwell Hall. He hadn't called the Lincolnshire estate home for almost twenty years but it was easy to resume his former life.

His *bachelor* life.

He studied the shelves lined with books, an empty space here and there where he had removed more beloved tomes to his London house. He took a draught of his brandy then watched the amber liquor slide back down, coloring the Greek key pattern etched on the outside of the crystal bowl. He had purchased the decanter with four matching glasses as a present to himself when he had reached his majority. Over two decades later, he should probably consider the set old-fashioned. Instead, reacquainting himself with such objects from his past filled him with nostalgia.

Even the library fireplace and the space before it elicited memories—sensual rather than nostalgic. It was where he and Joseph had shared their first kiss and where he and Henny had first made love.

Arthur swirled the liquor in his glass. He still missed Henny. What they had shared had proved impossible to replicate. Not just the spark of youthful lust but the joyous friendship, the depth of honesty, the absolute trust.

He downed his brandy. The night with the odalisque was the first time he had believed he could possibly share such intimacy again.

Except his parents had other ideas about whom he ought to marry.

Helena's wedding had brought with it the Harwell family reconciliation and now Mother and Father were nagging Arthur about his plans for the future, especially since both Sophia and Helena were pregnant.

The winter holidays at Harwell Hall had been replete with the young female relatives of neighbors and friends visiting at Mother and Father's behest. Had fecundity been a trait of his own family, there would have been legions of distant cousins to consider as well. Arthur had played his part, conversing politely in the drawing room after dinners, but was usually able to escape to the masculine refuge of his apartment with Joseph and Nicholas in tow and, if they happened to be present, Geoffrey and his son William.

The day after the Harwell Twelfth Night dinner, Arthur sorely needed a respite, ensconcing his friends in his library. Nicholas and William huddled on the window seat, discussing Nicholas' travels to the Near East and William's entering Cambridge that autumn. Geoffrey, Joseph, and Arthur lounged around the roaring fire.

"I should be glad William is talking to an illustrious alumnus of our alma mater," Geoffrey sighed. "He won't listen to any of my tales of university life."

"I don't think I want your son knowing about what you and I did outside the boundary of the college walls, Geoff," Arthur said.

"Oh, pshaw. I was hoping it might inspire him to get his head out of a book and kiss a girl."

"How do you know he hasn't already?" teased Joseph.

Geoffrey lifted a brow as he studied William's animated antics across the room.

"You can always regale me with stories of what you two did at university, Geoff," Joseph continued. "When Arthur tells such tales, somehow he comes off as less than heroic."

"The sexual escapades of a nineteen-year-old are never heroic."

"Speak for yourself, my lord." Joseph winked.

And as jesting camaraderie mellowed to an afternoon of reading and letter-writing, Arthur's valet Owens entered the library with a message from Father, inviting Arthur to tea.

Arthur had groaned at that. The interrogation could be avoided no longer.

Mother poured tea in the morning parlor while Father stood at the bay window, observing the dozens of snowscapes framed by the diamond-paned windows. Arthur sat in one of the bergères reupholstered at some point in the last two decades in a lush, chestnut-brown velvet.

Mother handed him his tea. Her hair was now solidly gray and her demeanor more subdued than twenty years ago. "Arthur, have you thought about any of your prospects?" She smiled sweetly. "For marriage, dear."

Father strolled to the fireplace and drummed his fingers on the mantel. He sported shocks of bushy white whiskers on his cheeks, a fashion Arthur swore he would never adopt even in his dotage. "You will be marquess one day, son. And you'll need an heir to pass the title on to."

"Yes, Father."

Mother offered a teacup to Father.

"Perhaps soon." Father stirred his tea thoughtfully.

"Don't be morbid. You're in fine health." Father looked well. Relief from the burden of recent financial difficulties had transformed dour wrinkles into the lines of a jovial grandfather.

"I'll be seventy this year."

"That's no reason to give up."

That got a chuckle out of him. "No, but it is a reason to start planning."

"Mother has already done some planning. Which one of the girls from this holiday season did you prefer?"

"Don't be an ass, Arthur. Your mother means well."

Mother took her seat in the matching bergère opposite Arthur. "They are each one of them fine young women."

"A girl of nineteen is not terribly interesting to me. Besides, I'm sure they all consider me some despicable, leering old man."

"Ada Brampton was at least twenty-five," Mother said curtly.

Arthur scowled at her.

"You know that means she's getting too old to find a husband—"

"So I'm her best choice? Fine. I'll be sure to chat her up this Season, if that's what you want. But keep in mind you can't force love."

Father moved to the corner of the sofa. "You younger generation and your insistence on love. It's maddening."

Arthur sighed. "I know, I know. In your day, you married for power and position, for land and titles." He swallowed a gulp of tea. "I don't want that. I want to marry for love."

Mother spread her palm over her knee and gripped the dark-green fabric of her skirt. "Arthur, son, you have to put Henrietta to rest." She looked at him with soulful eyes. "You can't possibly believe she would have wanted you to remain a bachelor forever?"

"No. Of course not." Arthur cleared his throat. "And it's not about that. I'm not trying to be faithful to Henny's memory. I just know that a marriage can be something other than a business relationship." He smiled weakly at Mother. "I'll meet whomever you want me to meet but I insist that I make my own choice for a wife."

"I'm sure you'll like one of them."

"And no one under twenty five."

"Arthur, that's a bit old—"

"Mother! I want to be able to talk to a woman as an equal not as a child."

She let out a beleaguered sigh. "All right. But at least be polite to the younger girls. Parents are often so full of expectations when a daughter comes out. It's impolitic to refuse a dance."

After that, as winter dragged on, Mother did not revisit the topic. Nicholas and Helena returned to St. Albans. Geoffrey's visits grew a little more infrequent. Joseph often joined Arthur in the evening but he and Sophia had rooms in the main house.

Which left Arthur alone, drinking brandy from an antiquated snifter, perusing forgotten books. It was an ideal existence. The only missing element was a companionable woman to excite his mind and satisfy his cock.

He simply did not know how to tell his parents he was sure he did not want children. Helena had been a darling child and Geoffrey's brood—William, Molly, and Lilly—were all wonderful, and he enjoyed playing the part of uncle as they grew up. But how could he tell Mother that when he had heard of Sophia's and Helena's pregnancies, his joy at their news was tinged with relief that the children would not be his to foster?

He let out a long sigh. Perhaps his parents were right. He had put off his responsibilities long enough, and with the familial reconciliation his responsibilities were quite clear. He would dance with girls half his age while searching for his far more mature odalisque. Why, Sophia had just had her thirty-eighth birthday—perhaps his odalisque would not be averse to having children late in life.

But perhaps the man she had been trying to forget was her boorish husband. Countess Winthrop's guests always had interesting stories.

Then there was Lady Foxley-Graham. Somehow he and Nicholas never got around to talking about her during Christmas. Joseph had said all he would and Arthur avoided Sophia, as she would probably divulge his curiosity to the lady in question.

Lady Foxley-Graham was most definitely unattached. The question was, would she be amenable to the prospect of children? Or was she more like him, jealously guarding her freedom?

Arthur shook his head. What the hell was he thinking? He'd have to say more than a few words to the woman before his fantasies got the better of him.

* * * * *

London

"*Cheese and crust!*"

Julius glanced up from his novel at the utterance of the Cockney oath. Grace had pricked the tip of her index finger with her embroidery needle and was sucking the offended digit. Normally he would chastise her for swearing in such an unladylike manner but she looked the picture of domestic incongruity as she sat in the parlor chair dressed in an elegant silk dinner gown, her embroidery frame before her, attending to her wound in a crude, childish fashion. She had wanted so much to learn to be a proper English woman and was trying so scrupulously that he simply did not have the heart to admonish the indiscretion, which admittedly was minor as he was her only audience. He hid his smile and resumed reading.

A minute later, Grace was standing at his side, his glass of port in her hand.

"Grace, if you would like port, please have the courtesy to pour your own glass."

"But I don't want me own—"

"*My* own, Grace, *my* own."

"*My* own," she exaggerated. "I don't want my own glass. I just want a sip of yours."

"All right," he relented.

She took a generous swallow, somehow managing to get a drop on her lip. Her tongue flicked to catch the liquor, followed by a graze of her teeth across her lower lip. She flashed an expression of amused guilt and put the glass down.

She was so utterly beguiling at times. Julius reached out. She took his hand and he pulled her onto his lap.

She rested her head against his chest, her hand wrapping around his waist, her bustled bottom nestled between his thighs. "I can hear your heart beat," she murmured. "Boom-boom, boom-boom."

His heart beat a fraction faster as blood pumped to his crotch. He kissed the crown of her head. "I'm glad to know I'm still alive then." It was she who kept him vigorous.

She giggled. "What are you reading?"

He held the book out to her. "You tell me."

She opened to the first page. "*Cousin Henry*, a novel by Anthony Trollope." Her voice rang clear and confident, stumbling only on the author's last name.

Julius grinned with pride.

"What's it about?"

"A missing will and a dispute over who will inherit an estate." A topic he should be contemplating in his own life with Grace's change of circumstance. But, like an awkward youth, he hadn't yet broached the subject of her pregnancy. It was just too damn difficult. He'd work up the courage tonight.

Her eyes widened in bemused disbelief. "Is it any good?"

He chuckled. "It is a welcome diversion from my usual medical treatises." He took the book from her and placed it on the side table then picked up the port. He sipped, watching her over the rim of the glass. She licked her lips delicately as she watched him drink.

He held the glass out to her. "And did you like the port?"

She took the glass. "I did." She placed the port back on the table. "But I think I might like to try it this way instead."

She stretched her neck and touched her lips to his, brushing the tip of her tongue along the seam of his mouth.

Every nerve in his body flared at the delicate caress. They rarely kissed. Or rather he rarely kissed her. He rarely kissed his lovers. The simple act conveyed so much meaning. A kiss was too emotional, too intimate, too revealing of one's secret longings.

And at that moment he longed for Grace.

He downed the rest of the port, letting the liquor dampen his lips and moisten his tongue. He cradled her head in his hand as he leaned over and crushed his mouth to hers, devouring her as a man hungry, she sucking his tongue, seeking sustenance. He would succor her, would sustain her, would nourish her body and soul.

She clung to him, spiking her fingers through his hair, curling against his chest needfully.

He needed her as well. As their passion cooled to languid nibbles, he knew it was she, rather, who would succor him. Remorse stung his eyes. Pride had starved him of love's banquet.

As he pulled back, she licked her lips and traced a finger around his mouth. "I love your whiskers. They tickle when we kiss. I like being tickled."

"Then we should kiss more often."

"We should."

He rested his forehead against hers. "Shall we to bed?"

Delight lit up her face before melting to misgiving. "Don't you have work? You always work into the night."

He cupped her cheek. "I can give it a rest one night."

He'd mention her pregnancy after they had made love; he swore he would. But he knew he wouldn't. She'd be too fragile and he'd be too spent. The topic would have to wait for another day.

CHAPTER SIX

St. Albans, March 1880

Lavinia stepped out of the carriage before Atherley Keep, the ancient home of the Earls of St. Albans, and breathed in the country air. The gravel drive crunched under her feet as she ambled away from the entrance to get a better view of the Gothic mansion. Nicholas had done a marvelous job restoring the estate to its former glory. Scaffolding covered the west side but the yellow stone of the façade gleamed gold against the pale gray of the cloudy sky, offering a welcoming elegance to visitors.

She had been invited by the Earl and Countess of St. Albans as a special request "before the hustle and bustle of Helena's birthday celebration" with an urgent "oh, you must say yes, Lavinia" scribbled hastily in Helena's feminine hand. The personal note was an obvious attempt to show that despite Lavinia and Nicholas briefly resuming their affair such facts did not much concern the earl's young bride.

Lavinia smiled to herself. Helena was going to be quite a force amongst the *ton* after putting a few Seasons behind her. And to think

Nicholas had once worked so hard to distance himself from such a life.

"Lavinia!" Helena came running from the entrance porch.

Or rather, she had the impetus to run but was held back by her very pregnant state. She stepped quickly and carefully, one palm spread across her belly, waving with the other hand. Lavinia strode forward swiftly to meet her more than halfway.

She kissed Helena's cheeks. "Helena, you look fabulous. Motherhood suits you."

Helena clasped her hands. "Oh, Lavinia! I'm so happy you're here." She linked their arms together for the stroll back to the house. "How was the journey? It's really not so far from London, is it?"

"Not really, no. I was worried Nicholas would find life out here a bit boring and rustic." She gazed around. "But I can see the attractions of the country."

"Vinny!" Nicholas stood in the entrance porch with a familiar— and very handsome—man.

She leaned in to Helena. "Is that the Earl of Petersham?" She hoped Petersham did not see her blush.

"Yes. You and Uncle Arthur are our special guests for the week before my birthday party."

"Really?" What she and Petersham had in common was anyone's guess. Unless Sophia had charged her daughter with a bit of matchmaking.

Nicholas met them. He kissed Lavinia's cheeks. "Darling, it's so wonderful to see you." He put an arm around Helena as they walked to the entrance.

"Nicky, you've done wonders. Your father would be proud. Louisa, as well."

Nicholas grinned behind a blush. "Thank you, Vinny. I just wish they were still alive to see."

Petersham leaned against a slim column of the stone arch of the portal. "Lady Foxley-Graham, what a pleasure." His gaze swept over her and when he met her eyes, one corner of his mouth curled upward, an action that only augmented his devilishly good looks.

She offered her hand, ignoring the heat prickling her skin. "Lord Petersham, the pleasure is all mine."

He took her hand and wrapped it around his arm. "I hardly think so," he murmured as they fell in behind Nicolas and Helena to enter the foyer.

She shot him a glance of surprise then turned away to hide her burning cheeks. She could definitely use a distraction from Nicholas. And Petersham seemed up for a game. What harm could a little flirtation do?

As an attractive footman collected her hat, gloves, and coat, she took in the sight of the Great Hall. The clean lines of the Neoclassical checkerboard floor and smooth plaster walls clashed with the exuberance of the Gothic fan vaulting. Lavinia smiled. She had always liked that the distinctive aesthetic taste of each earl was so conspicuously displayed but hated that the discordant elements were a reminder of the family's recent troubles. By restoring the building and grounds, Nicholas was restoring the family's legacy almost destroyed by debt and tragedy. Nicholas was never meant to be earl but he proved he was more than suited for the task.

Helena pointed to a staircase on the left. "Since we are such an intimate group…"

Did she emphasize "intimate"?

"We'll have tea in the solar." She turned to Lavinia. "You might remember it as the countess' summer morning room. Nicky's been doing loads of research about the estate—"

Nicholas colored.

"And we've decided to use the historical names when we can," Helena said.

Nicholas and Helena led the way up the stairs. Under the portraits of ancestors, the wood paneling glowed from recent waxing while the brass nameplates on the frames shone from recent polishing. Lavinia paused before the portrait of Robert Atherley, Nicholas' father, painted when he was in his late forties, the same age as Julius now but not nearly as good-looking. She snorted. Why the hell was she having such thoughts?

Petersham sidled up alongside. "You knew him, did you not?"

The warmth of his body and the oaky base notes of his cologne calmed like a comfortable fire on a winter's evening. "I did. There is some resemblance although it is difficult to tell from the late earl's expression." He wore that scowl far too often.

"I cannot imagine the current earl having anything but an expression of lovesick happiness." Petersham chuckled. He leaned in. "Do you know what this is all about, my lady? Our invitation?"

His murmuring baritone was so seductive she would have disrobed before him had he asked. "Not at all, my lord. I was hoping you would be able to provide a clue."

He offered his arm. "I'm sure we'll discover soon enough."

She smiled and laid her hand on his forearm to continue up the stairs to the solar. Lavinia gasped upon entering.

It was as if Louisa had never left or, rather, that she had never met her death and had continued to live in the space, rearranging furniture, adding and subtracting *objets d'art* as whim and fashions inspired her. The Neoclassical flavor persisted in the white plaster moldings but the furnishings added a touch of modernization with jewel-colored upholstery and drapes.

"Oh, Nicky," Lavinia sighed as she sank down onto the crimson sofa. "It's beautiful."

Nicholas beamed. "It's one of the rooms we've actually finished." He sat opposite her in a gold-brocade armchair. "We restored several of the guest rooms in the southeast wing and the public dining and drawing rooms downstairs." He gestured to indicate each location. "But this is the one private room we restored."

Lavinia lifted a brow. "I would have thought your bedroom more important."

Petersham chuckled and plopped down in the matching armchair next to Nicholas, crossing his legs casually, his gaze heavy in her direction.

Helena laughed out loud then quickly quieted as a handsome footman, carrying a silver tray laden with tea accouterments, glided in.

Nicholas cast a glance at his wife's rounded belly. "We wanted to have a party for Helena's birthday. So we concentrated on the public rooms."

The footman set the tray on a table in front of Helena as she took her seat next to Lavinia.

"Thank you, Roger."

Lavinia could swear Helena flashed the servant a look beyond simple gratitude. Or perhaps Petersham's beguiling presence was making Lavinia imagine such naughtiness as rogering the attractive footman. "Where's Mason?" she asked as Roger bowed and left.

"Didn't Nicky tell you?" Helena turned her attention to pouring tea. "He's been promoted to estate steward. He lives in the gatehouse, although there's no longer any gate." She handed a cup to Lavinia.

Nicholas watched as Helena poured. "And you should see it, Vinny. Mason's made it rather his own masculine refuge, but the historical elements have been much restored." He took his own cup. "The two of us have been exploring family records in the library—"

"And staying up very late some nights," Helena scolded.

Nicholas grinned. "Did you know each level of the house increases in privacy as you go up? The ground floor once housed the stables and the audience hall, the first floor held the rooms for entertaining other nobles, and the second floor was for the family. This hierarchy was undermined when servants' quarters were added in the seventeenth and eighteenth centuries."

Lavinia wiped away a tear threatening to fall. "Louisa would be so proud of you, darling."

He met her gaze. "Thank you, Vinny."

She put down her tea and arranged her skirts. "Now, Nicky, Helena. What is this all about? Lord Petersham and I are bursting with curiosity." She had to conceal her burgeoning suspicions. If the request for an early arrival was about her and Petersham, she wouldn't mind so much. Just that it was daringly obvious. She glanced his direction.

Petersham raised a brow with a smirk, surely harboring some vaguely naughty notion.

She turned her attention to Nicholas. "Well? What are we doing here?"

Nicholas chuckled. "Yes she is always this direct when in close company," he said to Petersham. "I will tell you after dinner, Vinny, dear."

Lavinia took a sip of tea, trying not to be obvious as she flicked a glance at Petersham. She hoped Marie had been a discerning lady's maid and packed some alluring gowns to wear at dinner.

Arthur had a difficult time of it during dinner. The food was superb and Nicholas and Helena were right to be proud of their polished silver setting and gilded porcelain. Nicholas had sent his steward around to pawnshops and auction houses looking for the St. Albans' heirlooms.

"Fortunately dishes garner the highest price when sold as a complete set," he said. "We found them in a shop in London. We're still looking for some of the silver though. That is valuable just sold on a piece-by-piece basis."

No it wasn't the food or the enthusiasm of the St. Albanses for their heritage. It was Lady Foxley-Graham's accursed dress.

She had dressed for dinner—they all had. But she had treated the occasion not as a country visit with old friends but as a fashionable retreat. Her fitted bodice, a shimmering shade of brown the likes of which he had never seen, was the perfect foil to her brown hair and brown eyes, and when she had met them all in the solar before dinner, Helena had effused over the riot of trim and tucks on her lavender skirts and bustle. The viscountess then proceeded to twist and pose for her hostess, unaware that the two earls present were held in thrall by the lady's charms. Arthur had the pleasure of escorting her down to dinner, holding his arm as rigid as possible as she wrapped hers around it, attempting to breathe normally as her scent—a subtle lavender to match her skirts—filled his senses, trying desperately to keep himself from encircling her cinched waist and pulling her into a nearby corner for a passionate kiss.

Then, sitting across from her, he had a perfect view of her neckline, shaped in a sort of triangle, the base at her bosom, the apex joining demurely at her collar, an effect that could only be described as a window onto her chest. Her very abundant chest. A spray of sheer lace trim strategically obscured the shadow between her ample breasts yet really only drew attention to the temptations that lay beneath. He endeavored not to stare at the enticing feature, to instead take in other bits of her, only succeeding in landing his gaze on her mouth while she ate, opening slightly to insert her fork, her lips closing around the silver tines as she slipped the length of the utensil out.

He was hard most of dinner except when mortification descended as his niece chatted away, asking him about this and that. But then Lady Foxley-Graham would add interest to the conversation and he was back to his aroused state.

If Lady Foxley-Graham was anything, she was the most elegant, sophisticated woman Arthur had ever met. Perhaps if he had decided to forgo middle-class mistresses and high-priced courtesans and attended a ball or two he would have met such women as she. But mistresses and courtesans didn't expect marriage proposals. Dance partners did.

Maybe marriage wouldn't be so bad after all.

Now they were in the drawing room, enjoying port, except Arthur was enjoying watching Lady Foxley-Graham sip her port, her lips on either side of the crystal, her tongue flicking ever so slightly along the edge to catch the liquor. Having studied her mouth intensely over the last few hours, something about it began to look familiar. Perhaps it was only because he had imagined her lips around his erection while he frigged himself—

He had to stop thinking about her.

He crossed one leg over the other to shield his crotch and gazed up at the painted octagonal coffers of the ceiling, the twin to that in the dining room, both superb examples of the English Renaissance— or so Nicholas had boasted. "Excellent port, Nicholas."

"Thank you." He blushed with pride.

"We almost didn't have drink in this house," Helena said. "Both the old earl and Nicky's brother were terrible drunks. But Nicky's quite abstemious when it comes to such matters. So I convinced him otherwise."

"If you want a cigar, Arthur, we'll have to do that outside. The smell bothers Helena."

"Perhaps another time." After his erection had completely slackened.

Lady Foxley-Graham straightened dramatically on the sofa across from him. "Nicky," she began in her melodious voice, "I think you promised to tell us the secret of why Lord Petersham and I are here."

"It's not a secret, Vinny."

The pet names were suggestive of something more than a mere friendship. But the lady had known his mother so most likely the names were remnants of a familial affection.

"All right then. It's not a secret. So tell us." She turned to Arthur. "Lord Petersham, surely you are on my side in the matter?" Her smile carried a touch of deviousness. Which made him think of her lips around his cock again.

He shifted in his chair. "Of course, my lady. I am positively eager to know why I have been summoned."

Nicholas sat on the arm of the sofa next to Helena and placed a hand on her shoulder. "The Countess of St. Albans and I request the Earl of Petersham and the Viscountess Foxley-Graham serve as godparents to our child."

Arthur gaped. Lady Foxley-Graham gasped.

"Oh, Nicky," she said, wiping a tear from her eye. "I'd be honored." Her words were strained, as if stuck in her throat.

The manly thing would be to offer a handkerchief. Luckily the shock of the request had stunned Arthur into the present and out of his lewd fantasies. He went to the viscountess. "I would be honored, as well." He offered her his handkerchief.

She smiled and squeezed his hand before she took the square of linen.

"Oh, Lavinia, don't cry." Helena reached over and patted her shoulder. "I want to explain why we came to this decision and why it is so important for us." She rested her head against Nicholas' hip in a daringly intimate move. "Each of you has been so important in our respective lives. Uncle Arthur, it was you who encouraged and protected Mama when she fell in love with Papa and when she was pregnant with me. You saw talent in Papa, seeing beyond the circumstances of his birth, and fostered his success."

"And Vinny," Nicholas said, "you never gave up on me. You kept in contact, being the intermediary between me and my family, being there for me when I returned to London." He gazed at Helena. "And although at first you tried to keep us apart, ultimately it was you, Vinny, who ensured Helena and I were united."

Helena smiled. "We want such family-oriented, honorable people to be there for our child. We want our child to have your good influences just like we had."

Lady Foxley-Graham continued to wipe her tears.

Arthur wanted to cradle her in his arms, kiss her hair in shared joy. "Is there anything we need to do before the child is born?" he asked.

"The Bishop of St. Albans wants to meet whomever we choose as godparents," said Nicholas. "Just a formality. He's new, I'm new, the cathedral, like this house, is being restored." He stood and paced slowly before the hearth. "I suppose you should meet with the bishop before everyone arrives for Helena's birthday celebration later this week. And then after that it will be Easter and I'm sure the bishop will be far too busy."

"Of course, Nicky." Lady Foxley-Graham had recovered somewhat.

Arthur beamed at Helena. "I remember the day you were born."

Her smile sent a pang of nostalgia to his heart. Her resemblance to a nineteen-year-old Sophia was striking. Despite all the heartache in their past he would not have acted differently.

He drew in a breath. "So, Lady Foxley-Graham, it appears the mystery of our presence has been solved. What say you to a stroll on the estate tomorrow to discuss this business of god-parenting? We can knock up Mason at the gatehouse."

"I would enjoy that immensely, Lord Petersham, if you would deign to call me by my Christian name."

He smiled. "Of course, Lavinia. And you must call me Arthur." His heart was pounding already at the thought of spending time with her alone.

* * * * *

London

Grace stared through the peephole at Julius and his pretty blonde patient splayed immodestly before him. It was the girl's third visit to his office. She had just turned eighteen and her mother had sent her to see Dr. Christopher, having heard about his "unusual and amazing" device at the teas and at-homes of Mayfair. And while the girl's mother was rather forward-thinking in her views on women's rights, she did not have the fortitude to teach her daughter about self-pleasuring. That, she had said in the initial consultation, she would leave to the good doctor, whose skills and knowledge were celebrated.

Grace had kept her proud amusement to herself at the last. Julius was most definitely skilled and now his reputation was legendary.

During the blonde girl's first visit alone, Grace had been in attendance. With some of his young patients, Julius preferred Grace to be in the room, acting as if she were an older sister or best friend rather than a doctor's medical assistant. She would claim she was nineteen, not much older than they, and would pull up a tall stool and sit at the head of the medical table and talk while Julius performed his expert ministrations, answering such questions as "Is it really supposed to feel like this?" and "Do you do it too?", offering encouraging words as they built toward their crises then soothing words as they came down from the heights, later assuring them that no one would know if they did it alone in their beds at night.

And for some of the more reticent girls it would be Grace who introduced them to the powerful orgasm achieved with the device. Julius was not insulted. No. It afforded him the opportunity to sit in the little room and watch through the peephole.

But the pretty blonde girl had never really needed Grace's support. In fact, it seemed the blonde ones always had a bit more self-assurance. This one, despite her fluttering lashes and large, innocent gray-green eyes, had no qualms about being alone with a man. She watched Julius with keen interest as he busied himself with the jar of oil on his medical cart.

Which meant Grace could take the opportunity to watch Julius pleasure the blonde in privacy.

Before she had left the examination room, Grace had checked that everything was in order and, finding it so, had joined Julius at the cart. "Dr. Christopher, will that be all?"

He had looked up quickly, uncharacteristically startled. Julius never let himself get lost in his thoughts when in the presence of a patient. He prided himself on being mindful of every detail of every visit, recording observations in his notebooks after a patient's visit, especially when self-pleasuring was concerned. He had glanced at the blonde lying on the table before him as if needing a reminder that she was even there. Her sweet smile was tinged with eagerness.

"Yes, thank you, Miss Danby. I will call for you if you are needed."

Grace had curtsied and scurried off to the little room under the stairs.

She let out a sigh at the view of Julius angled over the blonde, his hand poised over her mons, reminding her that he would be touching her there but in a different way this visit, that she would experience a far more wondrous feeling than what was effected with her own hand.

"It might seem overwhelming, almost confusing. But it is best if you set your mind to focus on a pleasurable thought," he said. "Perhaps if there is a young man you fancy?"

She had crimsoned at that. "Will he know?" Her lilting voice drifted through the well-hidden system of tubes and horns that carried sounds to the occupant on the other side of the peephole.

Grace chuckled at the question. A girl would always have this concern if there was a particular young man she fancied. Only a few of the patients were ever concerned their mothers or governesses might know.

"Absolutely not, my dear," Julius said in a calming tone. He would never state the obvious—that the young man in question was probably tossing himself off every night to a lewd fantasy of the girl.

Julius scooped a fingerful of oil and smeared it on the girl's clit, preparing her, subduing her.

Grace sank into the cushions of the wingback and hiked up her skirts, sliding her hand inside the slit in her drawers to play with her own clit. She was already wet. She smoothed the sticky arousal over her pearl of pleasure, matching her own ministrations with Julius' particular sensual rhythm. The girl gasped then moaned and wriggled her body. Grace understood. The familiar sensual warmth coiled between her legs, as well.

"Good, good, my dear. Now you will know the full emotion of which you are capable."

Julius took hold of the baton of the vibrating device and clicked on the motor. The gentle whirring of the machine sent a voluptuous anticipation to smolder in Grace's core.

He pressed the device to the girl's clit.

The blonde sucked in a breath then exhaled an "oh!"—a typical reaction.

Julius took the girl's hand and instructed her to grab hold of the baton. When she did, he lay his hand over hers.

Close above her ear, Julius murmured directions and encouragements to the girl, his gaze flicking between her expressions of surprise and their joined hands producing pleasure. And then he smiled, the signal that the girl understood what it was she was supposed to be doing. In a moment, he would take his hand away and simply watch, his cock growing hard, the struggle not to touch himself twitching on his face as the girl climbed to her orgasm.

Grace absolutely loved that expression, his struggle for self-control, his final mastery over himself. It was akin to his mastery over her when they made love at night.

She stroked more swiftly.

Julius lifted his hand from the device, remaining close by in case the girl lost her rhythm. Still leaning over her, he murmured something in her ear and she nodded. He straightened, dropping his hand to his side.

And then he did the most curious thing. He walked to the counter, opened the door to the cabinet, and began perusing the glass bottles of his medicines, jotting notes in the medical accounts register.

Grace stopped touching herself. Something was wrong.

Julius loved watching girls masturbate with the device for the first time, his erection tormenting him with the pain of unrequited release. By the end of the day, he was trembling with need for Grace's mouth or hand or cunt.

But he was ignoring the blonde. Surely he could hear the melody of her syncopated, quavering moans over the drone of the motor? Perhaps this was a new letch? Was he standing at the counter with his eyes closed, imagining his stiff cock at her yearning cunt, ready to deflower her when she screamed out for more?

No…no, he was not. He was bent in concentration over the ledger book, writing meticulously in the registers.

The blonde girl's yelp of climax startled Grace back to her own hand between her legs and her dashed climb to the peak. Julius walked over to the girl then soothed her and offered praise. The blonde's flushed skin and sparkling eyes showed how much she was under his spell. Most likely the first night she attempted solitary pleasure, it would be the pleased expression of the handsome Dr. Christopher that would dance through her dreams.

Grace removed her hand, her fingers cold from inaction. She'd be the one trembling with need that night. She wouldn't care if Julius was too tired or not in the mood or had work to do.

He would have to satisfy her.

CHAPTER SEVEN

Lavinia looked down from the landing to see Arthur waiting for her in the foyer for their planned midmorning stroll. He held his hat in his hand—or rather he tossed his hat back and forth between his hands. Perhaps the earl was as nervous as she. She sucked in a fortifying breath. She was acting like a schoolgirl. The earl was handsome and unattached but he wasn't looking for a mature widow as a mate. And if he were, it would only be for the Season.

But she had begun dreaming of him as her sultan. She had already begun thinking about this year's ball at Countess Winthrop's. If she wore the same costume—

"Lavinia." Arthur bowed as she approached the bottom stair. "You look gorgeous."

She was sure she blushed. He certainly did.

"I apologize." He gripped the brim of his hat. "That was perhaps too forward of me."

"Oh, no. Please do always flatter me. I fear I have only a few years left of such ardent flattery. After that it's 'you're looking good for your age'."

He chuckled. "I'm sure no one will ever say such a thing to you." He indicated the front door. "Shall we?"

It was a lovely day on the cusp of spring, not a cloud in the sky. She had decided against a parasol, choosing instead a wide-brimmed straw hat more appropriate for summer. And the neckline of her dress had a sheer lace insert that would shield her pale bosom from the sun. Like a gentleman, he allowed her to set the pace.

They chatted about the estate, Lavinia pointing out details and vistas she remembered—some fondly, some not so fondly. Nicholas' father and brother had been terrible at managing the grounds, and all over were the tell-tale signs of their inaction.

After a spell, Arthur slowed his pace and linked his hands behind his back. "Since we are to be godparents I suppose we should discuss our views on religion."

"Religion?" Lavinia turned to him, a little flustered.

"We have been chosen the spiritual shepherds of this child."

She stiffened. If he were some sort of evangelical, she'd have to be careful of what she said. But, little by little, his earnest expression melted until a twinkle flashed in his eyes and a smirk tugged at his lips.

Inwardly she let out a sigh of relief. "You're joking."

"Only just partly. We *are* meeting with a bishop. We should have something prepared."

His gaze flickered to the sheer panel covering her bosom. She swore she saw yearning in his eyes.

"Well then, I suppose I must believe in God. At least I don't actively *not* believe in Him. I rather think that makes me an agnostic. In the dispassionate sense, not in the Huxleyan sense. My position on God is rather ill-considered."

He chuckled. "It sounds more considered than you might think."

"And you?"

"Rather the same as you. Although I do maintain a strong streak of humanism, which would mean I place human endeavor above God. The bishop might not approve."

"A bit unusual for an industrialist, isn't it? I think of such men as self-interested rather than interested in the plight of other men."

"It's because of my industrialism that I became a humanist."

"Oh?"

"Joseph and I happened to start our venture just as the railway was becoming a major force in America. However, it was also at the very same time as their American Civil War. Being established in the north, we managed to avoid involvement, in battle action at least. One could not avoid the impact of slavery or the war on the whole of America. After the war, there were freed slaves who sought work in the north at manufactories like ours. Many companies saw the glut of workers as an opportunity for profit, to offer lower wages. Joseph saw it as an opportunity to acquire the most talented workers. He was adamant that we not exploit the black man."

"Joseph?" Lavinia lifted a brow. "Joseph Phillips?"

"Yes." Arthur chuckled. "He appears gruff on the outside but inside he has a heart of gold. He's from a laboring class background; he knows what it is to be exploited. We decided to pay according to level of skill and not color of skin." He sighed. "We lost some good white men that way but we also convinced others of the evils of such prejudice."

"And you made a handsome profit."

His grin showed off his pride. "We did, I will admit. But it got me thinking about what's been going on in my own country. So I read Marx and Engels."

"Oh my. Is the Earl of Petersham a communist?"

"I hardly think so. Perhaps a bit of a Radical. My association with Joseph changed me. It's definitely not in my blood. My father finds extending any sort of rights to the working man a bit shocking."

"As do many peers." She smiled. "But you'll discover that eventually when you join the House of Lords."

"I hope to delay that inevitability for as long as I can. I eschew politics. I leave that up to my solicitor."

"Mr. Peel?" It was very difficult to forget the excessively tall man.

"Yes. Geoffrey keeps the partnership abreast of any changes in the law we need to concern ourselves about."

"Well, I do know at least one Radical in Lords. The Earl of Ryburgh. I can make the introductions. He'll be a good ally when the two of you are colleagues."

"I take it you follow politics?"

"Oh, I do. Most assiduously."

"Ah. My father will be glad to know we are acquainted then. Perhaps you can be of assistance when I attempt to effect change in the hallowed halls of Parliament." There was that twinkle again.

She laughed. "So we are meant to discuss our roles as godparents. Have we decided what we shall tell the bishop, my lord?"

"That we shall guide the child to be one who will 'walketh uprightly, worketh righteousness, and speaketh the truth in his heart'."

"Very good. Quoting scripture should put us in his good graces." She boldly wrapped her arm around his. "Up ahead is the gatehouse. You can discuss your Radical politics with Mason. He's been very subtle in his strategy to gain power for the working man. Well, one working man in particular, I suppose." And Mason would be impressed to see her with a handsome man on her arm.

Lavinia sat on the window seat in the Atherley library, staring blankly through the stained glass. Here and there lost pieces of color had been replaced with clear, offering a view of the gardeners on the estate. Inside the vast stone room, the deafening silence was dampened by rows of bookcases where once were pews. It was brilliant how one of the earls had seen fit to recast the Gothic chapel into a library during the age of enlightenment and reason.

She had spent the better part of the day discussing religion, politics and history with Arthur and Mason. The former butler, now steward, somehow seemed younger than his sixty-odd years as he effused about the plans for the buildings and property, and especially about how clever and good-natured Nicholas was with the entire project. Mason had been waiting for the opportunity to bring life back to Atherley Keep. It was ironic that such life could only be effected by the deaths of the former occupants.

And over an impromptu luncheon, Mason had lauded the new countess and how eager he was to meet the rest of her family. Arthur seemed very pleased with the man.

Lavinia sighed. One problem with house parties, even ones as small as this, was that she never got sufficient time to be alone with her thoughts. And she needed to be alone with her thoughts after having spent so much time with Arthur. She was inexplicably drawn to him. Of course, he was handsome and witty so most women would find him alluring. But there was something else, something familiar, as if they had always known each other.

At least he was doing a very good job of distracting her from nagging memories of Julius and inappropriate thoughts about Nicholas.

The library door clicked open.

Nicholas entered, surprise flitting over his countenance when he spied her. "Vinny. I didn't know you were here. I can come back another time."

She patted the seat next to her. "It's your house, Nicky. Sit."

He thinned his lips. "I know that look. You want to be alone."

Funny how some memories clung to the minds of old lovers. "I can spare a few moments with you."

He sat next to her on the banquette a little too close for her fragile emotions. But his warmth was welcome nonetheless. She would simply have to deflect her body's stirrings with words.

"You and Helena appear to be happy."

He grinned. "It's glorious, wonderful. I cannot explain it. As if there's a ball of pure joy burning within me. Whenever I see her, it sparks and flares. When we're apart, it smolders, waiting for the next time I see her."

"So you're smoldering now."

"Ha! I am. And I have you to thank for it." He wrapped his arm around her shoulder. "She's in the solar with Arthur, writing to her grandmother."

"I've noticed you don't refer to him as Petersham."

"He insists on the use of his Christian name. And he's always been 'Uncle Arthur' to Helena." He chuckled. "But I can't call Mr.

Phillips anything but Mr. Phillips. There's something so formidable about him that inhibits me despite his urging."

"I heartily agree." *Formidable* was a good descriptor for the man.

He squeezed her shoulder. "I'm so glad you're family now."

The squeeze became a caress along her arm, the delicate strokes shooting straight to her sex. Against her better judgment she relaxed into him. "How do you mean?"

He burrowed his nose in her hair and breathed in. "The godmother of my first child." His exhale was hot on her neck.

"Nicky, don't." Her protest was meek.

He licked along her pulse point, his tongue cooling her heated flesh. "Don't what?"

She turned to face him. "Don't tempt me in the public rooms of your house."

His smile was devilish. "Like you said, it's my house."

His lips lingered over hers for the briefest of moments, his eyes gauging her reaction. But she did not flinch, much to her consternation. She wanted him. Wanted someone at least, and Nicholas was right there in front of her.

His mouth was warm and inviting, his tongue delicately probing. He knew precisely where to hold her, to stroke her, his hands spanning her back, his thumbs teasing her nipples, inciting them to harden under her clothes.

But his wife was upstairs and workmen were just beyond the window. She pushed him off gently.

"Nicky, please. I don't think we should continue our affair."

"I wish I could have married both of you." The furrow in his brow heightened the earnestness of his words.

"And you can erase any fantasies of having us at the same time. I'm afraid I harbor no attraction for feminine delights, even with a beauty like Helena."

That got a chuckle out of him. He released his hold and leaned back. "Arthur seems interested."

Heat flushed her cheeks. "Did he tell you?"

"He didn't have to. He couldn't stop staring at your plunging neckline last night. Although neither could I."

Lavinia pressed her palm to her chest in a vain attempt to quell her thrumming heart. "One does not simply start an affair based on physical attraction. There has to be more."

"And is there?"

"What?"

Nicholas smirked. "Vinny, you just spent practically the entire afternoon with him."

"So I did." And so everyone noticed. "On my part yes, I will admit to an attraction."

"Ah, of course. You prefer the man to take the initiative." He leaned in. "You prefer to be seduced," he murmured in her ear.

He knew her too well. She would only let her own flirtation go so far then would pull back to see if the man was interested. If he persisted, she would give in.

The smirk deepened. "I'll see what I can do."

She rounded on him. "Nicky, don't you dare."

He held up his hands. "Don't worry. I won't. I don't think he needs any coaxing. He's probably just being polite. Especially in front of his niece."

"Thank you."

He took her hand in his. "But there is something you should take note of. A peculiarity about the house. It seems there used to be quite a bit of bed hopping a hundred or more years ago. Especially amongst the guests."

"Oh?" Intriguing.

"You'll find a hidden door in the paneling of your room, which connects to the neighboring bedroom via a private passageway. What's most extraordinary about this arrangement is that the doors can only lock on your side. So while you have access to the neighboring bedroom, it is not reciprocated."

"And who, pray tell, is sleeping in the neighboring bedroom, Nicky?"

"Arthur."

"Of course. And does the earl know about this hidden access?"

"No." His lips twisted in mirth. "I leave it up to you to tell him if the occasion arises."

She grimaced. It was too obvious.

"Don't blame me, Vinny. Helena got the idea from Sophia." He drew a delicate circle in her palm with his finger. "My bedroom also connects to yours."

She jerked her hand away. "Nicky, stop."

He smiled and stood. "I'll leave you alone with your thoughts, Vinny." His gaze swept over her bosom. "I'll see you at dinner."

She watched as he left. Ever since her first affair—with Julius— she had never had to be the seductress. Even with the younger men she helped navigate through Society, something eventually ignited on their side and they were compelled to take her to bed. Julius had instilled the confidence in her to simply wait. Men would come to her.

This time though, she couldn't wait. Her heart still ached for Nicholas and that heartache had dredged up memories of Julius. She needed someone to take the heartache away.

She might have to seduce a man.

How on earth did one go about doing that?

London

Grace sighed heavily, breathing out the day, and closed her eyes, trying to imagine her limbs as buoyant balloons rather than the lead weights they actually felt like.

It was late. Afternoon had bled into evening. There had been too many patients and she had done what she could. She knew some basics—how to tell if a baby's cry meant the doctor needed to be seen right away or could wait another day. She could instruct in soothing simple rashes, could patch the scrapes on an overly enthusiastic boy. Simple tasks that left Julius with the patients most in need— symptoms of pregnancy, painful menses, women in hysterics, unexpected bleeding.

She still fielded the occasional query concerning Dr. Nicholas Ramsay. It had become rote to explain he had changed his name and become the Earl of St. Albans and, after a moment of surprise on the part of the patient, to go through a litany of affirmations, including how she was sure he was happy being an earl and living on his estate with his pretty wife.

Except Dr. Ramsay—or Atherley or whatever he preferred—had seemed so happy as a doctor. And Julius had never been overworked with Nicholas around.

Julius was with his last patient of the day in the smaller examination room, the room with his device. The main examination room had been left in disarray so Grace set about putting it in order. Julius had uncharacteristically left his notebooks strewn on the desk and jars of herbs on the counter. She stacked the notebooks in a neat pile and put the jars back into the cupboard. She'd have to check for needed replenishments in the morning. She didn't want to do any more work. She just wanted Julius to be finished with his patient so she could take him upstairs and make him eat something. Far too often he got so involved in his work he'd forget to eat.

From the next room came a woman's surprised yelp of sensual satisfaction. The whir of the vibrating machine stopped. Grace waited for Julius' "good evening", the rap of the patient's heels in the hallway, the click of the latch in the front door.

Grace found him seated on the low stool before the examination table, leaning against the end between the metal stirrups, his head resting on the padded top.

She offered a hand to help him up. "Jules, you need your supper."

He emitted a low chuckle as he took her hand between his. "I'll be fine." He rubbed her palm then brought it to his lips, his kiss sparking a much-needed jolt of energy. He patted the edge of the table. "Come sit with me for a moment."

She hopped onto the table between the stirrups. He bunched her skirts up over her knees then leaned back against her, wrapping his arms around her dangling legs.

"We should take a holiday."

"A holiday?" What a peculiar notion. "And what would your patients do while you're away?"

He chortled as he caressed her calves above her boots. "Have you ever been to the seashore?"

"No. Only the banks of the Thames." She bent over to stroke his hair. "I've heard stories though. I'd love to see the ocean one day."

He tickled the backs of her knees then circled his hands to tantalize the tops of her thighs. "I know a lovely place in Penzance, on the Cornwall coast."

She kissed the top of his head. "That sounds wonderful, Julius." It would be a dream come true.

He stood and gathered up her skirts farther then lifted one of her legs to settle it on the stirrup. "Just you—" He did the same with the other leg. "And me."

She lay splayed open before him, incredulous at the idea. Just the two of them. Alone.

He loosened the tie of her drawers then slid his fingers along the fabric of the opening to the crotch, pulling the two halves of the garment apart.

He stared at her sex and licked his lips. He saw women's privates all day yet would still look at hers with marvel. This time there was something else, his wide-eyed expression tinged with a ravenousness that sent a shiver of anticipation through her. He stroked the hair covering her mons then urged the folds of her flesh open with his thumbs. He sat on the stool, his face so close to her his breath blew hot on her quim.

He lowered his head even closer. And then he did something he had never done before. He licked her.

Grace jumped. He gripped her calves against the metal stirrups, holding her steady as his tongue slid through her slit. He teased her clitoris with flicks of his velvety tip, shooting shards of pleasure to stab at her core.

He feasted with mouth and tongue and she succumbed, melting before him in a sensual puddle. She writhed, encouraging him, his expert ministrations heightened by the tickling strands of his beard and his knowledgeable touch. He lifted his head with a groan of admiration then pulled back the hood of her clit and nibbled on the sensitive bud.

She thrashed on the table, jerking her hips. He answered by delving his tongue deep inside her, thrusting and licking, easing her into submission before he once again returned to tormenting the excited nubbin.

He knew how to take her to the peak, let her slide back down and take her to the heights once again. It was glorious but, oh, so maddening.

"Julius…please…" She pleaded for satisfaction. He liked it when she begged.

He plunged three fingers into her flexing cunt, palpating her slick walls as he sucked hard on her yearning clit. She was delirious from his touch, dizzy from lack of breath. Was she moaning? She must be. He loved her moans and he was chuckling against her, the vibrations tormenting her further, driving her more quickly toward culmination.

She screamed her climax and bucked up, but he persisted, drinking the wetness of her release, his hands under her butt, holding her against him.

She shuddered an exhale. He let her down gently onto the table.

She wanted to ask why he did such a thing when he had never done so before. But Julius was mysterious, impenetrable at times and often answered vaguely. She'd mark his words, his actions—maybe ask him later when they were lying in bed.

He circled around to the head of the table, wiping his lips, a faraway twinkle lighting his eye. "Now let's go see what Mrs. Jennings has prepared for our supper."

His countenance was that of a man already thoroughly slaked.

"Yes, Julius, let's."

CHAPTER EIGHT

St. Albans

Lavinia leaned her head against the wood paneling of her bedroom entryway, willing her nerve to quash her better judgment. Nicholas was beastly to have riled up her senses with a kiss that afternoon, to perpetuate the memory of his seduction in London over a month ago and the memory of their affair last year.

To have stirred up memories of her disastrous affair with Julius, a man she fell in love with so hard, she'd let him get away with murder.

She shuddered and pulled the collar of her dressing gown more tightly around her. She swore she would never let a man take possession of her emotions like that again, yet here she was gliding stealthily down a darkened hallway, hoping for a glimpse of one such man, a glimpse of that man and his wife. A glimpse, he had reminded her, of what she might have had.

A few lamps glowed in the corridor of the bedroom wing, enough to discern which door led where. Each suite had two doors.

The one flush with and matching the hall paneling opened into the sitting room. A set of slender, gilded double doors set back in an alcove marked entry to a bedroom. Not only did this ensure bedroom privacy by being separated by a public room, it seemed an ingenious way to mark an otherwise monotonous hallway with both decoration and practicality. Servants and guests would know exactly what to expect behind a closed door.

Or what to hope for.

The newly well-oiled knobs and latches would be silent should one dare to enter through the bedroom doors. Or open them just enough to engage in a bit of peeping on one's former lover.

Luckily the doors to Nicholas and Helena's bedroom had been left ajar. The newlyweds must have been in a hurry to further celebrate their wedded bliss.

Lavinia knelt down on the hall carpet and peered through the crack between the doors. Framed by the elegantly carved and gilded wood was a scene of beautiful sensuality. Haloed by the glow of oil lamps Helena rode Nicholas, straddling him back to front, her very pregnant belly protruding in Lavinia's direction. Nicholas pushed into her from below, holding her steady at her waist. She gasped and stilled then let out a little cry. He raised himself up to cradle her body in his finely sculpted arms, lifting her as he folded his legs underneath to gain more leverage. As he rocked into her from behind, one gloriously masculine hand cupped a breast while the other reached between her legs, his finger stroking as she writhed, his lips whispering unheard obscenities.

They were two people sharing love and joy, who were meant to be together, the joining of their perfect bodies utterly riveting, utterly engrossing.

Utterly private.

Still Lavinia could not rip her gaze away.

Guilt shirred her flesh as she slid her hand under her dressing gown, over her nightdress to fondle her clit, imagining Nicholas' touch, rocking her hips as if he were driving into her from behind—

"*What the devil is going on?*"

She jumped at Arthur's hiss, tumbling backward to the carpet. He grabbed her around the waist, lifting her quite readily, hauling her down the corridor. His anger was palpable, his fingers digging into her side, the knuckles of his other hand white as he clutched a book.

He slammed her against the wainscoting of a recessed doorway, threw the book to the floor and dug the heels of his palms painfully into her shoulders.

"What the hell do you think you were doing?"

His breath fanned hot on her lips, the hint of tobacco and brandy flaring her nostrils.

She struggled to extricate herself from his cruel grip. He ground a hip against her. Her bones ached against the hard wood.

"Do you make a habit of watching my niece in intimate situations, Lady Foxley-Graham?" His lips grazed her ear.

"Arthur, please, it's not what you think."

He grunted darkly. "Then tell me what it is I should think."

"I wasn't watching Helena."

He loosened his hold only slightly, his body still trapping hers.

"No?" His gaze darted back and forth as he searched her face barely an inch away. "Then what—?" His lips tightened. "Nicholas." It was a realization.

"Yes." She nodded.

He relaxed his grip and eased back. "You were his lover."

She couldn't look him in the eye. "Yes."

He lifted her chin and met her gaze. "Does Helena know?"

His expression had softened to one of concern. For his niece's heart perhaps.

"Of course. It began long before they met. Before he became earl. When he was just Nicky."

His hands trailed down her arms and stopped at her waist. "I should have known." One hip continued to pin her against the wall. Except the formerly brutal action blossomed with new intent.

His thumbs traced the curve of her waist, prickling the peaks of her breasts under the fine cambric of her nightgown. Unbidden she reached up to finger the slick satin at the collar of his smoking jacket.

"It was abhorrent, I know. Absolutely horrid of me," she babbled, trying to tamp down the heat welling between her legs. "I should not have violated their privacy. But their door was open and I just, I mean, when I saw Nicky, I, well, it's not as if I want him back, I—"

"Shh, shh—" He cupped her cheek and smoothed her hair. His gaze fell to her mouth.

"I just want to feel again."

His lips lay hot on her forehead. Tears burned down her cheeks as he continued farther, pecking tenderly at her mouth, softening her. She opened under him, needing him, wanting him, somehow remembering him. His tongue found its way inside her as he pulled her more closely to him. She clung to his strength, yielding to him, twining her tongue with his, mewling her satisfaction.

Abruptly he pulled back, staring at her incredulously.

"It was you."

"Me?" She gaped in distress. "What do you mean?"

"Countess Winthrop's." His breaths puffed raggedly. "My odalisque. My God. You're my odalisque."

Disbelief tightened her lungs. "The sultan." Her heart pounded. "You were the sultan."

He traced a finger around her lips. "You made that very same sound."

"What sound?"

"A moaning sigh when you kiss."

"I do not."

He chuckled. "We'll just have to ask Nicholas about that." He stroked her hair. "Or we could continue what we were doing and you could pay more attention."

His mouth descended on hers once again, sweeping her away to a blissful state of mouth on mouth, tongue tangling with tongue, his hands stroking and caressing everywhere, hers clutching and tugging, her senses reeling in satisfied indulgence, a moan rumbling within—

"Damn you, Petersham."

He grinned. "I swore I would find you." He unfastened her dressing gown, his fingers trembling. "I dreamed of this moment every damn day." He trailed kisses down her neck as he pulled the robe slightly off her shoulders and began unbuttoning the placket of her nightgown. "And I frigged myself practically every damn night, fantasizing about these glorious globes." He yanked aside the linen and lace to uncover one breast, gaping as he palmed it, sweeping his thumb over her nipple until it puckered in excitement. "Perfection," he sighed then drew the tip into his mouth.

She arched against the wall, allowing him more access, the wet heat of his mouth tantalizing more than just her yearning peak, its pleasure tugging and teasing her clit. He kneaded her other breast before attending to its crinkled tip, wetting the fabric of her nightgown as he sucked eagerly. She held his head steady, needing his attentions, needing the reminder of a memory that had thrilled her, left her satisfied, left her hopeful.

"What else did you fantasize about, my lord?" She rocked her hips, hinting at further fulfillment.

"I think you know, my lady." He scrunched up her nightgown, tucking it behind her.

She fumbled with his trousers, his drawers, pulled off his jacket and one strap of his braces to free his cock. He was iron-hard, as ready as she.

He rammed inside her in one movement, his groan mingling with her sigh. She gripped his shoulders and wrapped a leg around his hips, seeking purchase as he drove into her, his pace frenzied, a man in need of release. She climaxed around him, wanting more, undulating her hips to take him deeper, bracing herself against the wall.

With a gravelly curse, he crushed his weight against her and pulled out, splattering his emission on the paneling below. He scooped her up in his arms and carried her into the bedroom, her bedroom, kicking the door closed.

He put her down then slipped off her robe, letting it fall to the floor. He lifted the hem of her nightgown and pulled it off over her head.

Lavinia gasped. She stood bare before him.

He picked her up again and lay her on the bed, stretching himself over her.

"I fear I was overly excited, my lady." He kissed her face, her neck. "Will you forgive me?"

"I will grant you the opportunity to redeem yourself."

He chuckled as he tickled her with kisses over her breasts, down her waist, across her hip, along the top of her thigh. He licked his lips as he parted the thatch of hair before him. "My penance is your pleasure." He pressed the wet heat of his mouth to her clit.

Lavinia yelped in delight, wriggling her pelvis in encouragement. His tongue was absolute heaven and relentlessly sought to wrest her bliss. She speared her fingers through his hair, gripping the strands as he coaxed her toward ecstasy.

He was too good.

Her orgasm released a deluge of pent-up desire as she bucked against his greedy mouth. He stayed there for her as she came down from the heights then tore himself away from the bed.

He stripped completely. Impossibly he was hard again, his cock bobbing provocatively as he gazed down at her. "You of all women."

She offered a quizzical expression.

"I'm a lucky man."

"How so?"

"I rather like you out of bed as well." He stretched out at her side and skated his fingers across her flushed skin. "A man of my age is usually not so vigorous." He continued to the hair at her mons, delving into the sticky wetness to massage her clit. "But when given the opportunity to be with the woman of his dreams—" He lengthened over her, opening her thighs with his knees. "He becomes as a youth again."

He plowed into her, the force of his desire melting her into the mattress. This was the seduction she craved. With every plunge she forgot Nicholas, with every ragged breath she forgot Julius. With every groan she remembered the sultan, with every caress she remembered Arthur.

He pulled out, aiming at the mattress between her legs. She grabbed his cock, the ecstasy in his eyes fading to wonder as he came in hot jets on her stomach.

He crashed to her side, panting. "Good God, Lavinia. You are better than a dream." He wrapped an arm around her.

She nuzzled in the crook of his arm, his heart thudding in her ear, his seed oozing down her belly. "Stay with me."

He kissed her hair. "Unfortunately, I fear it impolitic for me to stay the whole night."

"Like in Countess Winthrop's library."

"I had to. You know that." His tone held regret.

"I do and I forgive you." She pulled away to scramble under the covers. "A few moments of indulgence before you leave. There's a secret passageway to your bedroom, you know."

His sharp guffaw pierced the air. "Truly?"

"The dream gets better, doesn't it, my lord?"

He adjusted the counterpane at her neck. "I shall leave through the front door to remove the evidence of our impulsiveness just outside. Before the maids discover the shocking sight."

"Ah yes." She giggled.

The book, the jacket and the proof of his desire were more new memories to dissipate the old.

For one brief moment the night before, Arthur had been utterly shocked to find the refined Lady Foxley-Graham peeping in on the privacy of a bedroom. Now his interest in the lady was thoroughly piqued. And his admiration for Nicholas deepened.

He was famished in the morning, as well as excited and nervous to see her. He was the first in the breakfast room, joined soon after by Nicholas then Helena.

Lavinia sauntered in a good hour later, smiling her "good morning" to Nicholas.

Admiration was tarnished by jealousy.

And then she met Arthur's gaze, her smile slimming timidly as her cheeks increased their rosy hue. She offered a subdued morning greeting before scooping out a generous serving of eggs. The jealousy dissolved.

He had to say something. He had to talk to her. It was killing him. "Lavinia," he managed, "it is such a splendid day. I thought we could take a stroll in the garden after breakfast. You know, to discuss our meeting with the bishop tomorrow."

"Oh, yes!" piped up Helena. "You must see the rose garden. The bushes are all pruned but you can still see the placards. Lavinia has a rose named after her."

"She does, does she?" He smiled at the viscountess, taking in her ensemble of yellow-orange, a jacket over a skirt with tiers and fringe. The buttons of the jacket only went so high, the neckline filled in with ivory lace.

Lavinia turned away, resuming her attention to her plate of food.

Helena continued, oblivious to the debauchery her uncle had been up to down the hall from where she slept. "If you want to see the rose in bloom, there's an etching in the library. It's lovely. A lavender purple variety."

"You may find it a bit rough out there," Nicholas said. "We're still completing some much-needed restorations to the formal gardens. In fact, darling," he said, turning to Helena, "I want your opinion on some plans from the landscape architect."

As the newlyweds continued chattering about estate renovations, Arthur stole a glance at Lavinia. Her lips curled demurely.

"Are you very interested in gardening, Lady Foxley-Graham?"

"Merely an amateur. I find it soothes me on those days when I feel slightly agitated." She flashed him a provocatively uplifted brow before returning to her breakfast.

The thought of soothing Lavinia made him incredibly hard. He cleared his throat and went back to his eggs, still surprised at his potency. "When can I expect to have the pleasure of your company?"

She smiled, her gaze flickering to Nicholas and Helena before returning to him. "After breakfast, I'll just need to retrieve my hat and gloves from my room."

Half an hour later, Arthur was walking arm-in-arm with Lavinia through the gardens of the Earl of St. Albans, well landscaped despite Nicholas' protests otherwise. And, indeed, there was a placard announcing the *Rosa Lavinia*.

"One day, I shall have the pleasure of seeing your rose in bloom. And what meaning does a lavender rose convey?"

Her lips twisted in some relived memory. "Enchantment and love at first sight."

"Really?"

"That's what the man who named it after me said."

"A man?"

"Absolutely. An earl I believe."

Oh she was cruel. He leaned in to murmur in her ear, "I'll have you know I will be marquess one day."

She did not turn to face him as a wicked smile curled her lips. "Which trumps earl."

Damn. Another lover. She was probably awash in them. But surely he was special?

"Lavinia, I meant it when I said I have been hoping to find you, find my odalisque. That night…I simply cannot express…" *God in Heaven* he could not express it. "You were so…the whole affair was so…perfect."

This time she did turn to face him, the wickedness replaced with delight. "It was, wasn't it?"

She had felt it too. His heart swelled. He wanted to kiss her but they were exposed. Beyond the garden was a stand of trees, offering more privacy. A bedroom would be best but how to casually saunter into a bedroom in the middle of the morning without raising suspicion? The trees would have to do.

As he steered her toward the copse, the delight in her eyes gradually darkened. She stopped and turned to him.

"My lord," she whispered, "please believe me when I say I don't normally have furtive encounters with strangers at social events. When I went to the masquerade I hadn't been with a man since Nicholas. Seeing him so happy with Helena at their wedding made me feel well, sorry for myself, I suppose. It was brash and daring."

Her remorse pierced his soul. "Tending to such needs is normal for those of us with lustful natures." He squeezed her arm.

She sucked in a shuddering breath. "It's acceptable for a man to feel regret when a lover leaves him and for him to act upon it." Tears glittered on her lashes. "But not for a woman. We're not supposed to even have lovers to begin with. Of course, we all do anyway. We just cannot be so open about it."

He fished for his handkerchief and handed it to her.

She accepted the small gesture and dabbed her eyes. "Thank you."

"The masquerade was brash and daring for me as well. Like you, I needed to feel something other than self-misery. The last mistress I had left me to care for her aging mother in her hometown up north where she eventually rekindled a romance with a childhood sweetheart. I just received notice of the christening of their first child."

She gaped at him. "You're serious?"

He smirked. "Yes, I'm serious."

She chuckled. "It's been longer for you than for me? And how is that possible for so handsome a man?"

He grinned at her flattery. "In truth? Because I'm tired of mistresses. I want a companion, a friend." He held her gaze. "A lover who is an equal."

"Arthur—"

He held up his hand. "I know what you are going to say, Lavinia. But I'm forty-four years old. I'm tired of the game. I want what I want. And I want you. I want to court you, to woo you."

"To court me?" Her cheeks colored.

"And everything that implies." Marriage. A life together. God his cock was hard.

She smiled. "Just remember I like roses. Lots of them."

"'Each morn a thousand roses brings'."

"Poetry as well? Such a gallant."

"We met over a poem. *The Rubaiyat of Omar Khayyam* if you remember."

"I will never forget, my sultan."

He indicated the clump of trees. "'With thou beside me singing in the Wilderness, Wilderness becomes Paradise'."

He offered his left arm and she took it with an uncharacteristically shy glimpse from under lowered lids.

Could she feel his heart pounding? She said nothing and stared straight ahead as they promenaded toward the grove. He wanted instead to grab her hand and run, to let the wind tear off his hat as they bounded through the garden, laughing.

Finally they were amidst the grove, in the shelter of birch trunks and their shadows. He pulled her to him, their bodies fitting together perfectly as he kissed her. She tore off her gloves and threaded her fingers through his hair, sending his hat tumbling to the ground. Could it be true that this woman wanted him as much as he wanted her? He pulled back from the kiss but she held his head steady as she leaned in for more, unafraid to take her pleasure. She tasted like…possibilities.

And then she gazed up at him, her eyes glassy, her cheeks pink, her features softened with contentment. "Arthur, last night was liberating."

Liberating was a good word. "I know. I feel as a man half my age."

She cupped his crotch, tracing the hard length within between two fingers. "Your body is responding like a man half your age."

He couldn't stop smiling. "I was prepared to kiss every English woman of a certain age and—" He glanced at her bosom. "*Shape* to find you." He fumbled with the ribbon of her bonnet.

"I knew Sophia and Joseph were acquainted with the sultan but I was too afraid to ask. What if you were a married member of Parliament? Or a Catholic priest?"

"Or the Bishop of St. Albans?" Her bonnet off, he smoothed his palms over her chignon.

She laughed. "That would have been awkward."

He leaned against a trunk and drew her to him, her back to his chest. He wrapped his arms around her and buried his nose in the crook of her neck. Her scent of roses and lavender was subtle; a man would have to be intimate to notice. That he was her intimate quickened the beat of his heart and tormented his prick.

"How should an earl woo a viscountess?" he murmured.

"We will make appearances at certain events this Season." She melted against him. "You will escort me to all the fashionable balls, the opera, the ballet, the Summer Exhibition. You will never be seen to leave my house except during regular calling hours. Our mutual intentions will be made clear by such discretion."

He trailed his tongue along the heated pulse point of her neck. "And when do I get to fuck you, my lady?"

She turned in his arms to face him. "Whenever you wish, my lord. Just not in public." She delicately sucked on her lower lip.

Finally a London Season where he would have some fun. He kissed her thoroughly, her mouth soft and acquiescing. He unbuttoned her jacket top. "'Ah, Love! could thou and I with Fate conspire, To grasp this Scheme of Things entire'."

"The *Rubaiyat* again?"

"Of course."

"Don't quote that around the bishop."

"I don't care what the bishop thinks now I have you." The neckline of her corset cover was not as plunging as what she wore to dinner yet offered enough of her to ravish. He cupped her breasts and lay possessive kisses on her shoulder.

She moaned his name as she unbuttoned his waistcoat. "Perhaps it was fate, perhaps it was destiny, perhaps—" She stopped undressing him. "Sophie," she drawled, devoid of sensuality.

He sighed. "I was pleasantly erect and you have to mention my sister?"

She thinned her lips. "Who chose your sultan's costume?"

"I did. I wore it the year before to the masquerade."

One corner of her mouth quirked up. "So the Earl of Petersham is a regular denizen of clandestine sexual festivities?"

"Countess Winthrop is a good friend of mine," he protested.

"You don't have to use euphemisms around me, darling. If she was your lover, just say so."

"And how do you know the countess is not currently my lover?"

"Because she only retains her lovers briefly and never continues with any of them after they've attended one of her balls. I also know she is not actually a countess."

"You seem to know a great deal about her."

"I made inquiries before I accepted the invitation. I am not generally acquainted with the habitués of the demi-monde."

"Have I just been insulted?" He feigned a pout.

"Not at all." She patted his chest. "You're a man. You're allowed a wide breadth of acquaintances. So you wore the costume the year before. Did Sophie know?"

"Yes."

She laughed softly. "It was she who suggested my costume, even helped with designing it. And it was she who invited me."

He grinned. "Then I will have to thank my sister for looking out for my interests when she arrives."

"Along with your parents."

"You really know how to thwart a man's ardor, don't you?"

"They may be somewhat shocked to discover their son has been carrying on an affair in their granddaughter's house."

"Ah, yes."

"So let's keep it secret until the Season. Your mother won't object to a formal courtship."

"You are good at this. I had only heard rumors."

She laughed and tugged on his now-opened waistcoat. "I'm a woman. I must abide by Society's rules." The heat of her hand surrounded his cock.

Shit, she *was* good. He had not noticed she had unbuttoned his fly. Her thumb smoothed over his glans, wetting it as she gripped the shaft.

"I'd rather be inside you," he said against her mouth.

She leaned in to graze her lips across his cheek. "And I want to frig you, my lord."

All sensation pooled at his crotch as she fingered him delicately. He grabbed her waist and rested his forehead against her shoulder. She pumped slowly, her touch steady, her strokes expert and when he murmured her name, her movements began in earnest, jerking him swiftly, rendering him insensible, his knees trembling to keep him from crashing to the ground. Her scent teased his nostrils, her rapid breaths taunted his ears, her very presence sent him to the realm of recent memory when her hot, wet mouth encircled his prick, when he fucked her on a red velvet divan—

Suddenly, he was with her in the present, in the moment before explosion. "Darling," he protested.

"Shh, shh. Let go."

He came in her hand, into his handkerchief she still clutched. He looked up to find her gazing at him with wide eyes and flushed cheeks.

He too was awestruck. This woman—where had she been all his life?

London

Julius leaned his head against his arm, resting on the mantel, and stared into the library hearth. One speck of coal still glowed albeit fitfully, in a valiant effort to not extinguish yet useless in the face of inevitability.

It had been precisely like that for his cock not an hour before.

Oh, he had been eager to fuck her, but deep inside nervousness had burbled until it boiled over into frustration. The last time he had experienced such a sensation he had been a green lad of sixteen. It had been his first time and the nervousness made him come too quickly. Over thirty years later, it meant he could not come at all. He could barely maintain his vigor.

And yet he still burned for Grace.

The door to the library clicked shut.

"Well, here you are then."

Grace strode forward to meet him and held out her hand. She wore a dressing robe over her nightgown and clutched a shawl over everything. He took her hand in his. Her fingers were frigid, like ice. Such a chill could be harmful to the—to her in her condition. He pulled her against his body, wrapping his arms around her, trapping her hands between them.

"You shouldn't be out of bed. It's too cold in the house at this hour," he murmured against her hair.

"Jules, you're ignoring me."

He pulled back. "I'm right here. How could I be ignoring you?"

"I don't like how you just got up and left." She sighed into his chest. "It happens to more men than you might think and more often than you might think."

Ah, yes. Grace was not without experience. That was putting it mildly. Grace had had far too much experience probably before she had turned twenty. "I don't want to talk about it."

"But we need to talk about it if that's how you're going to react."

"There's nothing to say, Grace."

"All right then, you listen. If you can't make love to me one night, then that's just how it will be that night. The more you try the worse it will be." She gazed up at him, her expression barely discernible in the darkness. "I want you in bed beside me, not brooding alone."

He touched her cheek, the wetness of tears surprising him. "I think I've been tired of late. Overworked perhaps."

It was only a partial lie. They had been seeing far more patients recently but that had been his fault. An attempt to drive his attention away from the reality he refused to face. As if treating mothers-to-be could really serve such a purpose.

It was more like a reminder. And then he needed more distractions.

It was a bloody vicious circle.

"Can you suggest a colleague to some of the newer patients?"

That was the obvious solution, wasn't it? But then he and Grace would be forced to spend more time together. Eventually she would expect him to say something about…about her.

Why did the words come so easily when it was another man's woman, another man's child?

"So many of the new patients are expectant young women. Surely you know of a specialist?"

But he wanted to save all the babies, all of them, make sure each one of them was born healthy. He couldn't do that if another doctor saw them.

"And you're seeing fewer hysteria patients."

She'd noticed.

"I think that's not helping your state of arousal. I think you need more stimulation not less." She squirmed against him, freeing a hand to cup his crotch, to toy with his still-flaccid cock.

"Grace, you can't force it." The moment the words left his mouth, his cock stiffened ever so slightly.

"Yes I can, Jules. You're not a dead man yet." She slid her hand under the waistband of his trousers and grabbed his burgeoning erection.

He lowered his head to kiss her, catching her nose with his lips before finding her mouth. She giggled as she opened for him, her infectious joy filling his soul with hope.

No, he wasn't dead yet. Grace's determined grip was proving that, while inside her grew the promise of continued existence.

And now he was achingly hard, desperately needing to spend. "Let's to bed, Grace."

She offered one final squeeze with her hand, now warmed from her efforts. "Yes, Julius, let's."

In so many ways, Grace held the keys to his salvation. He needed to find the courage to tell her.

CHAPTER NINE

St. Albans

Arthur was quite pleased the meeting with the bishop went well. It ended with him and Lavinia promising to comfort and encourage their godchild and the bishop somehow interpreting this as keeping the child on the straight and narrow path of faith. Nicholas and Helena were satisfied with the outcome and that was all that mattered.

Guests for Helena's birthday party began to arrive soon after. First was Nicholas' cousin, the Viscount Ravensburgh—Bertie, as Nicholas called him—along with an unexpected family friend, the Marquess of Norrington. The lack of refurbished bedrooms became evident but was quickly settled when the pair agreed to double up, a situation they both declared they were used to from their adventures abroad.

"Sometimes you simply cannot find a suitable set of rooms," Norrington had explained, "and you are obliged to sleep two abed in a farmhouse."

A few days later, Sophia and Joseph arrived, both glowing and happy, Joseph running after his very pregnant wife to cater to her every whim and need. It was endearing.

Sophia and Helena holed themselves up in the solar, chatting endlessly about baby clothes and names, pregnancy symptoms and changes. In bed one night, Lavinia grumbled how she was bored to tears.

"You could join the men in the parlor," Arthur suggested.

"Really? That would be so much more interesting. But I don't want to spoil your fun. You should feel free to talk about anything in front of me."

"I'm sure you imagine we talk about our former days as lotharios."

"Former?"

He chuckled. "Besides Ravensburgh and Norrington waxing poetic over the Italian sunshine, it's mostly business, or Joseph interrogating poor Nicholas about his plans for the future. They've bonded over the renovations."

Lavinia was grateful and Arthur was contented. It was the most comforting feeling in the world to have one's lover simply present in the same room, even if sometimes she read the newspaper or a book while he and Joseph discussed the business of railway parts and Nicholas and Mason poured over architectural drawings.

And then at night he would go to her room, a feat accomplished by the secret corridor and Nicholas and Helena's obvious strategizing. Their lovemaking was made all the more profound by the foresight of the ever-astonishing Lavinia. She had packed a Dutch cap, allowing Arthur to experience the full intensity of his crisis.

Arthur did not ask why the lady had brought the prophylactic to a family gathering. If she had thought to seduce Nicholas upon arrival, she had no notion of it now. Arthur saw to that every night as he worshiped her body, her fleshy arse like pillows under his kneading fingertips, her luscious breasts overflowing his palms and so succulent in his mouth, her breathy moans and restrained cries of ecstasy urging him forward, the rapid rhythm of her pounding heart mingling with his own as he collapsed over her body slaked and spent.

The words *I love you* dancing precariously on the tip of his tongue with every climax…

Despite having to arise and return to his own bed before the housemaid laid the fire, for a few days Arthur's life was pure bliss.

And then his parents arrived.

Helena, of course, was overjoyed to see her Grandmama and Grandpapa and Mother especially seemed to be in heaven among her fruitful progeny. But Father had different ideas about how one should spend one's afternoon and it wasn't with a lady present in the room.

As Lavinia read *The Herts Advertiser and St Albans Times* in the parlor, possibly looking a tad too comfortable on the sofa, Father scowled in her direction from his position by the window.

"Lady Foxley-Graham—"

Lavinia looked up from her paper.

"At the time of our introduction at the wedding breakfast, I had thought your name sounded familiar. It has taken me some time to remember how it is I might know you. You're one of those women's righters, aren't you?"

"My lord?"

"The women's property bill a decade ago. You and Ryburgh claimed it would help poor women."

"I believe the legislation has helped working women hold on to their income in the face of profligate husbands."

Father grunted as he returned to the view out the window. "Just don't expect me to give women the right to vote. That's what husbands are for."

Every man present in the parlor looked up at that.

Lavinia folded her paper deliberately. "And what about the women who lack husbands?"

"They can jolly well go get one if they want a say in politics." Father rocked on his heels. "A woman should know her place."

After a few private words between Father and Nicholas, the latter clearly trying not to unsettle the still-new familial accord, Lavinia was relegated back to the realm of the women.

That she hated it was terribly present in the bedroom. As Arthur cradled her in his arms during afterglow, his heart swelling with masculine possessiveness as he cupped a generous breast, he assured her he held no such outmoded beliefs. He refrained from stating the obvious: if he were her husband, he would rely on her good opinion and knowledge of politics for his vote.

Despite such disquietude, Helena's birthday party was a success. During the toast, she divulged that her birthday wish had been for her parents and grandparents—and uncle—to continue their efforts toward reconciliation and she was so happy her wish had been granted. Mother had stated that the impending births of their second grandchild and first great-grandchild would certainly lay to rest any remaining animosity.

Champagne flowed freely in the drawing room after dinner, lightening the mood of all present and loosening tongues. Mother's tongue especially.

"Arthur, the Season will soon be upon us. It's time you took the job of being a marquess's heir seriously." Her voice was far too loud.

Arthur cringed. This was either about politics or marriage. He glanced at Lavinia across the room laughing with Ravensburgh.

"How so, Mother?" He kept his voice low, hoping Mother would follow suit.

She did not. "Marriage and an heir."

Shit. Luckily Lavinia did not hear. "I don't think this is the proper time and place to discuss this, Mother," Arthur hissed.

"And why not? We're all family." She surveyed the room. "Or at least on intimate terms like family."

"I don't think the entire family needs to hear about your plans for my marriage."

"Nonsense. I've made up a list of some eligible candidates for you to meet during the Season."

Arthur downed his champagne.

"And I understand Lady Foxley-Graham has a wide circle in Society." She beckoned Lavinia over with a wave and a smile. "I'm sure she can be of help."

"Lady Richmond," Lavinia greeted, approaching in time to hear the last. "How can I be of assistance?"

"I was hoping you could lend your considered opinion on some eligible girls."

Lavinia glanced at Ravensburgh and Norrington—the only other unmarried men in the room. "Of course, Lady Richmond," she said politely. "For whom?"

Shit. Arthur gripped his glass.

"Arthur."

Lavinia paled.

Double shit.

All eyes focused in their direction. Arthur surveyed the room. Nicholas and Sophia looked the most distressed. But no one said a word.

"Now, my dear, I'm looking for well-connected girls, anything above a viscount's daughter. She must be pretty, educated and under twenty-five."

The room began to spin and it wasn't the champagne. Arthur sucked in a long breath.

And then Father approached. "And fecund." He turned to Nicholas. "You were once a doctor, St. Albans. How can we be assured a young woman is capable of providing us with an heir?"

Nicholas cleared his throat. "Well," he began slowly, "it is necessary to know if both parties are, as you said, fecund."

"Oh, but we know Arthur can sire children," Mother said with uncharacteristic vulgarity.

Arthur caught a glimpse of Lavinia. She was stoic, her expression unreadable.

Wide-eyed horror flitted across Nicholas' face. "I suppose most young women are capable of...of childbearing," he sputtered, collecting himself. "Although to be absolutely certain there would have to be children already, perhaps from a previous marriage."

"A young widow?" Mother said as if she hadn't actually considered all the possibilities.

"And if such a woman already had children," Nicholas added, "perhaps Arthur could adopt his heir."

As a new peer, Nicholas still had much to learn.

"Adopt?" Father barked. "Nonsense. The letters patent state 'heirs male of the body'. Succession by adoption may be allowed in those foreign lands you've traveled to, my boy, but not in England."

Lavinia's pallor turned absolutely peaked. Nicholas went to her side. "Vinny, you've finished your champagne. Shall I pour you another?"

She turned to him as if startled from a dream. "Thank you, my lord. But no. I fear I need a bit of fresh air."

She handed her glass to Nicholas then left the room.

Annoyance at his family and concern for his lover prickled Arthur's flesh. He couldn't follow her. It would be too obvious. He'd have to wait.

Mother was oblivious to Lavinia's emotions. "Your father was just reminiscing about the Earl of Ryburgh. If I recall correctly, he has five daughters. The middle one, Lady Beatrice Smythe, will be eighteen I believe."

He was going to be sick.

"This will be her first Season."

He had to get out of there. "Mother, thank you," he said dripping charm. "I'm sure Lady Beatrice Smythe is lovely. However I need to excuse myself for a moment."

Luckily a woman in a dinner gown was not as quick as a man rambling through Atherley Keep. Arthur spied Lavinia entering the library and followed.

He found her outside in the former porch of the Gothic chapel, now a forecourt with sweeping views of the grounds. She stood facing the vista, her arms wrapped around herself, her hands rubbing the bare skin above her elbows. He took off his jacket and placed it on her shoulders.

"Darling, that was inexcusable. I'm sorry you had to hear that."

"I should have known," she said hoarsely, containing a sadness that threatened to break forth. "Of course I should have known the bachelor Earl of Petersham needed to marry and produce an heir."

"Please don't."

"I was blinded by my own desires."

"I'll simply tell Mother and Father I have already made up my mind."

She rounded on him. "About what?"

"Marrying you."

She stared him in the eye. "Arthur, I'll be forty-six next month."

Shit. "I…I didn't realize. I had thought you Sophia's age. I suppose that's not so old."

"Trust me, it's old as far as this is concerned." She looked askance then closed her eyes and drew in a breath. "I've been spending quite a bit of time with Helena and Sophia and to be truthful, I cannot stand all the talk about babies and motherhood. And the more I listen to it the more I realize how ill-suited I would be for such a life."

"I suppose most women have those fears at first."

She glared at him. "You don't understand. I don't have any fears. I don't have any regrets. And I don't have any interest."

He wished he could be so unequivocal when it came to his parents. "What about marriage?"

She sighed. "I've always wanted to marry again. I just never found the right man."

"And now you have."

"And he is required to produce children." She shook her head. "Even if I did desire children I'm not sure I'm able to…" She trailed off with emotion.

He wrapped his arms around her. "Darling, I've found you. I'm not letting you go—"

"Arthur, your parents are against such a connection."

"There has to be someone somewhere in this blasted country in the line of succession."

Her forehead crinkled as her jaw dropped. "And?" She shook her head. "You are Richmond's heir. You cannot escape that."

She was his odalisque. There had to be a way. "I hate this. I didn't intend for this to be nothing more than an affair." He held her more tightly.

"An affair until you got married." Her voice quavered.

"No." He breathed her in, breathed in that scent only her lover would be privy to.

"But that's all it can be."

"Damn it." He huffed an exhale. "All right, an affair. A love affair." If that was all he could get, he'd take it.

"I need to think this through, Arthur." She stepped back and wiped a tear from her eye, her fingers shaking. "Lady Richmond knows something of your past," she said quietly, the quaver still clinging to her words. "Did the child die?"

A chill spiked his spine. "Yes. And its mother." He did not want to talk about any of that at the moment. "It was a very long time ago."

She smiled a thin-lipped smile, her eyes soft with her own regrets. "At our age everything was a very long time ago." She pulled his jacket from her shoulders and handed it to him. "And now I think I should like to hear about Viscount Ravensburgh's recent travels. You may escort me inside, my lord."

He shrugged into his jacket. "Of course, my lady."

He held out his arm and held his tongue. He was simply grateful for the warmth of her hand through his sleeve.

Lavinia dismissed Marie early. Once her corset was removed, she could finish undressing and dressing for bed by herself. Her lady's maid knew her moods by now. Lavinia just wanted to be alone with her thoughts.

That wasn't true. She wanted to be with Arthur. She needed to be with Arthur.

He should have been honest with her but then again, she was an experienced Society matron. She should have known familial duty would rear its ugly head at some point. Arthur had confessed months ago he had no children and she knew very well he was the heir to the Richmond Marquessate. She should have made the connection. Passion had blinded her.

More painful was that he was the best damn lover she had ever had. He lacked the wanton inventiveness of Julius, a lover whose excess could be painful to endure. Yet the creativity *was* there, mixed with all that was good about a man like Nicholas—a generosity toward pleasuring that did not forsake his own libidinous needs.

Arthur Harwell was the antidote to her melancholia.

But seeing him married would only plunge her further into despair.

Still, thanks to their host and hostess, they had the perfect circumstances under which to conduct an affair. For the remainder of their time at Atherley Keep, if all she could have was a love affair, so be it. Last year, she had done the same with Nicholas until he was married off. This time she would guard her heart while she was satisfied in bed.

She had left the party early, Arthur still seemingly agitated—with her or with the situation, she wasn't quite sure. The party would be breaking up by now—Sophia and Helena always retired early, as did the Richmonds. Arthur was probably having one final drink or smoke with the younger men.

She took off the rest of her underthings and put on a dressing gown. She opened the adjoining door and slid into the tiny corridor, offering silent gratitude to Nicholas for the arrangements. She listened at the door to Arthur's bedroom. It was quiet on the other side. If he was already sleeping or not yet in bed, either way it would be a surprise. He always came to her.

She opened the door slowly. The room was dark, the glow of moonlight and a sliver of light under the door to the sitting room announcing the bedroom was unoccupied. The indistinct words of masculine voices and the scent of pipe tobacco indicated Arthur was having a late night conversation with Joseph.

So she would wait for him. She slipped off her robe and stole naked under the covers. The sheets smelled like him, his soap, his cologne. She reached between her legs, stroking gently. Just the idea of him aroused her. She wrapped herself tightly under the counterpane then let fantasy overtake her as she fell asleep.

Joseph took a swig of brandy then rested his head in the crook of the wingback in Arthur's sitting room. Before him Arthur paced, his striped silk dressing robe flicking open every time he turned, exposing his flamboyant paisley pajama bottoms, the exotic flavor of his fashion at odds with the clean lines of the Neoclassical decor. Arthur toyed with his empty pipe then flung it onto the mantel with a huff.

Joseph understood his friend's frustration. Arthur's future was no longer his own. The Harwell legacy had finally come calling.

He crossed one leg on top of the other. It might be best to lighten the mood. "So…younger than twenty-five. That'll keep you busy."

Arthur rounded on him. "Don't you start too. I don't want to hear any of it."

Joseph sobered. "Okay." He placed his glass on the polished side table.

"I should have known my sins would come back to haunt me." Arthur resumed his pacing.

"Your sins?"

"Of letting you and my sister marry for love. Speaking of which, shouldn't you be in bed with her by now?" he bit caustically.

"Sophie is sleeping with Helena tonight. They wanted to gab. That's why they've been retiring early of late."

Arthur eyed him. "You're not expecting to sleep with me tonight, are you?"

He quirked a brow suggestively. "Are you inviting me?"

"No," he shot back too quickly. "I have my own outlets. You'll have to be satisfied with your hand."

"Speaking of which, do you have that issue of *The Pearl* I loaned you?"

That got a chuckle out of him. "And where do you expect to read such salacious material? Surely not in one of the public rooms."

"I've set up the daybed behind a screen in our sitting room."

"With your daughter just beyond the door?"

"She's generally not in the habit of wandering about in the middle of the night." And the exotic nightwear Arthur had introduced him to made masturbating all the more discreet.

Arthur hunched over the fire, one arm on the mantel, and heaved a sigh.

Joseph went to him. "You should try to get some sleep."

Arthur traced the delicate curves of the carved bellflowers and urns in the marble mantelpiece. "Yeah."

He tenderly brushed Arthur's hair behind his ear. Arthur raised his head. The whites of his hazel eyes were tinged pink with pent-up emotion. Arthur was keeping something to himself—or rather *someone*. His legendary odalisque, most likely, and if he knew who she was by now, it was possible the woman was not what the Richmonds wanted in a daughter-in-law.

Joseph grazed a thumb along Arthur's stubble-roughened jaw to his lower lip. "I'll have a talk with Sophie tomorrow and she'll talk to Helena. Your father practically worships Helena. If anyone can convince him and Lady Richmond to be more considerate of your emotions, it's her."

"Thank you, Joseph." His indebted relief heightened his vulnerability. And his attractiveness.

Joseph leaned in. If Arthur wasn't in the mood, he'd push him away. But he didn't. Instead he waited for Joseph's lips to skim against his then flicked the tip of his tongue along the seam of Joseph's mouth.

The sign that Arthur wanted a bit of play. And Joseph could do with a bit of brown.

He plunged in, grappling Arthur around the shoulders to secure him for an open-mouth exploration. Arthur relented in his arms, offering himself like a virgin on her wedding night, gripping his torso for purchase, letting Joseph do what he wanted, what he desired. And what he wanted was the feel of hairy, muscular flesh.

Joseph untied the sash of Arthur's robe then tore away at the buttons up the front of his pajama top, revealing the sculpted form beneath. "I've missed this," he breathed as he ran his hand over the rippled abdomen, around the waist, sliding under the silk of the pajama bottoms to grip his firm butt.

Arthur gave a low chuckle and started in on Joseph's robe and pajamas, untying and unbuttoning. "Well you certainly know how to raise a man's spirits."

"Let's see what else I've raised." Joseph skimmed his hand along the ridge of Arthur's hip to find his cock. The smooth shaft was hard as stone.

Just like Joseph's.

It had been too long since their last fumble in the dark, although if he were being honest with himself it had simply been too long. He let go of Arthur's cock and rested his palm on the finely honed hip, leaning his bared chest against Arthur's, the feel of heated skin against heated skin lulling. Joseph muttered a satisfied oath.

"I take it your hand isn't quite satisfying?" Arthur said in amused sympathy.

"No." He slowly fisted Arthur's cock. "I haven't had a decent fuck in at least a month."

Arthur stilled his hand then leaned his forehead against Joseph's. "Look, if this were my house—"

Joseph let go. "Yeah I understand. I wouldn't want to shock the housemaid."

Arthur grinned.

"Except the housemaid has already been shocked by the likes of Ravensburgh and Norrington."

Surprise lit up Arthur's eyes. "You're joking."

"According to Sophia. She heard it from Helena who heard it from Nicholas."

"They are quite a pair, are they not? Young, handsome, full of adventure."

"How we used to be." Joseph grasped Arthur's butt and ground his hips against him. He glided his tongue along the heated pulse in Arthur's neck, the fragrance of arousal filling Joseph's nostrils.

Arthur gently pulled free. "How we're not going to be tonight." He patted Joseph's cheek before turning back to the fire. "*The Pearl* should be on the bedside table." He pointed to the closed door.

He'd definitely need a toss later.

Joseph exhaled his temporary frustration as he opened the door to the bedroom. He crossed the carpet to the nightstand where the magazine lay neatly. The lamp and fire from the sitting room illuminated the unmade bed—

Which was odd, since Arthur hadn't had the chance to rumple the covers yet.

Joseph looked more closely. The bed wasn't unmade. There was someone in it. A female someone.

She was curled up in a ball, her back to him, her long dark hair spilling across the pillows. One very shapely leg poked out from beneath twisted sheets.

Arthur, you dog. No wonder he wouldn't give in.

But who? A servant? Had to be. Nicholas had hired a household full of beauties. The handsome Earl of St. Albans seemed to have attracted the cream of Hertfordshire to work at his estate.

She moved, stretching her nude foot out and in the process pulling down the covers, exposing a stunning curve of a backside and the swell of a breast half-hidden by her bent arm.

His waning cock stirred back to life and he adjusted it down the leg of his pajamas. It had been years since he and Arthur had shared a woman but that didn't mean they could never do so again. Surely Sophia wouldn't mind just this once. He could even run down the hall and ask her.

Or he could simply retrieve the magazine from the bedside table and tease Arthur mercilessly.

She stirred again, the arm shielding the breast slipping to her side as she turned onto her back, revealing a gorgeous tit. *Shit.* She was spectacular, he just wanted to—

"Arthur?"

Holy fuck. Lavinia.

"Joseph?" she squealed. She grabbed the covers and clutched them to her as she sat up in the bed. "What the hell are you doing here?" Fear colored her words.

"I could ask you the very same thing, my lady."

Arthur stumbled in. "Joseph, did you find— Shit." He stood stock-still then dragged his fingers through his hair. "Lavinia, I had no idea you were in here. Otherwise I wouldn't have let Joseph come in."

"Well, Lord Petersham," she said succinctly, glancing back and forth between the two men, "you could ask him to leave."

"Ah. Right." He motioned toward the door. "Joseph, after you."

Joseph chuckled as he exited.

Arthur followed him to the sitting room and closed the door behind him. "Yes, it is everything it looks like. And no, nobody knows. Well, they may suspect but we're being discreet."

Joseph slapped his shoulder. "That is one hell of a woman in there."

"Oh, God. You saw. How mortifying for her."

"I'll keep it a secret. I won't even tell Sophie."

Arthur glared at him.

"I won't, believe me. But I urge you to think about telling her yourself. She wants to know her brother is happy."

"Yeah, all right. She probably already suspects."

"So she's the reason you're upset with your parents." Joseph scrubbed a hand down his face. "Geez. Lavinia was right there with all that talk about marriageable girls. No wonder she left."

"It just about killed me, seeing her reaction." Arthur sighed. "Joseph, she's the woman from the masquerade." There was sorrow in his eyes. "Lavinia's my odalisque."

"Of all the women in the world." Joseph shook his head in disbelief. "Congratulations." He nodded toward the bedroom door. "What are you waiting for?"

Arthur offered a wan smile as Joseph left. Book in hand, Joseph slinked down the hall to his bedroom, a bedeviling thought needling his brain. What if he had worn a mask to Countess Winthrop's masquerade? Would he have been so lucky?

Arthur returned to the bedroom. Lavinia was no longer naked under his covers but wrapped in her robe, pacing the carpet at the end of the bed, an oil lamp sputtering weakly on the nightstand.

She practically jumped when he clicked the door lock.

He went to her but did not touch. "Darling, I didn't expect to see you like this again. You cannot know how happy this makes me."

She reached for him, wrapping her fingers around his. "I apologize for being upset earlier."

He rubbed his thumbs on the backs of her hands. "No need."

"If a love affair is all I can hope for, then I'll take it." She met his gaze. "But just for the duration of our stay here in St. Albans."

Arthur suddenly had the notion to never leave the sprawling estate. He pulled her to him. "Darling." He enveloped her in his arms, gazing at the desire on her face before taking her in a deep kiss.

She kissed him back, her passion laced with desperation as she tugged at his opened robe and pajama top.

Shit. She had seen both himself and Joseph in a state of half-dressed dishevelment. Did she take note? Or had surprise clouded her assessment of the scene?

She pulled his robe off slowly, carefully avoiding contact with his naked torso. "The night is not yet over, my lord," she said, a devious gleam in her eye.

"I see you have something in mind, my lady."

"Perhaps, my sultan." She tossed the robe on the low bench at the foot of the bed.

"And what is it you desire, my lady?" He leaned toward her ear. "Your predilection, as it were?"

Her lips curved at some unspoken fantasy as she removed her own robe and tossed it over his. "I prefer to be seduced, my lord." Her nipples hardened in the cool air.

"Hmm, like what you are doing to me right now?" It was near impossible to keep up the fantasy with her naked before him.

She bit her lower lip briefly, letting it slip from her teeth plumped and reddened. "Am I seducing you, lord sultan?" She pulled the paisley top from his shoulders then inexplicably put it on herself, covering her luscious breasts. "And what is it *you* desire? A harem to slake your lust?" She fastened two buttons just below her bosom.

"Just one odalisque with a wicked tongue skilled in the ways of carnal desire."

She untied the drawstring on his pajama bottoms. "Are you certain an odalisque is what you crave at the moment?" She knelt before him and tugged on the silk trousers, sliding them down his legs to his feet. One by one, she lifted each foot to remove the garment pooled at his ankles.

His erection jutted between them. "Suck me, my lady." He jerked his hips forward, his cock grazing her lips. "Then I'll think about fucking you."

She opened her mouth and flicked her tongue under the shaft, shooting chills of pleasure along every nerve. He sighed his satisfaction and prodded forward a little more. She drew the tip between her lips, squeezing him, her tongue stroking, her fingers teasing the muscles along the backs of his thighs.

He cupped her head in gentle gratitude. No twenty-five-year-old would be like this. Hers was the mouth of experience. A mouth that could make him forget all his cares and worries and send him into bliss.

He rocked his hips gently, fucking her mouth, letting her take him to the moment before the brink, forgetting he really wanted her cunt because he was prepared to spend in her mouth.

But then she drew away.

He looked down at her as she stood, pulling the silk bottoms up her legs as she did so. She stood before him. Dressed.

Like a man.

Except the trousers slung low on her wide hips, the fabric baggy around her legs. Her breasts strained the buttons of the top and her unbound hair cascaded over her shoulders. Far too feminine for a man.

"I think perhaps my lord sultan wants something a little different tonight." She brushed the faintest kiss to his cheek. "Something Greek. Perhaps a stable boy."

But not too feminine for a boy.

Arthur swallowed. So she had taken note of his and Joseph's partial nudity. Instead of being disgusted, she was willing to play the proxy. He had never wanted to fuck her so badly than at that moment.

She climbed onto the bench and positioned herself on all fours, the perfect height for his cock to enter her from behind.

He untied the drawstring and pulled the silk trousers to her knees, the pale curves of her buttocks inviting touch. He knelt behind her, pulling the cheeks apart to expose the crinkled hole of her arse fringed with downy curls. It flexed provocatively.

He fingered the swollen folds of her cunt. She was wet, ready for him in that orifice but not the other.

He scooped the dewy moisture and drew it up, spreading the honey of her excitement to lubricate the forbidden hole, slowly massaging the unyielding muscles to surrender. He leaned forward, touching the tip of his tongue to the aperture.

Lavinia gasped.

He dived in, lapping, licking, prodding, swirling, loosening…her breathy moans and rolling hips encouraging him. Slowly he inserted a finger, finding the tightness within, stroking until it relaxed. He removed the digit, the tightening upon his exit a reminder of the snugness that awaited him.

He stood, his iron-hard cock prodding impatiently. He stared at the forbidden hole, wet and glistening. There would be pain at his entrance, the muscles would feel as if they were being torn apart. But the pain would be exquisite. He knew that from experience.

And if they were going to end their affair with emotional pain, at least the physical would be remembered otherwise.

He fingered her cunt, so deliciously ready for his prick. He plunged inside, moving in and out until he had lubricated the shaft thoroughly. At his final withdrawal he aimed at the tighter hole, pressing in slowly, excruciatingly so, as he reached around and thrilled her clit.

Her breathing quickened then hitched with a gasp and continued raggedly.

He focused on her pleasure as he slowed his own. "Breathe, love. Relax on the exhale."

He pushed forward with each release of breath, murmuring praise as she worked through the agony. And then he was embedded to the hilt, the exquisite tightness almost his undoing. He commenced the rhythm of lovemaking, furiously rubbing her clit, willing her toward climax.

She cried out her orgasm, her cunt clenching air, the contractions reverberating in her arsehole, her wetness drenching his hand. He bent over her, burying his head against her shoulder, slamming inside her, no longer holding back, intending to make his mark deep within her so she would never forget him.

With one final thrust, he emptied himself, snarling his satisfaction into the night.

His heart pounded in his head but could not drown his thoughts. There would be no other like the woman beneath him. Did he really have to compromise? Did he really have to doom himself to a lifetime of unfulfilled desires, of bitter disappointment?

He slackened, falling from their joining, and she fell forward. He lifted her in his arms and lay her on the bed, under the covers, holding her, kissing her hair as she cried silently.

"Shh, shh. Darling, was I such a brute that you shed tears?"

She wrapped her arms around him, clinging desperately. "No. No, Arthur it was wonderful." She sniffled and wiped her face on the sheet. "Too wonderful."

He understood. "We're good together."

"We are. Let's make the most of it during the remainder of our time here."

And after that? He knew she'd save a dance or two for him during the Season. April would be interminable before he would see her again in May.

CHAPTER TEN

London, April 1880

Julius turned to a fresh page in his patients notebook. It was out of the ordinary for Clarisse Chadbourne to have made an appointment. He had no record of ever having seen her before, except at the occasional social event he felt compelled to attend. She was the wife of his colleague, Dr. Gilbert Chadbourne, a surgeon, a well-made man still of a vigorous age. Perhaps despite his good looks and apparent virility he lacked the ability to please his wife. Perhaps she sought Julius' talents in relieving frustration.

But when Mrs. Chadbourne arrived, her countenance suggested not sexual deprivation but just the opposite, mixed with a bit of panic. She wore a dark, hooded cloak, only taking down the hood and removing the garment when she was in the examination room and the door had been closed behind her. Her dress hugged her generous curves perfectly, hinting at the sensual woman within, but its high neck and dark plaid were at odds with the spring weather.

"Mrs. Chadbourne," Julius said, indicating she sit on the examination table. "How can I be of service?"

"Thank you for seeing me, Dr. Christopher. I hope I am not being too forward when I say I have heard you offer unusual treatments for women."

He lifted a brow. "I wouldn't call them unusual. My practice is in step with current medical theories."

She met his gaze briefly. "Yes, well, I have heard that you are of a more modern disposition than some," she said quietly.

"I take that as a compliment. How does this apply to you?"

"Dr. Christopher, I'm pregnant—"

She did not look happy about the news.

"And I do not want this child."

A chill prickled his spine. It had been a long time since he had heard those words. The last time it had not been a woman who uttered them.

"Gilbert and I have a vigorous intimate life. And we already have four children. Neither one of us wants any more. We've been using various methods of…of prevention." She hushed the last word as if it were iniquitous. "It appears one of those methods failed not too long ago."

Ah. "And how long has it been since your last menses?"

"About three months."

"The menses can cease for a variety of reasons. Have you been experiencing typical symptoms of pregnancy?"

"Yes. It's been difficult to keep them secret from my husband and my lady's maid."

Secret? That was indeed surprising. "So your husband does not know?"

"I think he suspects. He's a doctor so he's more attuned to the physical than other husbands might be. But the less he knows the better." She looked at him beseechingly. "I want it to seem natural. Many of Gilbert's colleagues are men with very traditional views. If they thought he might be involved it would destroy his career."

Julius cleared his throat. "And a charge of murder would not destroy mine?"

Mrs. Chadbourne blanched. "Julius," she began quietly, tears forming in the corners of her eyes, "I know I am putting you at great risk. If you cannot help, I'll look elsewhere. I've seen advertisements in magazines—"

"Quackery, Clarisse. All those advertisements are quackery." He heaved a sigh. She was better off under his care. "I can prepare an emmenagogue—an herbal remedy to restart the menses."

"Thank you," she exhaled.

"But I warn you: there will be cramping and bleeding. Your condition won't go unnoticed by the household or your husband. You'll have to go away."

"I'll make arrangements to go abroad on holiday. I have a dear friend in Belgium."

He glared at her. "Your friend will have to be aware of what will be happening to you and be able to offer succor."

"I understand. She's a trusted confidante."

"All right. I'll label the mixture as a remedy for dysmenorrhea, painful menses. That way your symptoms of cramping and bleeding will draw less suspicion."

Clarisse reached out and squeezed his hand. "Thank you, Julius."

He nodded sullenly then went to his cupboard and pulled out a locked box. "Make your arrangements as soon as possible," he said as he fished for the key. It hung on his key ring but he rarely used it. He had given Grace a copy so she could restock the box with fresh herbs, with herbs that would still hold their potency. He hoped for Clarisse's sake that the mixture would be potent enough.

"This may take a while. Would you like to return later today?"

"If you don't mind, Doctor, I would prefer to wait."

"All right."

Julius rang the bell pull. A moment later, Grace knocked on the door.

"Come."

She entered timidly. "Dr. Christopher?"

Her obvious pregnant state was suddenly alarming. He wanted to shield her, to protect her. Instead he shunted aside his emotions as a professional ought to do. "Yes, Grace, please come in." He went to his desk and pulled out his recipe book. "I need you to follow this list and carefully and precisely measure out these herbs." He pointed to the recipe. "Label each jar with the name and amount. I'll prepare the instructions."

He meticulously transcribed the instructions for use, noting probable side effects. He knew all too well what a woman would have to endure. When he was finished, he inspected Grace's labels and amounts, placing each jar in a box. He closed the lid and handed the box to Grace to wrap up.

He handed his instructions to Clarisse. "You must follow these instructions to the letter or there may be horrible consequences. I have detailed the usual side effects: heavy bleeding, cramping, nausea, dizziness akin to a fever. Please have your friend read and understand these instructions, as well. I strongly urge you to have a sympathetic doctor at the ready in case the event does not go as planned."

She glanced at the note. "A tea? What does it taste like?"

"Bitter and herbal. Something like a digestive liqueur."

He helped her with her cloak then she took the box from Grace. "Thank you, Julius."

He gripped her arm. "Clarisse, you must write me to let me know you are well." He tried to quell the anxiety in his voice.

"I will, Julius."

And then she left, cloaked and hooded, Grace leading her to the front door.

Julius locked the door to the examination room, sank against it and let the tears fall uncontrollably.

Lincolnshire

Joseph gazed down at Sophia lying in the bed beside him, her respiration edged with the wheezes of one who had just gone through great physical exertion. Her body curled awkwardly around the fruits of her labors, shielding and protecting the bundle as if it were the most precious object in the world.

Because it was—*he* was. A son. Their son. Joseph quietly snorted his amusement. After nineteen years, Helena finally had a brother.

Before the day had come, Lady Richmond had sent for the doctor and midwife so they would be at the ready at Harwell Hall. And when Sophia went into labor, Joseph insisted on being present at the birth as he had been for Helena's. He held Sophia's hand, reciting poetry and singing songs, until the moment arrived and the doctor insisted upon her full attention. Joseph remained at her side, letting her grip him, hit him, listening to her screams as if music to his ears.

And then the child came. Fat and bawling, healthy despite Sophia being thirty-eight years old.

They had agreed upon the name Henry Abraham Phillips. The first in honor of Arthur's deceased beloved, Lady Henrietta Langley. The middle name after the American president who freed the slaves. Both namesakes had left indelible impressions on the first years of *Harwell Phillips & Company* as the partnership struggled to gain traction in the American railway industry.

Then while mother and son slept that first night, Arthur got Joseph drunk in celebration, reminiscing how the birth of Helena had been mired in solitude and secrecy. Leaving Joseph wondering why the hell it took so damn long for him and Sophia to have another child.

They had purposefully refrained because of his too-frequent absences on business. In New York, Sophia had had the benefit of his mother's assistance and advice. Yet whenever they were in England, she had to rely on nurses and nannies—and Anna Peel, if she was not busy with her own brood. Besides, Joseph hated that he had missed so much of Helena's growing up. That would change now. His son would have the benefit of his experience and the joy of his love every damn day.

As he looked down upon mother and child so serene, so contented, he wasn't so sure he did not want to have a third. They would be old parents, but not so old as others.

Not as old as Arthur if he went through with Lady Richmond's plan to marry a debutante. What was worse than Arthur not wanting such a marriage was the possibility he would distance himself and consider the brats to be merely his expected duty.

He would probably spoil his godchild and nephew more than his own children.

Joseph would see to it that Arthur found joy in parenting—even parenting children he might not think he wanted at first. Joseph had been too much a part of the Harwell family discord. No more. There would be no more acrimony in the family. He would make sure of that.

Henry gurgled.

Joseph touched his son's soft cheek. He would show Arthur by example what a blessing it was to have a child one did not expect, how, despite a man believing there was no more room in his heart, there was always room for a child.

And one's grandchild, expected a few months later.

Joseph chuckled audibly. Sophia stirred next to him, surprised to see little Henry still in the cocoon of her body.

"The nurse hasn't taken him yet?"

Joseph smoothed the hair from her brow. "I told her to wait a while."

"He's going to wake up at any moment and be hungry," she chastised. "You're not going to like it."

Joseph kissed the crown of her head. "I'm going to love every minute of it, darling."

He lay a comforting hand on his son, his palm and fingers almost as large as Henry's entire body. As Henry wakened noisily to the astonishment of hunger, Joseph laughed out loud.

London

Julius leaned his elbows on the desk in his study and held his head in his hands. The lamp burned dully, like his mood. He had thought old memories dead and buried, but when Mrs. Chadbourne made her request, he realized how close to the surface they lay.

Lavinia had been an innocent in the whole affair, unaware of the evil his mind considered. The image of her sprawled on her bed, bloody and crying, had burned into his brain. And then he had rejected her, left her to fend for herself emotionally and physically after the devastation wrought by the end of their affair.

He was a monster. He hadn't been thinking of her at the time. He had thought only of himself.

How did one purge oneself of a nightmare?

Monks and penitent sinners did such things as self-flagellation. Some were roused by the acts of violence, no doubt, as a sort of masturbatory release. But Julius needed something different. Not an act of self-abuse where his own hand would be stilled by the fear of pain, but an act by another who would not feel the pain and hence, have no qualms.

Grace.

She had it in her—he knew she did—yet she had always held back. When they had performed erotic flogging she dampened her enthusiasm partly so he would not be exhausted. It was an act of selfishness on her part, she had once said, as she wanted him to have the strength to perform. But what if the act were not erotic? They had never done such a thing, not together. And, despite Julius' vast experience, he had never done anything like it with another.

Grace was in the library, curled up on the couch with a book, her lips moving as she read, a dictionary on the seat beside her. Once she had learned how to read, she took to the diversion with alacrity, thirsting for the meanings of new and strange words. She thoroughly enjoyed novels, plus serialized stories in magazines and penny dreadfuls. It was really quite endearing.

He watched her from the doorway for a minute before she looked up. She smiled, her face glowing with contentment. She must have read something in his expression, for her brow furrowed.

"Julius? Is something wrong?"

"Grace, I've done a bad thing."

She closed her book. "Oh?" She untucked her legs and put her feet on the floor and stared at him, waiting for him to say something.

But he couldn't. How could he tell a young woman who carried his child the horror he had done to another such as she?

She stood, her hand holding her belly. "If you can't tell me then I don't want to know." She came toward him with open arms. "I know you can't always tell me about your patients. But I'm here to comfort you."

He fell into her embrace. "I don't deserve you." He held her tightly. "I need you to punish me for what I have done."

She pulled back, horrified. "Jules?"

"Please just do this for me, Grace. Please."

She searched his eyes. "Yes. What is it you would like me to do?"

"The room under the stairs…I need you to…flog me."

Surprise flashed on her face then deepened to understanding. "All right. Let's go downstairs."

Once in the room, she lit the lamp.

"Get the vectis," he said.

She left to retrieve the obstetrical instrument from his examination room while he undressed.

He waited for her, naked under the shackles. When she returned, she placed the vectis on a stool then proceeded to bind him, first his ankles, his legs forced to spread to reach the manacles on short chains, then his wrists, his arms also spread wide for the shackles on the ceiling. He ignored the cool bindings prickling his flesh. Instead he stared at the vectis, the ebony-handled instrument with its metal loop at the one end mesmerizing him. They really should just leave it in the room under the stairs. He never used it as a birthing instrument and since he had used it on Grace the first time last year, he found it more useful as a flogger. At this moment, in his state, it was heavily symbolic.

She went to the cabinet where they kept a few supplies. "Shall I gag you?"

He would need the release of the screams. "No."

"Then are you ready, Doctor?" She stood before him, holding the vectis in one hand, her other hand stroking and fondling the curved metal loop with the delicacy of a lover.

Julius closed his eyes and drew in a long breath, exhaling it slowly through his mouth. "Yes, Miss Danby."

She knew precisely what to do. Her first swats were gentle, letting the chilled flesh of his buttocks and thighs become used to the cold metal. He flinched not from the pain of impact but the surprise.

She stopped, letting him gather his courage or perhaps drawing out his apprehension. She walked around in front of him, lay the vectis on the stool and stared at his cock, hanging flaccidly. She grabbed it, pulled cruelly and slapped the head. He recoiled with a yelp, the restraints tugging at his limbs. She repeated the assault, briefly studying his slowly burgeoning prick as it lay in her palm before smacking the glans one more time. Julius sucked air between gritted teeth, exhaling slowly to dispel the lingering sting.

Grace picked up the vectis and went behind him to resume her punishment.

This time she held nothing back.

She struck with the fury of a woman wronged, the fury he needed to expel his demons, slapping his buttocks, his thighs, his upper back. With every hit, her grunts of exertion grew louder. He swung on the shackles at the impact. His balls flew up and slammed back between his legs.

Which must have given her the most incredible idea.

With a strength she had never shown before, she swung the vectis between his legs, hitting his stones, the impact forcing him to double over, the restraints preventing him from doing so.

The pain was glorious.

"More!" he croaked.

She granted his wish, her abuse varying its focus—his butt, his thighs, his balls. With every hit he was cleansed, with every cry he was purged of his sin. Behind closed eyelids he saw Lavinia in her pain. He would never make such a mistake again.

Grace would make sure he did not.

She slammed the vectis one more time against him then stopped. A warm rivulet of blood cooled his burning thigh. Julius gulped air to satisfy his enervated lungs.

She came around his front and knelt before him. She once again grasped his cock, now hard from the stimulation it had misinterpreted as erotic, and stroked, her movements determined, frantic, willing him to come.

She knew him better than he knew himself.

It was easy to surrender his fate to Grace, to her ministrations, giving her control of his body. She gripped his balls, squeezing harshly in rhythm to her strokes before shoving her fingers in his arse to massage his prostate, coaxing his lust, drawing it out of him until he exploded. She milked him of his sinful seed, determinedly working inside to force the release of every drop. He came on the floor, expelling the evil from his body with each spurt of his emission, the pools of semen widening with every release.

He wanted to crumple but his restraints prevented such reprieve.

It was only the first step. It would have to suffice until he could gather courage to meet with the wronged lady herself. To confront the memory of what he had done and complete his atonement.

Grace sat back on her heels, panting, as exhausted as he.

"Thank you, Grace. Thank you."

CHAPTER ELEVEN

London, The Season, May 1880

"The Royal Academy Banquet is tonight."

William Peel looked up from cutting his chicken. "Do you think the food is as good as Mrs. Chiswick's, Papa?"

Papa guffawed and Mama laughed. Molly and Lilly dared not, except William made such a face at them from across the dinner table that they both giggled then quickly bent their heads over their plates, pretending to eat.

"I'll tell Mrs. Chiswick you like her cooking, dear," Mama said. "I'm sure you'll miss it this autumn."

When he left for Cambridge. One of Papa's memories of university was being hungry most of the time, partly because he was so tall and required more food than the other students and partly because the food was awfully bland.

"I wasn't thinking about the food, Will," Papa continued, "but how the occasion marks the beginning of the London Season."

"Oh," was all William could think to say.

Mama gave him one of her pretty smiles. "Your father often receives invitations to Society events. We thought perhaps you'd like to join him."

"You mean like teas and balls and such?" With girls? Girls who understood the conventions of polite chitchat and the latest dance steps?

"Yes, dear." Mirth twinkled in Mama's eyes.

William glanced at his little sisters, both of whom stared in awe at him. He scowled back. Last year his attendance at such events had been an utter disaster. And while since then Molly had helped him improve his dancing, and meeting so many important people at Helena's wedding had forced him to learn how to navigate social niceties, he wasn't quite sure he was ready. He'd rather be at home, reading the latest issue of the *Journal of the British Archaeological Association*.

"But isn't that the sort of thing girls do?"

"Yes. And it will be Molly's turn in about five years." Papa winked at her before turning back to him. "Girls do it so they can meet young men, Will. Which means young men are expected to be there."

William was certain he paled.

"It's not really all about finding a wife." Papa gave Mama one of those leers that always made her blush. "You'll fall in love one day—"

Lilly giggled. William shot her a withering look.

"There's no hurry. But Will," Papa said more soberly, "you're becoming a man. While part of becoming a man is his higher learning, another part is meeting the right sort of people who can further you in your career. You'll make friends with the boys at university and learn from the professors. However, it is the aristocracy who have the resources to fund your archaeological expeditions."

"But you and Uncle Arthur and Uncle Joseph have loads of money to finance my tours."

"We don't have the reputation in the field. You'll want to get your funds from a collector or noted gentleman scholar."

"Uncle Arthur has an interest in the Near East and other things exotic."

The corner of Papa's mouth quirked upward. "Yes, yes he does. Always has. And now that he's quite settled in the railway business, perhaps he'd like to dabble in archaeology. But I think you'll help him best by establishing your reputation first."

"Yes, Papa."

"And now you're going to university, dear," Mama began, "it is time you referred to your 'uncles' by their proper titles. You should call them 'Lord Petersham' and 'Mr. Phillips' except when in the most intimate of settings."

"Yes, Mama."

"We simply want to send you out into the world as prepared as you can be." Papa chewed thoughtfully on his mutton. "In fact it would behoove you to get in the good graces of someone like Lady Foxley-Graham."

William almost dropped his fork. Lady Foxley-Graham was quite possibly the most beautiful woman in the world. Not that Mama or Aunt Sophia or Helena weren't beautiful. They were…but Lady Foxley-Graham had a charm that was positively bewitching. After Helena's wedding, William had spent quite a few nights pleasuring himself to the memory of her smile as she placed her hand in his at their first meeting.

Papa turned to Mama. "What do you think, Anna? She chaperoned Nicholas during the Season last year."

"Yes, Geoffrey, but Nicholas was older and already embarking upon a career as a doctor. I believe the idea was to help him find a suitable doctor's wife amongst the girls still on the shelf."

Papa grinned. "And look how that turned out."

Mama giggled.

Were his parents daft? Lady Foxley-Graham had been more than a mere chaperon to Nicholas; she had been his lover! Helena had told him that while she taught William all about necking during Christmastime. Helena practically worshiped the viscountess and said Nicholas was a wonderful lover because of the lady's instructions. And then Nicholas taught Helena how to kiss and then she taught him—

Why it was as if he had learned how to kiss from the very lady herself!

William's trousers suddenly became uncomfortably tight.

Luckily dinner wouldn't be finished for a spell. And Mama was already asking Molly and Lilly what they learned from their tutor that day.

If he could be chaperoned by Lady Foxley-Graham it would be a dream come true.

He would continue with that thought in his bed later that night.

Lavinia lay on the morning room couch in far too comfortable a position. She should have just stayed in bed really. She could read the damn newspaper and drink her blasted tea in her bedroom just as well.

But the light was better for reading in the morning room and being in bed alone was simply too depressing.

Her perusal of the "Imperial Parliament" columns finished, she flipped through the pages of the *Morning Post*, ignoring sporting news then skimming the foreign briefs before poring over the notes in the "Fashionable World." She stopped cold on page six.

There at the top of the far left column was the notice of the Royal Academy Banquet held Saturday night at Burlington House, the event that signaled the opening of the London Season. The president of the art academy, Sir Frederick Leighton, had given the opening toast. The Prince and Princess of Wales had been there. The Prime Minister, Mr. Gladstone, fresh from winning the election for the Liberals, "was received with great cheering" before giving a speech.

The art academy's affair was, in fact, well attended by everyone who was anyone. Well, men of importance at least. And their wives would have been in attendance at the Royal Academy's Private View the previous afternoon, hobnobbing with the royal family.

But not her. No. She even grabbed Friday's *Post* to peruse the list of those in attendance at the Private View and, no indeed, Viscountess Foxley-Graham was not among them.

Lavinia sighed and threw the *Post* on the carpet. The Season of 1880 was destined to be the worst ever.

It was her first Season alone. She simply could not remember a time when she wasn't shepherding a young man through the rules and vicissitudes of Society. She hadn't prepared this year. She had been too immersed in her failed fantasy of Nicholas to have found another. His last letter had said he hoped she had a grand time this year but that as his wife was due to give birth in June, he would be infrequently in London. He would let her know if he felt compelled to be there for a Parliamentary matter. They could have tea.

And probably end up in bed.

At least it would take her mind off Arthur. Except she'd probably close her eyes and fantasize about him while Nicholas lay between her legs.

A knock resounded politely on the morning room door.

"What is it, Sims?"

The butler entered and shifted uncomfortably in the doorway. "Flowers, my lady."

"Oh?" She lifted her head. "Can you bring them in here?"

Sims glanced behind him. "No, my lady. While it would not be too impossible a task, it might require more of the staff."

How very odd. "Shall I visit the flowers then?"

"That might be the better approach at the moment, my lady."

Lavinia got up and followed Sims to the foyer. It was an astonishing sight. The space was filled with basket upon basket of roses, pink and white, red and yellow, evoking a memory of a line of a poem recited by a lover: *Each morn a thousand roses brings.*

"Sims?" She looked helplessly at the butler.

"This note came with a solitary rose, my lady."

Sims handed her the note and a lavender rose—*her* rose. The note held but one word, a word that set her heart pounding uncontrollably and a smile to tug on her lips.

Arthur.

Lavinia tried not to sag against the wall of Lord and Lady Wrexham's ballroom but between enervation and boredom, sagging came naturally.

She kept her eye on the interstices of the gilt-topped columns separating the entrance lobby from the ballroom, watching to see who arrived and with whom. Charlotte, the Countess of Banbury, had a similar idea but had positioned herself closer to the receiving area, holding court with the matrons of Society and their various charges, offering thin smiles and the occasional wave of her fan. The matrons would be gossiping in the abstract about which young girl should marry which older man, and there would be plenty of "oh, no, my dear, the marquess prefers a more buxom sort" or "he's a dour man and needs the mitigation of a gentle soul".

What all the biddies did not seem to understand was a proper match could not be made in the abstract. One needed to actively nurture and promote connections and to best do so, one needed to know the parties involved on a far deeper level than mere casual acquaintance.

Charlotte understood this and was, therefore, greatly sought out for her advice. Lavinia understood this but was always so difficult to pin down as she found it far more productive to be in the thick of things, matchmaking face-to-face.

Except this Season. Instead of being caught up in a whirlwind of introductions and character assessments, she stood against a wall, her only company a potted palm.

And then *he* walked into the ballroom.

The Earl of Petersham was eye-catchingly handsome in a pale-green and gold waistcoat and matching tie under his evening jacket. The green would pick up the color in his eyes, the gold, in his hair. Of course it was done deliberately. Lady Richmond understood how handsome her son was and, for the first time in over twenty years, she would get to show him off.

It was simply maddening.

He searched the room, sidetracked momentarily by greetings or small talk. He would nod politely, perhaps offer a slight smile, say a few words but his attention would not loiter. Once relieved of social obligation, his gaze would wander.

Lavinia shrank back to hide behind a frond. Still somehow he found her from across the room.

His gaze was penetrating, piercing her heart, scorching her core. She looked away but could not do so for long. He said a few words to his mother, patted her hand, then left her side. He was before her too quickly.

"Lavinia."

She offered her hand instinctively. He took it and kissed her fingers. The moment he did so the world melted away.

"Lord Petersham," she managed through her rapidly pumping pulse, "how very wonderful to see you."

"The pleasure is all mine." Somehow the vague pleasantry seemed lewd.

The marchioness appeared at his side. "Lady Foxley-Graham."

She nodded. "Lady Richmond."

"I'm very glad to see you. I'm sure you know some of the young ladies on Arthur's dance card. Perhaps you can offer a word or two of advice on their prospects?"

Lavinia tamped down her seething jealousy. "I'd be delighted, my lady."

Arthur gave her a suspicious look as a sly smile curled his lips. "Perhaps we can discuss my prospects while we enjoy a waltz, my lady."

She wanted nothing more than to be in his arms. But it would be cruel to her heart. Best she stayed against the wall.

"Yes, Arthur, what a wonderful idea," Lady Richmond chimed. "Lady Foxley-Graham, it seems the next dance is about to begin."

Arthur held out his hand and against her better judgment, Lavinia took it.

His carriage was strong, guiding her through the waltz, commanding her body to move as he wished but not necessarily as she wanted. He noticed.

"Your heart is not in the dance, I fear."

"How did you know, my lord?"

He leaned in. "Because I know how your body responds when it takes pleasure willingly."

He was cruel. "Perhaps I should leave you to find a willing partner."

"Perhaps we should get a breath of fresh air."

Before she knew it he was whirling her toward the French doors leading out to the terrace. He broke the waltz stance and took her arm. He smiled and nodded pleasantly to passing guests as he led her outside into the cool night.

They did not dawdle on the terrace. Instead he kept going, over the flagstones to the lawn, by which point he was no longer leading her but dragging her. A folly loomed ahead, a diminutive classical temple, the entrance lit by lanterns lining the path.

He steered her around to the back where it was dark, the garden wall only a few feet away. He trapped her against the temple, his hands flat against the concrete and stone on either side of her shoulders.

"I sent you flowers."

"I received them. Did I not send a thank you note?"

"You did. It was very formal."

"How else should I respond when an unwanted suitor sends me a foyerful of roses?"

"Unwanted?"

She strained against the tears threatening to fall.

"Lavinia, please let me endure this Season. Let me humor my mother. I will find a way for us to be together." His voice held frustration and need. He released her from the cage of his arms and turned away.

The cold concrete chilled her to the bone. "Seeing you smiling while you dance with other women, chatting in the refreshment room." She drew in a shuddering breath. "It will kill me."

He spun around and faced her. "This kills me as well. I'm on display, an object, like some painting at the Academy a buyer inspects to see if it pleases." He ran his hand over the back of his neck. "I burn for you."

"Then burn for me, my lord."

"What will it take?"

"Arthur, it's hopeless. You need to accept that I cannot give you what you need. I cannot provide you with an heir. If that is what you require, then you must look for it elsewhere."

"You're not too old, Lavinia."

"But I am!" She exhaled in exasperation. "Even if I were able to carry your child, what if it were not a boy? I assure you, my lord, I really will be too old after that." She steepled her fingers and pressed them to her lips, trying to calm herself. "Arthur, I've come to terms with not ever having children and now I do not want them. You must understand this."

His silence was oppressive until he slapped the wall of the folly. "I do understand. Unfortunately, I understand all too well. When one makes such a decision, eventually the decision becomes a fact beyond which one cannot imagine any other future."

She stared at him. He understood. He really understood. "Who was she?"

He sucked in air, exhaling through pursed lips. "Lady Henrietta Langley, the daughter of the Earl of Bloxholme. Henny." He smiled. "We were to have lots of children. Well, one only imagines such things when one is young." His inhale shuddered. "She miscarried just before she died. It was how I found out she was carrying my child."

Lavinia's heart clenched. A horror much like her own. "Arthur, darling, I had no idea."

She reached out her hand and he took it, his gaze cast to the ground.

"Her death left a hole in my heart. I was simply not motivated to marry and have children. I could only imagine such a future with Henny because I was in love with her and that was what she wanted."

Lavinia squeezed his hand.

"I cannot see myself marrying a woman simply for the sake of producing an heir. I fear I would grow to resent the child. My father was a stranger to me for most of my life. I do not want to be such a father."

She had never seen him so melancholy. In the moonlight, the mood suited him. It softened his features to their true handsome aspect. And made her want to divulge her secrets as he had divulged his.

She inhaled her courage. "His name was Julius Christopher—"
Arthur furrowed his brow.

"You'll recognize the name as being your sister's lover last Season. He's extraordinarily charismatic and I do not begrudge Sophia for falling under his spell." She relaxed her hold on his hand and threaded her fingers through his. "My husband was so much older than I. I was twenty when we married. He was fifty-five. It was an arranged marriage; there was no real love between us. No animosity either. Just a mutual understanding of the way things were."

Arthur drew closer.

"My husband became ill and we sent for the doctor. It was Julius who came to call. He was young, ambitious, and unmarried. I was young and unsatisfied. We began our affair soon after. Julius was a remarkable lover—creative, potent, seductive. I fell hard for him."

She leaned into Arthur as he grazed her cheek with the backs of his fingers.

"I had never become pregnant in the five years of my marriage with my husband. Of course, he was practically impotent and often uninterested. We assumed—as is always the case—that the problem lay with me. He had been married before and his first wife was also thought to have been barren. When Julius and I began our affair we were careful. Eventually we became careless, conveniently forgetting that infertility can be the problem of the male and not just the female."

His thumb delicately caressed the hollow of her palm.

"I became pregnant with Julius' child. I could have kept it. I was married, young, expected to have children. But Julius was so unlike my husband physically that the child might have resembled him and drawn gossip."

Lavinia looked away. She couldn't tell Arthur the truth. She just couldn't. He had a similar experience. He would attempt heroics. Another day when he had forgotten her in the arms of a younger woman she would confess all. Just not now.

"Four months into the pregnancy I miscarried, discharging blood and gore, vomiting from the nausea. I fell into a fever. Julius, as our family doctor, was at my side, probably too often. When it was finished he told me the bad news. I had lost my child and he wasn't sure I would be able to carry another."

"Oh, darling."

"The guilt was unbearable. I had failed as a wife and I had failed as a woman. I distanced myself from him, from my husband, from everybody. Three years later, my husband died. I was left a wealthy widow. Julius and I found ourselves back in each other's arms. He was a vastly successful doctor by then." She drew in a bolstering breath. "And then he confessed. He had felt relief I had miscarried. The scandal of a bastard would have held him back and he could not have lived with that. He apologized, hindsight showing he could have had me as wife with his very own son at his side. Still he felt no regret. Julius had become a hard man, his ambition focused, singular." She looked at Arthur, banking back tears. "When one thinks one can never have children, one becomes accustomed to the idea. Eventually I realized I like my life without them." She closed her eyes as exhaustion overtook her.

"I would never force the issue, Lavinia. I only know I want you."

"Arthur, it is different for a man. You may have children—provided you are capable of course—until you are in old age. Men don't make a decision not to have children. They either do or they do not. And they are no less a man for either choice. Society tells me I am less of a woman for mine. What would Society say about you if you made the choice to be with such as I?"

"Society would say I must be profoundly in love with you and they would be correct."

He was so close the heat of his body warmed the bare skin of her décolletage. He rested his hands on her shoulders then skimmed down her arms to her waist. He pulled her against him with a jolt, letting her know he meant it, before covering her mouth with his.

It was a kiss like no other. Honest, brutal, the physical deepness approximating the emotional depth. He was slow, deliberate, forceful, and unyielding. He held her to him with an assuring strength yet with an acquiescence of her freedom to leave.

But she wanted to stay. She could think of nothing more she wanted than Arthur Harwell, the Earl of Petersham. She kissed him back hungrily, letting him know of her desire. He urged her against the folly, grinding his crotch against her. She cared not if the peach silk of her dress would be stained green by the moss on the wall. She wanted him.

She cupped his groin. He wanted her just as much.

He unbuttoned his flies and freed himself. With a growl of need, he lifted her skirts and petticoats, holding them determinedly as he nudged open her legs. He swore an oath as he searched for the split in her drawers then moaned in relief when he entered her. He filled her perfectly. They were meant to be together, meant to be as one.

She climaxed around him, whispering his name. He began his journey to ecstasy in earnest, driving into her with a harsh beat.

With a clipped grunt he pulled out, spewing his seed onto the ground, his ragged breaths slowing to a more even rhythm.

Tears burned her cheeks.

"Shit. I'm sorry." His words lay hot and wet on her nape. "That was bloody brutal. But it's been forty-one days."

Lavinia bristled. He'd counted the days? "Arthur, you're not a monk. I don't expect faithfulness."

"Damn it, Lavinia! I'm in love with you." He looked up at the night sky and sucked in a mouthful of air.

"Arthur, don't…"

He returned his gaze to her, tears mingling with the sweat sheening his clean-shaven face. "I love you."

She couldn't say it, she couldn't. Even though the sentiment ripped at the sinews holding her heart together. She looked away, too many emotions twisting her face.

He offered his handkerchief. "Please, Lavinia. Trust me. I will find a way for us to be together."

She wanted so much for that to be true. She wiped her eyes.

He pecked her lips tenderly and smoothed down her skirts then attended to his own state of dishabille. He cupped her cheek, his expression serene as he gazed into her eyes.

She wanted him, wanted to love him, wanted to share her life with him. Wanted so much for that to be possible. "All right, Arthur. But you must find a resolution before Lady Richmond finds you an innocent for a wife."

He chuckled, the response offering much needed relief to her heightened emotions. "I will, darling, I will."

CHAPTER TWELVE

Grace walked along the corridor to the bedroom. It wasn't *her* bedroom, it was *his* bedroom but he usually referred to it as *the* bedroom. Julius wasn't in the bedroom very much anymore. Lately he had been holing himself up in his study, at times falling asleep on the couch and not bothering to come to bed at all.

And tonight, as she passed the study along the corridor, the door was closed. The pale glow of light within bled through the sliver of space between the door and the floorboards.

She had no idea what kept him up until all hours of the night. He hadn't been doing any experiments but perhaps he was planning new ones. Perhaps it had something to do with Mrs. Chadbourne's visit as he had been spending a great deal of time in his study since. Perhaps the medicine he gave her needed to be perfected. He had said it tasted bitter.

She pressed her ear to the door, not quite sure what she hoped to hear. There was nothing but silence.

The angle of her vision pointed down toward the knob, under which more light came through.

The keyhole. Julius must have taken the key from the keyhole.

Grace got on her knees, thankful the hall carpet extended almost to the wall. It would muffle any sound on her side of the door. She peered through the hole, her gaze darting about to take in the unusual perspective.

He was behind his desk, reading, the halo of a lamp illuminating his somber countenance and the document he held in his hand before him. He may have been crying, she couldn't be absolutely sure.

He lay the document down on the desk and stared at it for a moment before covering his face with both hands. He rubbed his eyes then speared his fingers through his hair, gripping the strands as if he wanted to pull them out at the roots.

And then he sucked in an audible breath and his body shook as he sobbed.

Bad news. He had received bad news. A death maybe.

Grace stood with effort and continued to the bedroom. He wouldn't want to talk about such things but she could be there for him with a smile and a gentle touch.

Whatever it took to make her Julius happy again.

Arthur stared into his teacup, the delicate white bowl half-full of tea edged by the blue and gold of the saucer underneath. If he blurred his eyes just a little, the set would appear as two concentric circles, brown within white within blue—

"You're being far too introspective, my lord. It is distinctly out of character."

Joseph's voice tinged with playful mocking took him out of his reverie. He refocused his eyes on his friend sprawled out on the sofa in his drawing room. "Sorry. I should pay more attention to you."

"I can amuse myself. Your father, however, will not stand for such disregard."

His father. That's why Arthur was in a mood. Father was expected at any moment. Arthur had invited him and Joseph to tea at his Belgravia house. He had a proposition.

"Until Richmond arrives tell me how the Season has been. Surely you've been dancing with plenty of lovely young ladies."

"Girls, Joseph, girls. They practically left their pinafores at the coat check."

Joseph chuckled.

"Although there was one young woman. Hardly the sort my mother would choose for me. But she was older at least. Well into her twenties. Miss Penelope Hardcastle. Mother pointed her out while she was dancing with Ravensburgh. They looked as if they were flirting quite heavily."

"Interesting. Could he be looking for a wife?"

"Possibly. But when the young lady in question was introduced to me I realized it was rather what she did."

Joseph shot him a querying look.

"Flirting. Heavily. I recall her words as I danced with her, 'Lord Petersham, I do believe the third floor has some amusements you might appreciate'."

Joseph grinned. "No subtlety there. And how was the third floor amusement?"

"You'll have to ask her. I declined the offer, although I let her know I was utterly flattered. I said something poetic like the affections of another was the wax in my ears to her siren song."

Joseph groaned a laugh.

"She was really quite charming. I dare say, were my heart not occupied she would have easily seduced me, and I wondered if my mother had put her on my dance card for that very purpose. But during the whole incident, Lavinia was dancing with Ravensburgh. I could barely keep my eyes off them."

"Was he flirting with her as well?"

Arthur smiled. "She was rather talkative. I suppose she knows about him and Norrington."

"Undoubtedly."

A light rapping resounded on the door before it opened and Wittering stepped through. "My lord," the butler began, "the Marquess of Richmond."

Joseph sat up and straightened his clothing.

Father entered, surveying the drawing room with a critical eye.

"Thank you, Wittering. A fresh pot of tea, if you will."

"Good, my lord." Wittering bowed before he left.

"Good afternoon, Father." Arthur led him to an armchair.

"You've changed the decor since last I was here."

"Fashions change in twenty years, Father."

"I suppose." He glowered then softened. "You have fine taste, son." He nodded to Joseph. "Mr. Phillips."

Joseph nodded back. "Lord Richmond."

Wittering came in with the tea and tended to Father's cup.

"Arthur, what's this all about," Father asked after Wittering had left.

Arthur breathed in fortitude. This was not going to be easy. Neither man before him knew what he was about to say.

"Father, Joseph, I would like to propose we seek a special remainder for Henry Abraham Phillips to be placed into the line of succession as my heir to the marquessate."

The oppressive split-second of stillness was shattered by "What?" squawked simultaneously by both men.

Father looked askance at Joseph. "Arthur, you can't be serious."

"I can, Father, and I am being serious."

"The boy is half American."

"The Phillipses have only been an American family since the eighteenth century. Prior to that they were English."

Father grunted. "Can you prove this?"

"Wait a minute!" Joseph stood. "My ancestors did not fight a fucking revolution so my son could become a peer of the realm!" He threw his hands in the air. "This is preposterous."

"You forget that my grandson has noble blood in his veins, Phillips."

Joseph rounded on him. "You forget, my lord, that my son's veins also course with the blood of freedom-loving patriots and honest laborers."

"Gentlemen, can we please refrain from such grotesque metaphors?"

Father and Joseph both aimed their ire at him.

"You're asking the impossible, Arthur." Father's tone was implacable. "You know damn well the letters patent stipulate succession through male heirs born from my body. Which means you had better produce one yourself. Collateral heirs cannot be considered. It would take an act of bloody Parliament to make such a change." He scowled. "You'd need a damn good reason and not wanting to get married is not a damn good reason."

"Father—Papa, I know you married for duty. But I cannot do that. I've danced with every young woman Mother has chosen for me. Not one of them excites me—"

"Arthur, this is not about sex."

"But it very definitely is!" Arthur balled his hands and ground them into his hips. "Even if I were to marry one of these young women, I would have to perform with her—"

Father snorted.

"I would have to care for her, care for our children. I don't want to be in a marriage with a woman who, whenever I look at her, dredges up regrets. Or, to look at other women and wonder if that one would have somehow been a better match."

"A man can take a mistress, Arthur."

Arthur stared at him incredulously. "Did you?"

Father paled in shock. "Of course not."

"And I don't doubt that. I'm tired of mistresses, Father. Believe you me. After a spell it just becomes…rote." The last thing he wanted was an inexperienced debutante supplemented by a mistress who refused to suck his cock, much less perform anything more deviant. "That is exactly what would happen in a loveless marriage such as you are expecting for me."

"I wouldn't say my marriage was loveless, Arthur." Father's tone was edged with vulnerability.

"Allow me this. The first time around you were willing to let me marry for love."

"Henrietta was young with a fine pedigree."

"But I was in love with her. Let me marry for love. You have your grandson, Father. Why not make him your heir?"

Joseph barked a complaint. "I've already done my duty to this family. I gave you Helena. I would like Henry to make his own way in life. Like I did."

Arthur sighed. Joseph was shocked and upset. It was too much of a surprise. "I need not remind you that Helena married for love, Joseph. It just happened to be with a peer of the realm."

"And that marriage healed the festering wound killing this family."

Arthur locked eyes with him. Obstinacy from shock was one thing. But forgetting all Arthur had done for him was quite another.

"Isn't there a blasted cousin somewhere?" Joseph growled.

"No," Father snapped.

Arthur bit back a retort. There probably was, somewhere, maybe even in America. God that would be ironic. But Father was adamant the line go through him. Stubborn pride ran deep in Harwell men.

Father caught his eye. "There's a woman, isn't there?" he asked quietly.

Arthur had hoped to keep the conversation general and not bring her into it.

"Arthur." Joseph's tone was admonishing.

"Yes, Father, there is a woman."

"Who is she?"

Arthur ran his palm down his face. "Lady Foxley-Graham."

Father frowned. "So what is the problem?"

"She's unable to have children."

"Ah. I see." Father sipped his tea thoughtfully. "You've defied me at every turn, Arthur."

"You've forced me to, Father."

"It's time you thought about the family and not about yourself."

Joseph plopped back down on the sofa and shot him a sympathetic look.

Arthur drummed his fingers on his thigh before seeking solace in his teacup. Was he defeated? Poetic words haunted him—

'Tis all a Chequer-board of Nights and Days, Where Destiny with Men for Pieces plays.

No. Destiny would not win. He made his move. It had been simply unexpected. He would have to give Father and Joseph time to think about it.

"Yes, sir." He would wait.

Lavinia knew she shouldn't continue her affair with Nicholas. But there he was, draped over her bed, naked, slumbering, an occasional snore the mark of his utter relaxation and lack of concern that his wife was about to give birth thirty miles away. Of course, his wife probably knew exactly where he was and what he was doing and didn't give a fig herself. Not even a year since their wedding and already theirs was an exceptional marriage.

Nicholas stirred, tangling himself in the sheets. Lavinia watched from her vantage point seated at the dressing table, a smile curling her lips. Since he had been spending time with her after Parliamentary business, she had finally found a peaceful resolution to the disquiet over her foolishness of falling in love with him a year ago. She still loved him and he her, but it was different this time around. Instead of a love fraught with anxiety over its finality, their relationship had moved forward in an unexpected direction. He would always want her, always desire her, always love her. Most importantly, he would always be there for her.

It was so much better this way. And surprisingly there were no regrets.

Their relationship had matured. No longer was she the experienced paramour instructing him in the ways of the heart and the bedroom. Instead they shared frustrations and needs. He had eased her guilt over the furtive fuck with Arthur the other night, had listened to her pour out her emotions over her infatuation for the man, had sympathized with her reticence of falling further into love's oblivion.

But there was one secret from her past she could not confide, for which she could not seek his counsel.

What really happened with Julius.

Not because of Nicholas' twisted history with the man, but because even Nicholas could not offer any real consolation. What she needed only Julius could give.

She needed his sincere apology and remorse. Until then, there could be no resolution to their affair. That was why she couldn't let him go, why she kept allowing him to torment her, perpetuating the endless cycle of their unsatisfactory tumbles stained by bitterness and sorrow.

Why she kept seeking the comfort of the one memento she held on to. Perhaps she hoped every time she looked at it she would see something different. That the past would somehow be changed.

It was hidden under lock and key in a jewelry box her husband had given her, a gift, once presented, he had never inquired about again. Lavinia went to the wardrobe and took the rectangular box from the shelf at the top. She smoothed her hand over the buttery-soft vermilion calfskin and drew a finger over the gilt-bronze studs lining each edge. She sat at her dressing table to fish the key out of the small drawer on the right. She kept it on a red ribbon.

She unlocked the box.

The rumble of a groan emanated from deep within Nicholas as he turned onto his stomach. Late nights with peers were exhausting him. No one would think to find him in her bed though. He was safe for the moment from politics.

As long as he slept, she could be alone with her memories.

The box held no jewelry. Instead it held a slim volume of verse and a letter.

A love letter.

Her husband had fallen ill—the beginning of the end of his life although she hadn't known it at the time. His doctor—Julius— recommended a holiday to the seashore, that the viscountess should join her husband to nurse him as only a wife could. Richard had no idea she and Julius were lovers. Ingenuously, Richard had invited Julius to accompany them. Richard decided upon a cottage owned by a friend along the coast near Penzance, as his own at Exeter was too far inland.

She and Julius were almost never separated. They were young, brimming with a surfeit of insatiable passion. As doctor and patient's wife, no one questioned their continued society. They were audacious and imprudent, sharing a bed at times across the hall from Richard's room while he slept under the spell of laudanum. At the end of the fortnight, they made love utterly nude on the shore at midnight.

And when they returned to their dull lives in London, Julius wrote her his only love letter. Poetry was not a talent but the fervency was clear.

She unfolded the paper, taking care with the creases.

Vinny, my love,

The memory of you plagues me, your sighs in my arms, your eagerness for my touch. The taste of you lingers on my lips, your fragrance is the air I breathe. A zealous ardor swells my heart, my soul to bursting. The unrequited fire of my desire consumes my very being. I long for the next moment we are together.

Yours,

Jules

Three months later, he would renounce every sentiment. And Lavinia would come face-to-face with hate and fear.

She couldn't do that again. She couldn't fall in love with a man, knowing it would destroy her.

And a continued affair with Arthur would most certainly be destructive.

The purr of Nicholas' snoring revived her. She would have to be content with the occasional romp with Nicholas. Possibly seek out someone new.

And before she ever fell in love again, she would make certain there were no impediments.

CHAPTER THIRTEEN

Lavinia kept her composure in Lord and Lady Shotwick's ballroom as she watched Arthur dancing with Lady Ida Beeston, a pretty little thing whose dress was clearly designed to accentuate her bosom. It was an enviable bosom, to be sure, and it seemed Arthur was having a difficult time of it, trying to focus on her face. Dancing with the young lady seemed to be secondary to chatting her up and the pair stayed on the fringes of the fray rather than trip over dancers in the middle. What they had to converse about was something of a wonder. Lady Ida was not known for her intellect.

And when the dance was finished, Arthur bowed politely then headed for Lady Richmond's small circle of friends.

He stopped when he spied Lavinia. Her face grew hot. It was too obvious she had been watching him.

And then he was coming toward her and not his mother.

Lavinia fanned herself. She had just sworn to guard her heart. But there he was, all handsome and smiling, and she glued to her spot, willing him to join her.

She offered her hand and he bowed over it.

"My lady."

His smooth baritone melted her resolve.

"Lord Petersham, how was partnering Lady Ida?"

"Delightful. Light on her feet. Light in her mind."

Lavinia laughed softly. "It seemed you had plenty to talk about."

"Ah yes. She asked what it was I did as an earl. I told her I build railways."

"Oh my, that must have been confusing. Not all earls hold positions in industry."

"She lamented that it must have been so very grand and romantic to travel by coach on dirt paths everywhere."

Lavinia started. "You mean before the railway."

Arthur smirked. "Yes."

Oh dear. Lady Ida really was that dense. "Ponderously slow, I should think."

"Then she asked me what London looked like before the railways took over—"

"Oh my."

"Because it must have been terrifically bucolic in my youth."

Lavinia whipped out her fan to hide her growing smile.

"I feared she would next ask me if wigs were ever so uncomfortable."

She could not stop the guffaw and slapped the fan over her lips in mortification.

Arthur grinned then leaned in enough that his scent teased her senses. "Are you free for the next dance?"

"You'll have to pardon my ineptitude. I fear we did not have the waltz in my youth."

He grinned wider and surreptitiously squeezed her hand.

Mr. and Mrs. Peel approached, accompanied by a young man who, from his generous height, lanky frame, and reddish-brown hair could only be their son. William, if she recalled correctly.

"Arthur," greeted Mr. Peel. "My lady."

"Mr. Peel, Mrs. Peel." Lavinia nodded her greeting. She smiled at the young man.

He blushed, his sheepish expression matching the slight slouch in his posture, as if standing straight would draw too much attention to him.

"Lady Foxley-Graham," Mr. Peel said, "I dare say you may remember my son from the St. Albans' wedding last autumn, but perhaps a reintroduction is in order. May I present my son, William Peel. William, the Viscountess Foxley-Graham."

"Yes, I remember." Lavinia held out her hand. "Mr. Peel."

He grasped her hand, his confident grip discordant with his apparent demeanor, and bowed quickly. "My lady." He stood to his full height as he loosened his hold and met her eyes. "I remember you from the wedding. How could I forget?"

Now it was her turn to blush. In less than a minute the awkward boy had become a man. And an attractive man at that.

"William will be attending Cambridge this autumn," said Mrs. Peel. "We thought we'd give him a Season. So when his sisters are of age he can properly defend their honor."

"I'm sure even the Prince of Wales would shrink from a rebuke from so tall a man."

Mr. Peel the elder chuckled.

"My lady," began the younger Mr. Peel, "if it is not too forward of me, I should like to ask you to dance."

Lavinia shot a glance at Arthur before nodding to Mr. Peel. "I would be honored." She once again offered her hand.

He took it, his glove a little warmer than before. The waltz had already begun so they found their rhythm and joined. Mr. William Peel was master of their steps, his carriage strong, his direction assured. In no time they were one with the swirling mass of couples on the ballroom floor.

And far away from his parents.

"My lady, I know the dance is already almost over. I offer my regrets for my lack of planning but wonder if I may beg a second dance?"

Despite Lavinia's stature she was small before him. His head angled down, his eyes focused on hers, his gaze not flickering to her cleavage as another man's would.

"Or perhaps a walk in the garden?"

He was bold.

So was she.

"I think we are near the doors to the garden and I could use a breath of fresh air. Let's take a stroll."

He smiled as the music ended, wrapping her arm around his. They strolled through the French doors to the terrace, his step on the flagstones as unfaltering as on the dance floor. He slowed as they reached the carved balustrade at the edge of the terrace.

He turned toward her, his arm still the support of hers. "I've overheard the Earl of Petersham sing your praises, my lady. They are true indeed."

So Arthur did think of her when she wasn't around. That was heartening. "I'm flattered, Mr. Peel."

"I understand you are a good friend to Helena's husband, the Earl of St. Albans." He leaned in just a bit more. "A very good friend."

Her skin prickled. Was he attempting seduction? "I have known the earl since he was a boy. I was a close friend of his mother's."

"Yes. I've heard that." He squeezed her arm. "Shall we take a walk in the garden?"

The prickle chilled. He couldn't be much over eighteen years of age. Yet, he was progressing as a man far beyond his years.

"As you wish, Mr. Peel."

He led her out onto the lawn, down a path lined with mirrored glass lanterns aglow with candles. The setting was romantic, with lovers all around.

It appeared he understood that fact precisely.

He steered her a little off the lighted path to a parterre garden, their footsteps crunching on the gravel as they strolled between the manicured beds. Before them loomed a row of tall squared boxwoods, an archway cut into the hedge.

Lavinia swallowed. A man hoping to get her alone was predictable but a boy? And one she barely knew. "Mr. Peel," she said, trying to convey a warning.

He directed her through the shrub. Lavinia did not resist. Instead curiosity overwhelmed her.

He stopped just on the other side, close enough to the archway so she could easily escape if she felt that were necessary. He released her arm, and took her hand instead.

"My lady, I know I am too forward—"

"You are, Mr. Peel." His confidence was shaking. Hers was resolute.

"I've heard—well it's not like gossiping, just overhearing—that you sometimes take young men under your wing. Offer them guidance, for their careers and such."

And such. Her stomach clenched. She would have to make him see the foolishness of his actions. "And what sort of career were you considering?"

"What? Oh. Archaeology I suppose."

"How romantic."

"Do you really think so?"

"Why yes, in the sense of the exoticism of it all." Her voice conveyed a serenity at odds with the agitation rising in her body. His closeness was unsettling. "And where will you go? Persia? Greece? China?"

"I rather like the idea of the Levant, you know, biblical sites."

Agitation burned slowly to arousal. "So then you'll be learning Greek and Hebrew."

"I already know Greek—" He shook his head. "I didn't really mean to discuss all this."

"I understood you wanted guidance in your career."

He gazed at her. His hand tightened around hers. "I was hoping for another sort of guidance."

He dipped his head and slid his free hand around her waist, holding her fast as he pressed his lips to hers.

It was wrong, terribly wrong. Not the kiss, *that* was…quite expert for one so young, but the whole situation, his relationship to Arthur, the fact they barely knew each other…that she was over twice his age. Everything.

Lavinia flinched and pushed away but he gripped more tightly, steadying her as he tantalized her lips with his tongue, teasing patiently until she softened under him, letting him plunder her depths. Her body weakened, relaxing in his arms, molding to his provocatively. He would be as hard as she was wet.

And she was very wet.

He pulled back slowly. Her heart pounded, playing a syncopated beat against her ragged breaths.

"I hardly think you need any guidance, Mr. Peel."

He brought her hand to his lips. "My lady, please forgive my impetuousness. I didn't mean to alarm you. I was overcome. Your closeness, your perfume, your beauty."

"Mr. Peel, believe me I am entirely flattered a young man deigns to give me such attentions."

"I'm a virgin," he blurted.

What should one say to such a confession? "One would not know that from the way you kiss, Mr. Peel."

"Thank you, my lady. Thank you." He let go of her hand. "I had hoped I might receive some guidance from you before I enter university." He drew in a breath and let it out slowly. "Guidance about how a man can be with a woman."

"Ah. Thank you for your honesty." Now free of his grasp, her hands trembled. "I am not a courtesan, William. Nicholas and I may have been lovers but it was from a mutual attraction, deep friendship, and shared experience."

He covered his mouth with his hand. "Please believe me, I didn't mean to imply such a slanderous notion." He shook his head again. "I know you are connected with my father's business associates, that you are a trusted member of their circle." He twisted his fingers. "And I've heard you've helped other young men, not just Lord St. Albans."

That was not slander. It was the truth. "I didn't sleep with all of them."

"Oh God, you must think me a barbarian."

"No I think you are an honest young man with a promising career before you. If you would like me to discreetly arrange for you to meet with a courtesan—"

"No," he said with surprising abruptness. "It has to be you. Helena speaks the world of you."

That was a surprising reference. "Helena?"

"She doesn't know about any of this. I just got the idea from talking to her one day. We're very close. Almost raised together. She thinks you're marvelous."

He *was* attractive and a good kisser. "If we were to attempt such a venture, I'm not at all certain where we would meet. You might be noticed arriving at my house."

"I thought we would pretend to meet by chance then I would take you home in a cab or maybe even walk you home…then you would invite me in."

"Oh my. You have put some thought into this, haven't you?"

"I thought it might be easier for you to make a decision if all the details were worked out."

And what a decision it was. She could do it. She needed a lover and if William was as good in bed as he was a kisser, it would be worth it. At the very least, his skills at gamahuching would be unsurpassed. If Arthur found out, he could say nothing. He had no hold over her. Well, he had no right to claim he did.

"William, what sort of library does your father have?"

"Library?"

"Books."

"I don't understand."

"Does he even have a library? Does he collect books of a particular nature?"

"Not really. He has some law books at home and books on birding, maybe hunting, that sort of thing. Mother loves novels. She keeps everything she's read. She likes to loan them to her friends. She seems to know exactly what her friends need and want to read."

"So if you wanted to begin a study of ancient languages before you left for university, you could not do that at home. Is that correct?"

' "Yes. I'd have to go to a lending library or buy them myself. Possibly Mr. Phillips or even Lord Petersham would have something like that."

"Let's leave them out of this." She wrapped her arm around his. "I have a spectacular library. My dead husband fancied himself a scholar. Included in my library are grammars and study guides for Persian, Turkish, Arabic, and Hebrew. You said you know Greek and I presume you already know Latin." She walked him a little farther into the darkness. "We'll do it this way. We'll meet by chance, on the street in public, near my house. We'll have a conversation about your studies. I'll offer my library at your disposal. You will come home with me, get to know the place and borrow a book or two. When your parents inquire, which they will, I'll say I've offered you an opportunity to use my library whenever you want. This way we have a reason for you to be at my house. You will have the responsibility of learning some useful language however, in addition to whatever else you learn at my house."

"You're really good at this, aren't you?"

He was so innocent. She laughed softly. "I've been doing this sort of thing for longer than you can imagine. One gains an understanding of how it all works."

"Thank you, my lady."

"You're welcome, William. Now there's a milliner's on High Street in Kensington near my house. Madame Colline. Why don't you plan to run into me at three o'clock next Thursday?"

"I think I can do that."

"Good. If I don't see you, I'll know you were caught up elsewhere so you needn't send a note."

"My lady, is there anything I should do to prepare? For you?"

So sweet. "Let's see how this first clandestine meeting works out and we'll make arrangements from there."

"All right."

"Now, Mr. Peel, we've been in the garden far too long. People will begin to talk. The last thing you ever want is for people to talk. You must take me in. We'll say we talked about your future and your dream to become an archaeologist. But we're just laying the groundwork so we won't mention the library just yet."

"Yes, my lady."

And like a proper gentleman, William Peel returned her to the ballroom.

* * * * *

Seated on the slipper chair before the bedroom fire, Julius had a view of Grace's back as she pulled off her chemise. She turned to the bed where her nightgown lay, the generous curve of her belly deeply shadowed with the firelight behind her.

She was really beginning to show.

He should really say something.

She slipped her nightgown over her nude body, hiding her condition under the voluminous white cambric skirt. She flashed him a smile. He extended his hand and she went to him.

"How are you feeling?"

She sighed. "Tired. Happy." She nudged his thighs to make space for her knees then straddled him.

Her belly was at his chest. "Happy?"

"It was a good day. It was lovely to see Mrs. Vickers and her twins today. They're adorable." She combed his hair with her fingers. "The twins I mean."

He laughed. "Mrs. Vickers is adorable as well." She was petite and fussy and always coordinated her clothes to the matched outfits of the twins.

Grace giggled. "Yeah."

He placed his hands at her waist, his thumbs stretching over her fullness. They had yet to discuss the child within—was it a girl or boy, what name should they choose, what room would be used as the nursery, would there be a christening, would they hire a nanny?

"But really I'm happy because I'm with you." She tugged up the hem of her nightgown to uncover her sex. "I get to see you all day long." She unbuttoned his fly. "And that keeps me happy."

She rubbed the wet heat of her quim against his drawers as she slipped off his braces. She teased his neck with tender nibbles as she freed his stiff cock from his underclothes. She held his head steady as she assaulted his mouth with an insistent kiss and lowered herself onto his prick.

He groaned in satisfaction. Now was probably not a good time to have a domestic discussion.

She rode him slowly, excruciatingly so, fluttering her expert muscles around his length, squeezing the tip before sliding down. She gripped his shoulders, propped her forehead against his. Their breaths mingled hot and humid in the pocket of space between their bodies.

"Darling…Grace…"

She increased her speed just a hair.

"Yes…"

She undid the buttons of his shirt then plucked at the linen cloth. "Take it off, Jules. I want to see you."

He tore off the garment. She gripped the strands of his chest hair, pulling until the point of discomfort, only to relax her hold then pull harder still.

Just how he liked it.

Under her nightgown, her full breasts swayed tantalizingly. He palmed the demi-globes before smoothing the fabric over her belly. Her shape aroused him as he'd never thought it would. "Now I want to see you."

He held her as she complied, struggling a little with the nightgown. She tossed it behind her.

"Fuck me, Grace."

She bobbed up and down, her breasts undulating to her sensual rhythm right before his face. He reached out his tongue, flicking the tip over her hardening peaks as they bounced before him.

She pinched his nipples. He jerked at the delectable pain.

"Suck me, Jules."

He lay kisses on her breasts before drawing in an areola, sucking hard until she gasped. Her body was his to do with as he pleased for only a few months more. He would make the most of it.

He plowed into her from below as he bit the sensitized tip. She squealed an oath before dissolving into giggles.

She matched his pace, her rhythm faltering in impatience, distracting him from his imminent climax. "Come inside me," she urged. "I want to feel you come deep inside me." She grinned devilishly and slammed down on his shaft.

Her horrified shriek pierced the air. She pulled up quickly, his tip still embedded in her warmth as she remained poised above his lap.

"I can't. You're too big." Her gaze held panic. "It hurts."

His chest clenched in mortification. "Then don't. I'll be gentle." He eased her down his shaft. "Let me make love to you."

She exhaled a sigh as she wrapped her arms around him and settled her cheek on his shoulder. He resumed at a languorous pace, one arm holding her securely as his other hand stroked her clitoris. She reacted as she always did, melting into him with a contented moan, the melodic sound stoking the lust in his loins back to burning.

This was their new life…mellow, languid, loving. He didn't need the taunting and teasing, savagery and ferocity, he could climb to the peak with just him and Grace, their bodies in tender union, each nurturing the other to culmination.

She came on his hand, her wetness soaking into his trousers, taking him to the edge. He closed his eyes, expanding his senses. Her flesh was hot under his fingers as he breathed in the aroma of her arousal, letting it swirl within and transport him. He spent his seed with restraint.

He kissed her cheek. "I'm happy too."

Arthur had ignored the note from Father all morning, wanting to simply drink his coffee and read the newspaper in silence. No doubt Mother was haranguing Father to prod Arthur into choosing one of the beauties he had been introduced to. He needed a break.

He hadn't even had a chance to dance with Lavinia the other night when she returned from far too long a stroll with William. Mother had whisked him away to dance with a young girl whose name he had utterly forgotten.

Father's folded letter mocked him from the center of the silver salver, the butler having just set the whole lot down on the breakfast table instead of hovering in hopes Arthur would pick up the missive.

He sighed and reached for the letter. It was not in Father's hand. Father's loyal secretary Billings had written the note. Either the factious formality had returned or something was wrong.

He unfolded the page with clammy hands and began to read.

Shit. Father was ill. Arthur was required immediately.

Except "immediately" was over two hours ago.

And by the time he was greeted by the family butler Cawston at the front door of the Mayfair residence "immediately" had turned into at least three hours.

Geoffrey approached from the direction of Father's office, his sullen face brightening when he spied Arthur.

"Geoff, what are you doing here?" He tried to keep the horror from his tone.

"Your father wanted me to review his will before he meets with his solicitor. Said he trusted me to give an honest opinion."

"His will?"

"I don't know if it is all that serious, really. He's ill, yes. But St. Albans is with him now. I would have assumed his regular doctor would be looking after him."

"And his regular solicitor."

"Yes, that too. So Richmond is keeping the illness mum. Private family business and all that."

"I'm sure he has his reasons." Perhaps an unwillingness to come to terms with his mortality.

"Arthur, I have to leave. Joseph and Sophie and your mother are with him now."

Which meant Father and Joseph must have reconciled. Perhaps it *was* serious. "Helena?"

"She's expected later. St. Albans was already in town. She's still at the Keep."

Arthur squeezed Geoffrey's shoulder. "Thank you, Geoff."

"My pleasure and privilege. Now get upstairs. They've been wondering about your absence."

A flurry of excuses flooded Arthur's brain as he mounted the stairs two-by-two. Yet when he opened the door to Father's bedroom he was not greeted with the expected chastisement but expressions of relief instead.

Mother went to him, gripping him by the arms. "Arthur!"

"My apologies, Mother," he said, kissing her cheeks. "I had business."

He nodded to Sophia, who reclined on a day bed, and to Joseph, who stood nearby. He approached Nicholas, who sat by Father's bedside, jotting notes in a journal. Father's eyes were closed, his face pale, his breaths huffing with irregular respiration.

"How is he?" he said quietly in Nicholas' ear.

Nicholas offered a weak smile. "Pneumonia. It's an inflammation of the lungs. I'll keep an eye on him for the next few weeks."

"So it's not serious?"

"Yes and no. In healthy adults, it can be combated. In children, the aged, and the sick, it can be fatal."

"The aged?"

"That's why I want to keep an eye on him. He's rather robust for a man of seventy. However I've written Helena to stay at home for the time being. And I don't want little Henry in this house. Lord Richmond is calling for all his family so it has been difficult to keep supplying excuses. Your presence will liven and distract him."

Father stirred under his covers, his eyes fluttering open. "Arthur? Is that you?"

Nicholas got up from the chair to let Arthur sit. "Yes, Papa."

Papa. He shouldn't have called him that. Father would think he was dying.

"Arthur, so good to see you. I'm dying."

"Balderdash. I've been informed by your personal physician—" He winked at Nicholas. "That you are merely temporarily ill and will regain your health in no time."

"That's what we have all been trying to tell you, Papa," Sophia said from the daybed.

Mother had joined Sophia and sat twisting her hands fretfully.

"I'm an old man. I think I know my body better than any young doctor."

Arthur sighed. Father was stubborn and no doubt believed every one of his own thoughts. Best keep his mind off such thoughts before they became prophetic. "I suppose you won't be dancing too much this Season, Papa. We'll have to bring in a theatrical troupe to entertain you."

Mother glared at him. Joseph chuckled.

"I'm not having some bloody drawing-room comedian recite Shakespeare in my house."

"Harold! Language!" Mother tipped her head in Sophia's direction.

Sophia was trying very hard not to laugh.

"Lord Richmond, you cannot expect to go out in your condition," Nicholas offered. "Definitely not to your club."

That got a rise out of the old man. Arthur grinned inwardly. Nicholas certainly knew his grandfather-in-law's habits.

"Well, then, Doctor, you damn well better take good care of me."

Mother once again scowled at his profanity.

So Father expected to get well after all. "Joseph, I need to speak with you briefly," Arthur said. "About my business meeting this morning."

Joseph quirked a brow. "Okay."

Arthur exited and Joseph followed him into the hallway, closing the bedroom door behind him.

The quirked brow did not waver. "And?"

Arthur grabbed his arm and drew him against the wall, tucked behind a cabinet-on-stand. "Father is playing some sort of game."

"Arthur, Richmond is ill."

"Yes, yes, of course he is. I'm afraid, though, he is forcing his hand with this marriage business."

"So he's in cahoots with the marchioness?"

The Americans had such freedom in their language. "Something like that. They want me to hurry it along." He slouched against the wall and stared up at Joseph. "Shit. I really wanted to marry for love."

Joseph offered a weak smile. "You deserve nothing less." He placed his hand, warm and comforting, on Arthur's shoulder. "And you don't need to talk to me about expected duty. I almost married my daughter off to the highest-ranking peer last Season, whoever he might be."

"Thank God my sister is insatiable and instead tried to marry Helena off to her lover."

Joseph chuckled with a bend of his head. "I never thought I would be able to laugh at that." He met Arthur's gaze. "But, yes the unexpected can happen."

Arthur tilted his chin with a dark smirk. "Like a barren woman giving birth?"

"Now you're being unnecessarily dramatic and morose. And no, I was thinking you might find a compatible young woman." Joseph's smile thinned. "You really are in love with her, aren't you?"

"I am. At least I think I am." He slid farther down the polished wood wainscoting. "Damn it. I'm desperate. She's all I ever think of."

"Collect yourself, Arthur." Joseph skated his palm down Arthur's arm to squeeze his hand.

"Thanks." He freed himself. "But have a care that we could be seen."

Joseph pulled back. "Of course, my lord."

"I hate when you call me that."

One corner of Joseph's mouth twitched upward with meaning. "I know you do. Now come back inside and humor Richmond."

"In a moment."

Arthur watched as Joseph returned to Father's bedroom. He was in far too black a mood to humor anyone, much less the man sending him to his doom.

Lavinia stopped at the top of the stairs just before the landing of the second floor of the Richmond London residence. There before her were Arthur and Joseph in something more than just a friendly position. Joseph angled over the earl, leaning in slowly as if he were about to take him in a passionate kiss. It didn't help that he drew his hand down Arthur's arm to squeeze his fingers. She stayed as still as a mouse before the scene. They didn't notice her.

And then memories blazed in her mind's eye, vivid and telling. The sultan casually fending off amorous advances by the American revolutionary at Countess Winthrop's masquerade. Joseph and Arthur comfortably disheveled from an evening of drinking spirits in the latter's sitting room at Atherley Keep.

Her suspicions about the two men were confirmed. They were lovers or had been at one time.

The thought was greatly arousing.

Both men were endowed with a charismatic potency. Joseph had a rough edge, bordering on coarseness that intrigued rather than repelled. Arthur was more refined, his sensuality intellectual rather than crude. They were broad-minded in their sexual predilections. The masquerade, Joseph's marital arrangements, and Lavinia's experience in Arthur's bed were proof of that.

Together the men would be the very definition of lust. It would be amazing to simply watch.

And then Joseph left Arthur's side and stepped through the first door on the left. According to Cawston, that was the marquess's bedroom and where he was expecting her.

Which meant the marquess had requested more than just her presence. Something was wrong. A thought confirmed by Arthur's downcast countenance.

"My lady! Oh, I do apologize."

Cawston's voice disrupted the stillness. Arthur jerked from the wall to stand upright, staring at her, his eyes wide in astonishment, then softening with need. Arousal fluttered anew.

"There was a reporter, my lady," the butler puffed from running up the stairs. "It will be difficult to fend them off what with rumors flying about concerning the marquess's health. I'm terribly sorry to have had to send you up alone."

So Richmond was ill. "I took my time, Mr. Cawston, and almost found my way." She indicated Arthur. "Lord Petersham would have put me on the correct path had I been lost."

Arthur cleared his throat. "Lady Foxley-Graham. What a surprise." He still stared, his eyes questioning.

"My lord." She nodded her greeting. "Lord Richmond requested my presence."

"You?" He swallowed. "Of course…you are family now." His brow twisted as if still not quite convinced.

Right. Godparents. The two of them together.

Cawston led the way to the same door Joseph had just used and ushered her in, Arthur in their wake.

"The Viscountess Foxley-Graham, my lord," Cawston announced.

All present stared at her in stunned disbelief.

"Lady Foxley-Graham," Richmond called out, before a fit of coughing took over.

Nicholas went to the marquess but Richmond waved him aside and beckoned to Lavinia.

She approached. Nicholas quirked a brow as he offered her the chair at the bedside.

"I can tell from your expressions you all think I'm mad as well as ill."

"*You* sent for the viscountess?" Lady Richmond's voice was edged with concern.

"I did." He motioned to a stunned Arthur, who approached. "Arthur, in the event I die—"

Lady Richmond gasped.

Lord Richmond ignored her. "In the event I die, if not from whatever this blasted ailment is, then from old age—" He directed that to Lady Richmond. "I will need my successor to be prepared to assume my regular duties. You know nothing about what it is I do in Parliament."

Arthur's shock melted into sheepishness. "You know I don't, Father."

"I would wager Lady Foxley-Graham knows precisely what it is I do in Parliament."

So that's what the display was all about. Lavinia's laugh was most inappropriate but heartfelt. "I know your opponents, my lord. They follow your every move."

He winked at her. "And I'll wager Arthur has no idea who my opponents are."

Arthur gaped with a touch of annoyance. "All right, Father, I get your point. Is that why Lady Foxley-Graham is here, to illuminate my shortcomings?"

"No. She is here to arrange for your instruction in the matter."

"My instruction?"

Lavinia tried not to look as surprised as she felt.

"It's about time you took an interest, Arthur. You are privileged as a peer to have a say in running this country. You should not be so dismissive of this honor and responsibility."

"Yes, sir."

The whole situation was a bit bizarre. Surely there were more suited mentors? "Pardon me, my lord," Lavinia dared. "If I may inquire as to why you do not entrust Lord St. Albans to do the honors? He has been negotiating the maze of Lords quite admirably."

"Ah yes. St. Albans has been having a time of it, haven't you, son?"

Nicholas blushed. "Yes, my lord."

Richmond eyed her. "I understand he has been relying heavily on your counsel as well, my lady."

That and so much more. "Yes, my lord. I see your point."

"You have quite a reputation, my dear lady. I would like to see it used to great advantage."

"You mean to your advantage, Lord Richmond."

He chuckled, which set off another coughing fit. Nicholas went to his side but Richmond waved him off.

"Politics is politics as you know. Whether in the central lobby or my sickroom."

Or her bedroom. "Yes, my lord."

"The members to whom you are acquainted may be my opponents but they are each one of them respectable men. I would like it if you would introduce Arthur to members of both houses and every party."

"Even the Radicals, my lord?"

That got a smile out of him. "Even the blasted Socialists. The ways of politics make for strange bedfellows." He finally addressed Arthur. "I want to believe you've formed all sorts of opinions from your business with Phillips. It may not be easy but sometimes you will need to bend those opinions for the betterment of our country." He nodded Lavinia's way. "I learned that from the viscountess."

"Yes, sir." Arthur shifted his weight like a chastised schoolboy.

Richmond waggled his hand in Lavinia's direction. "You two can work this out between yourselves. I suggest Arthur read the newspaper accounts and sit in the Strangers' Galleries."

"Of course, Lord Richmond."

After that, pleasant chit-chat, led by Sophia, ensued.

Lavinia caught Arthur's eye. He offered a sympathetic smile and a relieved expression. She let out an exhale. There had been no talk of his marriage prospects, only politics. She had feared that her presence had been requested to offer an opinion on pedigree. But talk of politics meant a wife had not yet been chosen for him.

Which meant there might still be a shred of hope.

The ballroom at Lord and Lady Quimby's Belgravia house was overflowing, making it difficult to distinguish anyone amongst the mass of faces. Only when Lavinia stood on tiptoe did she spy Charlotte along the fringes. She caught her eye and waved her over.

"My dear viscountess." Charlotte kissed both her cheeks. "Good to see you. Not many interesting people here tonight, are there?"

"You mean not much to gossip about, Lady Banbury?"

Charlotte unfurled her ivory fan with a flick of her wrist. "I feel a bit off my game this Season, what with no one to take under my wing."

"You should rest on your laurels. Helena made a fabulous match."

"She did, did she not?" Charlotte hid her broad smile behind her vigorous fanning. "And how is the Countess St. Albans? Has she had her baby yet?"

"Not yet. Very soon. I'm to be godmother."

Charlotte squeaked excitedly. "Oh, how lovely for you." She beamed and grasped Lavinia's hands. "And in eighteen years, you'll have someone to introduce to Society."

Lavinia laughed softly.

"Is there a godfather as well?"

"The Earl of Petersham. Helena's uncle."

"Ah yes, wasn't he involved in Sophia Phillips' scandal? Hiding her away while she was enceinte."

"I suppose he acted as any older brother would." Lavinia fanned the heat flushing her face. "He's quite the gentleman."

Charlotte eyed her queerly. "Ah. So there's my match."

"Charlotte—"

"I see interest and I know enough to know he's unattached. Infamously so." She grinned. "Which means only one as incomparable as you could sway such as he."

If only Charlotte were correct. The elation of a momentary imagined future was quickly quashed when she spied the Marchioness of Richmond. Lavinia stepped back, trying to hide behind Charlotte's generous skirts.

But Lady Richmond had already seen her. The marchioness waved with an affected smile and joined them. Lavinia let her kiss the air above her cheeks.

"Lady Foxley-Graham, just the woman I wanted to see tonight."

She feigned a smile. "I'm flattered, Lady Richmond, really."

"If anyone knows about one of our debutantes, it is you."

Lavinia's lungs clenched. A debutante for Arthur. "Lady Richmond, may I introduce my dear friend Charlotte, the Countess of Banbury. Charlotte, the Marchioness of Richmond. I believe you two met at Helena's wedding last year."

"Why yes, of course. Lady Banbury, a pleasure."

"Lady Richmond, the pleasure is mine." Charlotte nodded a bow.

"Lady Richmond, if anyone knows our debutantes, it is Charlotte. Who is the young lady in question?" Lavinia grabbed a glass of champagne from the tray of an obsequious footman.

The marchioness surveyed the ballroom then smiled with a squawk of recognition. "The pretty blonde thing over there. In the magnificent gold and olive dress with the fringe."

Lavinia knew the girl and she most certainly was a pretty blonde thing. Her curls framed a sweet face, radiating innocence. Her figure was statuesque and stunning. But as her father was one of the few Radicals in the House of Lords, a man who vociferously supported women's rights and Irish nationalism, most likely the girl's pedigree was not quite what Lady Richmond had hoped for her Arthur.

"I understand that is Lady Beatrice Smythe. The middle daughter of the Earl of Ryburgh." Lady Richmond's tone carried a hint of victory.

"She's just turned eighteen, my lady." Charlotte raised her eyebrows. "Would you be considering her for your son?" She flashed Lavinia a look of pure shock.

The marchioness sighed. "Lord Petersham—Arthur is being very stubborn. He won't look at anyone under twenty-five—"

Charlotte's fan flew to cover her gape. Lavinia deposited her empty glass on a passing tray.

"But there are so many wonderful girls who just came out this year." Lady Richmond turned to Lavinia. "I don't know the girl. Can you make the introductions?"

What harm could it possibly do? At the very least Arthur would meet Beatrice's father and learn a thing or two about politics. "I'd be delighted, Lady Richmond."

Just as the words left her lips, the Earl of Ryburgh saw her and waved. He came over, a blushing Beatrice in tow.

Standing side-by-side before them, it was apparent from whom Beatrice had received her pleasing good looks. Ryburgh's once-blonde hair had darkened and grayed with age but his countenance still retained its boyish appeal despite the laugh lines crinkled around his blue-gray eyes.

Ryburgh took her hands in his with genuine enthusiasm. "Lavinia, it's been too long." His eyes twinkled.

She smiled back. "Yes, Felix, it has."

He glanced at Charlotte and Lady Richmond. "Lady Banbury." He nodded.

"My lord," Lavinia said, "may I introduce the Marchioness of Richmond. Lady Richmond, the Earl of Ryburgh."

"My lady." Ryburgh gave a courteous bow. "And may I introduce my daughter, Miss Beatrice Smythe." He held his hand in presentation.

Until that moment, Beatrice had hung back shyly. She came forward and curtsied to Lady Richmond and Charlotte then smiled warmly at Lavinia.

"My, you've grown into a lovely young woman, Beatrice."

"Thank you, my lady." The color rose in her cheeks.

Lady Richmond pursed her lips. "But surely, Lord Ryburgh, your daughter should be styled Lady Beatrice Smythe?"

Beatrice stood a little straighter. "I have chosen to disregard my title and employ the common epithet, my lady."

Ryburgh stifled a grin.

Lady Richmond offered a specious smile limned with shock. "And how is it you two know each other?" she said, turning to Lavinia.

The earl spoke first. "The women's property bill ten years ago. Lavinia was marvelous with garnering votes in both houses."

Lady Richmond lifted a brow. "Oh?"

"Beatrice was a darling child back then," Lavinia added, hoping to emphasize how youthful the girl was. "I helped introduce her older sister Olivia that Season, if I recall."

"You came to our house for tea quite often. I always looked forward to your visits, my lady."

At her words, all eyes focused on Beatrice and she blushed again.

Lady Richmond turned to Ryburgh. "I've just learned recently of Lady Foxley-Graham's interest in politics. Lord Richmond speaks highly of her accomplishments."

"She's positively magnificent!" Ryburgh exclaimed. "She knows absolutely everybody in Lords and how best to sway them to her causes."

"Felix, you flatter me too much, I'm sure."

"And what are your causes?" Lady Richmond asked her.

"I feel it is my duty to help those who have no voice, my lady. Women, the poor, the working class."

"I dare say, we've given the working man the right to vote, Lady Foxley-Graham." Ryburgh winked at her. "It is their own fault if they do not make use of that right."

"True, my lord, but so many still remain disenfranchised. Why should lack of property or gender be impediments to democracy?"

Ryburgh discharged a sharp guffaw.

Lady Richmond stared at him and Lavinia, aghast. She recovered and turned to Beatrice. "I hope to see you at more of these events, Lady Bea—Miss Smythe."

"Thank you, my lady. It's my first Season out so I hope to attend as many as I can."

"Lady Ryburgh and I are taking turns showing her off." Ryburgh beamed at his daughter. "However I've discovered ballrooms are nothing like parliament. Different politics altogether."

"I'd be delighted to step in, my lord," offered Charlotte.

"Truly?" Ryburgh brightened. "Then why don't you stop by tomorrow, Lady Banbury? We have absolutely loads of invitations. It would be marvelous if you could sort out the best."

"It's settled." Charlotte smiled at Beatrice. "I'll call on you tomorrow, Miss Smythe."

Beatrice curtsied, her cheeks flushed.

"Fabulous," Ryburgh pronounced. "Then we're off to find Beatrice's next dance partner. A duke I think." He nodded at Lady Richmond and winked at Lavinia. "Until next time."

Lavinia watched as the earl attempted to navigate the crush. His attentions had always been generous—and welcome. Had he not been utterly smitten with his wife, she would have tried to get him into bed. But it was best, sometimes, simply to be just good friends.

Given the current circumstances such a thought was dispiriting.

CHAPTER FOURTEEN

Grace found Julius sleeping in a leather club chair in his library, an old and well-worn copy of *The Obstetrical Journal* open on his lap. It had been a busy day again. They really needed to hire another doctor. Julius could barely keep up with his patients.

So his sherry would have to wait. In the meantime she figured she'd straighten up his study. She'd already cleaned the two examination rooms. She was tired too, but maybe it was the baby. She had been experiencing a surge of energy at the end of the day recently that made napping difficult despite the enervation. The mornings were the most difficult. She dreaded getting up from the cocoon of their warm bed.

She went down the hall to the study, closing the door behind her so any noise she made wouldn't disturb him. He was a light sleeper, tightly drawn and ready to act, a habit developed after too many late-night doorstep emergency calls.

And he had been so secretive of whatever it was he had been doing in the study that she absolutely did not want him waking up.

She lit the oil lamp. The room was an uncharacteristic mess, the desk anyway. Papers were strewn about in a disorderly fashion, pages from letters bowled and curled from their creases. A blank page sat in the middle of the blotter, above it the inkwell sat uncapped. The pen had bled out onto the blotter in a sickly fashion, resembling a human organ rather than something pleasant like a butterfly.

The letters were not new, the stationery darkened from a color, perhaps lavender, to something more akin to spilled tea, the handwriting no longer crisp but blurred along the edges of the pen strokes. The folds were well worn, as if the missives had been read and reread over and over again.

The hand was feminine. So not correspondence from a colleague about medical concerns but from a woman—a lover? A family member?

Curiosity spiked inside. It would be wrong to peruse Julius' private correspondence. They had known each other barely a year. He had had a life before her, as had she before him. They each had had a string of lovers, luckily from differing classes. She would hate to be in a situation as one patient had intimated to her, of a friend who had begun an affair with a man whom she did not know was her cousin's new lover and ended up pregnant with his child.

Grace sat in the desk chair and surveyed the pages, mentally putting them in order, as she did not want to touch too much. Julius would know. He knew when something was out of place but usually it was because his space was ordered. Any deviation was noticeable. Although where chaos reigned it was uncertain if he could tell if it had been further disturbed.

A date caught her eye, at the top of the first page of many. The pages were still attached where the creases held them in place.

Exeter, 21 August 1859. Over twenty years ago.

Grace had been a child then. She barely remembered it. There had been happy memories to be sure, but most memories were of a wretched existence—her mother's fear they would be caught stealing an apple, her father's disgust at having to sell a man's fine leather coin purse after he had emptied it of the few coppers and shillings encased within.

"The poor robbing the poor," he had said.

Grace focused on the page before her. "In for a penny, in for a pound" was another aphorism voiced by her parents.

She continued reading.

My darling,

Julius, it seemed, was carrying on a love affair at that time. How strange to realize one's lover had been an adult when one was just a child. How humbling to realize she might be just the latest of his affairs. Would he one day be rereading her letters to him?

Would she feel compelled to write letters to him?

A woman only did such a thing if she was tortured by love and unable to see her lover, or remorseful and wanted to apologize, or felt wronged and needed an answer. Had Julius been wronged? Or was he the villain?

Grace read further.

I've recovered. I mean to say my body has recovered. My heart is still in tatters, bleeding for you. Richard was so worried for me, insisting he call a doctor. I finally convinced him sometimes women just have these spells...that their courses take a bad turn...and I lied that I had experienced it before. My lady's maid was shocked and horrified by the amount of blood, for there was an absolute deluge.

Still it did not compare to the deluge of grief I still harbor for the loss of your child.

Grace's heart clenched. Twenty-one years ago, Julius was going to be a father. He had never mentioned it. Why should he really?

I fear you are wrong when you claim my husband would have known the child was not his. In the delight of fatherhood, Richard would not have noticed. And if gossips had commented on the black hair of the son of a ginger-haired man, he would have laughed it off ingenuously. For who really understands these sorts of things but doctors and men of science?

So Julius' paramour had been married. Grace herself had never inquired about the marital status of the blokes she lay with. If a handsome lad was willing, it was often hard to resist, especially if he was willing to pay.

> *But to have given me a "tonic" without my knowledge is absolutely unconscionable. I know you've never wanted the "inconvenience" of a child, but I have been longing to provide my husband with the one thing I was supposed to give him. You would have had no responsibility whatsoever. I have heard endlessly how my predecessor failed to provide a son and now I share in that failure. It kills me to know I may never be fruitful and to know the innocent we created has been slaughtered by your ambition.*
>
> *And now I no longer have you either, Julius. You could have at least left me with your child, a memento of our love.*

The words stung like pin pricks to her flesh. *I know you've never wanted the "inconvenience" of a child.* Grace had not thought to even ask Julius. She just thought whatever happened, happened. She would take care of the child, even if Julius put her out on the street. She too only wanted a memento of their union.

But he didn't want a child even if he did not have to take care of it. His lover had been married, had been willing to raise the child with another man's name, and still he did not want it.

He had given her a tonic. Grace knew exactly what that was. Julius had provided it to Mrs. Chadbourne.

Well if Julius did not want the child, then she knew what had to be done.

Curiosity compelled her one last time. She leafed through the pages until she reached the signature at the end. A flush of surprise washed over her. She knew of the liaison yet she had no idea of the depths of the connection.

She did know one thing: the Viscountess Foxley-Graham never did have any children.

CHAPTER FIFTEEN

William stood on Lady Foxley-Graham's front porch and rang the doorbell. Like all the other days he had stood in the very same position he hoped maybe this would be the day.

He sighed.

Propelled by his desire to learn lessons of love he had enthusiastically dived into his language studies with alacrity. He would not give anyone any reason to believe Lady Foxley-Graham was doing anything for him other than lending books. He impressed Mama with the Persian conjugation of the verb "to see". He had thought to demonstrate with "to love" but then it would have been all so painfully obvious.

Well, probably not, but he didn't want to take that chance.

He had already been to the lady's house several times but nothing had happened—well, nothing like he had wanted to happen had happened. They would have tea, talk about his life, about her life, then he would go to her library and pick out a book or two. Although it all proved far more interesting than he thought it would be. Not only was there an astonishing array of written material on any subject one could possibly think of, after he had spent time with the lady he invariably was incredibly hard. Choosing a book became an erotic act, an act whose completion could only be effected alone in his bed at night.

Then one afternoon, while he had been paging through what he determined was a volume of Ottoman poetry, the conversation took a decidedly different turn.

"William," she had said from the window seat as she watched him, "I presume you pleasure yourself."

He stood stock still for a moment, trying to anchor his suddenly foggy brain before he turned to her. "My lady?"

"Oh, I've shocked you. I do apologize but we must discuss it some time. Now I assure you all men pleasure themselves, even though you'll all swear to your pastors that you do not. I want to know a little more about how it is you go about doing it."

He stared at her with wide eyes. "With my hand, my lady?"

She laughed, a sound so sweet it softened the tension in his muscles.

"How very droll, Mr. Peel. I meant the sensual thoughts you might have while you are touching yourself."

He inhaled and tried to dismiss the flush of shame stinging up his neck. "Lately, my lady, I've been thinking of you."

She smiled and a bit of color rose in her cheeks. "I am flattered, William." She looked down at her fingers, perhaps in an act of collecting herself. "I have the first lesson for you in our study of the ways of love. Next time you are pleasuring yourself—"

Most likely it would be the very moment he got home—

"I would like you to pay attention to what it is you find most arousing. If you indeed think of me, what specifically are you imagining?"

"I think, my lady, it's really never very specific. It's more just the idea of you."

She colored again. "Well try to be more aware. Perhaps there is an aspect of me you prefer the best."

"Yes, my lady." Everything, from her hair to her legs—if he ever got a chance to see them.

"It is very important for you to understand your sensual predilections. Once you understand yours, you can help your lover understand hers."

And thus ended their afternoon a couple of days previous. He frigged himself probably too much during the intervening time but had some success in discovering what it was about the lady he preferred. Her lips, of course, and her bosom. He so wanted to mold his hand to a breast, to smooth his palm over its luscious curves, to squeeze. To hear her response to his touch. Just thinking of such a thing made him hard.

And, unfortunately, he was still standing at her front door. He shifted his weight, hoping his cock would shift to a less obvious position in his drawers. It did not.

The surprise of Mr. Sims answering the door and ushering him in dissipated his ardor somewhat. Still the butler surely noticed. The old man must have known all of Lady Foxley-Graham's "students". A flush of abashment crept along his scalp. What must the butler think of him?

"The viscountess wishes for you to meet her in the library, Mr. Peel."

"Thank you, Mr. Sims."

He marched up the stairs, his nerves slowing his pace. It would be rude to keep the lady waiting though, even if they were only to talk about his masturbatory habits. He stepped more lively.

She sat in the window seat, a vision of loveliness, gazing down on her garden below.

"My lady."

She turned. "William. Come here." She patted the empty space next to her.

He sat. And then she put her hand on his thigh.

Every nerve in his body fired at the touch. His prick forgot its earlier abashed state.

But she didn't just merely touch him: she *stroked* him. Her fingers traced along the inner seam of his trousers slowly, her warmth seeping into his skin. If it were possible, his prick hardened even more.

Her gaze flicked to his crotch. "I see my touch excites you."

He flushed. "Very much so," he croaked.

She smiled. "I think we've had sufficient introductions over the last several visits. We've got to know each other, we've shared stories and laughter." She leaned in. "One needs to have such a foundation for an intimate relationship. It's not just about physical release. Although as you get older and have more experiences, you'll find there are a great many vagaries with regards to sex."

She still touched him. He swallowed but his mouth was dry.

"I wanted us to start in the library so you can say you were in the library today and it would not be a lie."

She stood and offered her hand. He took it.

"Now we'll go to my bedroom. You don't have to tell anyone about that."

She led him up the stairs to her room. Lace curtains allowed the afternoon sunlight to stream in but, he hoped, obscured his presence. She let go of his hand and they stood in the middle of the room. Her ornately carved bed loomed large against a wall.

"Have you ever undressed a woman, William?"

A thrill tingled up his spine. It was happening. "No."

"You most likely will not have to but you should watch so you'll understand what we wear. That way you won't be surprised when it takes simply forever for a woman to divest herself of her clothing."

He chuckled nervously.

She indicated a chaise longue. "Have a seat."

He sat. And then she began removing her clothes.

The spectacle was fascinating and arousing all at once. So many buttons, so many layers, the structure of the dress revealed to be padding and drapery, the form of the woman revealed to be achieved by cinching and plumping. His cock throbbed to the point of delirium. He wanted a frig so badly.

She stripped down to her underthings, her stockings and a garment she called a "combination", which served as drawers but with a top. It was not quite sheer but the roses of her abundant breasts darkened the fabric. She stepped toward him.

"Now it's your turn."

Bollocks.

"Why don't you let me sit on my chaise? You can drape your clothes on that chair there." She pointed to a stuffed armchair. "You only need to go to your drawers."

He undressed slowly, methodically, draping each garment on the chair, unable to meet her eyes. At first. While he unbuttoned his shirt, he glanced at her. She was smiling, a genuine sort of smile, not something false one might encounter at a tea party. She relaxed on her chaise, as if she were enjoying herself, one hand absently stroking her thigh. She emboldened him. He stripped off his braces, pulled off his shirt, and started in on the fly of his trousers, all the while holding her gaze. He had to look away to take off his trousers and socks but when he was wearing nothing but his drawers, he stood before her less ashamed than when he began.

She raised an eyebrow. "Magnificent. I see you are an athlete." Her gaze studied his chest, shoulders, and arms.

He flushed. "My father loves the outdoors. We hike and fish. It's really quite brilliant."

She stripped off a stocking. "Keep it up." And then another. "The male physique is a wonderful thing if treated properly." She stood and came toward him.

His cock sprang to life. Thank God he was wearing his drawers.

She drew her hand across his chest, tracing the lines of his muscles, staring at him with wonder. "You'll have hair one day soon."

He could barely stand it. His nipples hardened. His skin prickled to gooseflesh.

She stood directly in front of him, smoothing her palms down his arms, breathing approbations. If he looked down, he could see the crack of her bosom. Beyond that the bounty was covered by a thin piece of fabric. He tried not to look down. His hands ached from restraint—from not touching her or not touching himself, he wasn't sure.

She searched his face then drew her lower lip between her teeth. "You want to touch me, don't you?"

Oh God, yes. "Please, my lady, don't..."

She waited. "Don't what, Mr. Peel? We are both standing here in our drawers. I think that is permission enough for you to touch what you want."

Her. He wanted to touch her. He already knew what his achingly hard cock felt like.

His hand remained poised in front of her while his mind tried to think of the best angle. And then her hand was on his, directing him to cup a breast.

So soft, so weighty, so yielding under his hand. He stopped breathing…until he had to. She let go, leaving him to explore on his own, to smooth over the beauteous mound, finding the taut nipple. Placing a finger and thumb on either side.

"Go ahead."

He pinched. Her sigh sent more blood rushing to his cock and his other hand to explore the breast before it.

And then he was lost in a frenzy, his hands squeezing, his mind uncomprehending, his balls tightening. He palmed the demi-globes but it wasn't enough. He needed to taste them. He bent his head—she did not object—wrapped his hands around her waist and pressed his open mouth against a nipple.

"Oh, William. Oh, yes." Her words fell in a breathy sigh as she stroked his shoulders.

He licked through the fabric, wetting it until it was soaked, then sucked.

She moaned.

He sucked harder.

She arched her back, moaning his name, rubbing her hips against his.

He came in his drawers.

He jerked back, mortified.

She was breathless, flushed, one breast visible through the wet fabric.

"My lady, I…I…" He glanced at the stain at his crotch.

She lay a finger on his lips. "I wanted that to happen. You'll be more relaxed now."

"I don't understand."

She smiled sweetly. "You're eighteen. You're very potent. And very excitable. Your next crisis will take a little longer." She drew a finger from his sternum to his crotch. "Which means we'll have longer to play."

"There's more?" he blurted.

She laughed softly and tugged at his waistband. "Yes, there's more." She unbuttoned the waist. "I want to show you how to use that magnificent tongue of yours to please a woman." She continued unbuttoning his fly. "Take them off. I want to see you."

He did as bidden then stood for her perusal. She circled around, tickling with a featherlight touch, swatting his butt, cupping his stones, encircling her hand gently around his cock, which stirred once again to arousal.

"See. Like I told you. You're very excitable."

"I want to see you, too."

She grinned. "Of course." She let go of his prick to take his hands. "Why don't you unbutton and I'll take it off."

His fingers trembled as one by one he unfastened the buttons of her undergarment all the way to the split in the crotch. Her thatch of dark hair surprised him—he had thought it only on the male. One never saw hair on women in paintings or sculpture. Her pale skin peeked through between the open placket, enticing him. He drew a finger from the hair covering her sex up to the dip under her neck.

She licked her lips. "Now pull it off my shoulders, slip my arms through."

Moments later, she stood naked before him. He simply had not imagined such a magnificent sight.

A slender waist and hips were topped by a splendid bosom at which the underwear had only hinted. She was soft, sensual curves all over.

"Would you like to kiss me while we're nude?"

"God yes." He reached for her.

She took his hand. "Let's get on the bed, shall we?"

She led him to the bed, lying on it first, beckoning him beside her. Overcome with desire he clambered on the mattress and pulled her to him.

He knew how to kiss; he'd done it a great deal. But this…this was different. She was warm and willing underneath him, his rampant cock poking and prodding against not his trousers and drawers but the flesh of a woman. He had a vague idea of what a man and woman did and sought the entrance between her legs.

She grabbed his cock. "Not yet."

Disappointment bled into mortification. "Please forgive me."

She patted his cheek. "We'll be doing something else today. Something for the woman. Once you've learned that, then we can proceed."

He rolled off her. "I forgot I was a pupil for a moment."

She laughed. "William, you have already discovered the wonders of a woman's breasts, how they are sensitive to a man's kiss. There is another place on a woman that is sensitive to a man's kiss."

She took his hand and placed it over the hair of her crotch. She spread her legs slightly then directed his fingers between.

She was sticky and wet and warm. He hadn't expected that. Of course he wasn't quite sure what to expect.

"Gently stroke me. Become familiar with how I feel."

He probed and caressed until his fingers seemingly lost all sensation and his mind took over, fantastical notions of what a man might do to a woman taunting his needy cock.

She stilled his hand. "There is a spot on a woman that gives her as much pleasure as your cock gives you." She directed a finger through her cleft. "There." She flinched ever so slightly. "A bit of hard flesh. Like a nipple. Do you feel it?"

He did. "This?" He poked.

She flinched again. "Yes. Draw the wetness up and stroke me on that spot."

He kept slipping but she was patient, helping him, until he was pretty sure he had got it right.

She sighed. "Yes, dear. Like that. Just like that." She closed her eyes as the lines in her face softened. So beautiful. He had to give her what she wanted.

"A little faster."

He obliged. Her mouth fell open, the muscles in her neck ticked.

"Faster. Harder."

He crushed the nub and rubbed vigorously. Her breaths raced, punctuated with moans, her head pushing into the pillow.

She bucked her hips against his hand and cried out. He continued his ministrations. She slapped his hand away with a laugh.

"That is the result you want to achieve. A woman's pleasure. Her crisis. Like what happens to you when you masturbate."

He flushed.

She cupped his cheek. "And now we've each had a crisis."

He grinned. "You said something about a kiss."

"I did." A naughty gleam twinkled in her eyes. "What you just did with your finger? You'll do that with your mouth."

His eyes widened. "Down there?" He flicked his gaze to the hair of her mons.

"Yes." She smiled. "Start your kisses at the lips." She tapped her lips in invitation.

He touched his lips to hers, caressing the seam of her mouth with his tongue until she opened for him, letting him dally for only a moment before she pulled back.

"Then proceed down the woman's body with gentle pecks, stopping at her breasts momentarily."

He lay kisses on her neck, her shoulders, admired her beautiful breasts before kissing those and flicking his tongue on the erect nipples. She writhed and moaned under him.

"Continue to the swell of her belly, all the way to the hair of her motte."

He grasped her waist as he kissed down her middle, the soft skin of her belly so tantalizingly erotic he dared to lick and nip the tender flesh. She gasped then groaned her approval. He had surprised her. Could he surprise her more?

He kissed down to the dark, wiry hair at the apex of her thighs then licked back up to her belly, ending with another nip.

She threaded her fingers through his hair. "Oh God, William. Lower, lower."

Lower? In the hair?

"Where your finger played." She opened her legs.

Before him was the sticky flesh he had only felt. It looked…complicated.

"You already know how to pleasure me with your finger. Now use your lips and tongue. As if you were kissing my mouth."

What an absolutely amazing idea. Her sex did resemble lips.

He bent over, her feminine scent filling his nostrils and engorging his cock, seeing the little nub that before he had only felt. He ran his tongue over it.

"Yes. Kiss me."

He dived in, kissing, tonguing, sucking. She writhed under him so he held her steady, gripping her hips, his fingers pressing into the pillowy flesh of her buttocks. Her taste, her scent, her moans filled his senses, arousing him beyond his expectations. His prick ached with excitement, wanting its own pleasure. He undulated his hips against the sheet, the soft fabric chafing his sensitive flesh.

His tongue explored, finding the opening to the depths he had only ever heard about. He plunged in, tasting her heat. She gripped his hair, pulling the strands, moaning his name, rocking her hips to allow him deeper access.

This, this is what it was to fuck a woman.

He imagined he was extended over her, lying between her legs, not his mouth and tongue inside her but his cock. He ground his erection into the mattress as he thrust deeper with his tongue, matching the rhythm of his rocking hips to the cadence of her cries.

Deeper, deeper, searching for that place, that feeling where his body tensed, struggling for its sensual release, and then he was there, the moment before explosion.

He came on the sheets, growling his release into her quim, then stilled.

This was better than masturbation.

She tugged at his hair. He lifted his head, shame descending when he met her eyes.

"I see pleasuring me was as pleasurable for you."

"I'm sorry, my lady." Was that supposed to have even happened?

She laughed softly and motioned for him to lie alongside her. "Don't apologize. You are supposed to be aroused by the act."

"But I…all over your bed."

She wrapped his arm around her. "And when you are an older man, you will wish for a return of such exuberance." She drew a line down his torso to his groin. "Enjoy it while you can."

"Thank you, my lady."

She kissed his chest. "You're welcome. Now I shall give you another lesson to practice before the next time we meet."

"Oh?" Anything. Anything for her.

"I want you to masturbate—"

He laughed.

She smiled. "This time it will be different. What I want you to do is to mark the changes in your body, the course it takes before you have your crisis."

"How do you mean?"

"What are the physical changes? Such as, do you move from a relaxed state to a state of muscular tension? What happens in your mind?" She tapped his temple. "Do you lose yourself for a moment? Especially mark what happens right before you spend. This is important for you to know when you are with a woman not your wife."

"Not my wife?"

"Your mistress, if that has to be the case. Or your lovers before you get married."

"Like you."

She smiled. "Like me. So this means you might have to masturbate several times before you truly understand your body."

He laughed. "I think I can do that."

"Good." She gave his hip a little swat. "Now get dressed. You've been here long enough."

Time with her was never long enough.

* * * * *

From the bustling foyer, Arthur scanned the crush of guests in Lord and Lady Roxton's ballroom. The event was well-attended as it was the first held by the viscount and his wife after the double wedding of their twin daughters. It seemed all of London was in attendance.

Which meant Lavinia would be there. Eventually. So he kept searching, knowing the ever elegant and dynamic lady would stand out in a room full of dull aristocrats.

"Arthur, Lady Banbury says the Smythe girl will be with her here tonight," Mother said at his side. "You do remember Lady Banbury from the St. Albanses' wedding, do you not?"

"I do. She is a dear friend to Lady Foxley-Graham."

"Good. Then keep an eye out for Lady Banbury. Or for Lady Foxley-Graham for that matter. She might know where her friend is."

"Yes, Mother." Arthur would be very willing to keep an eye out for Lady Foxley-Graham.

They filtered into the ballroom, nodding and smiling to people of importance or social survival. Arthur was as polite as any infatuated man could possibly be. He almost heaved a sigh when he saw her. She was with Lady Banbury and a lovely blonde-haired girl.

"There they are." Mother practically dragged him toward the threesome.

Lavinia immediately offered her hand.

"My lady," he greeted with a kiss above her fingers.

"Lord Petersham." She casually slipped her hand from his. "I trust you received the books on parliamentary procedure I sent over?"

"I did, thank you. And I have been diligently reading reports on Parliament in the morning and evening papers."

She beamed. She looked spectacular in her tight-fitting gown of burgundy and umber trimmed in copper, the colors of sunset over a sultan's desert palace.

Mother greeted the blonde girl as if she had met her before, which raised his hackles. The girl was simply too young. Far too young.

"Lord Petersham," Lady Banbury said, "may I introduce my charge for this Season, Miss Beatrice Smythe."

Arthur bowed and took the girl's proffered hand. "Miss Smythe. Delighted to meet you."

She curtsied with a blush. "My lord."

He felt like an East End whore. It was too obvious.

"I've known Beatrice's father for years," Lavinia said, surely taunting him with the reference to time. "The Earl of Ryburgh."

Curious, then, how she was not *Lady* Beatrice. Arthur held his tongue on the matter. "It seems I am unfamiliar with him."

"You should pay more attention to your instruction from Lady Foxley-Graham," Mother scolded.

He raised a brow at Lavinia. "We should discuss all your political associates over tea, my lady."

She smiled a wicked smile. "We should, my lord."

"Arthur, the music is about to start," Mother said. "Why don't you ask Miss Smythe if she would like to dance?"

He wanted to simply storm out. But a gentleman did no such thing. A gentleman asked a young lady to dance.

She was a pleasant girl and an especially skilled dancer. Miss Smythe—who, he learned, eschewed her title on political grounds— kept rhythm for both of them as most of the time Arthur was distracted by Lavinia talking to his mother and Lady Banbury. A very handsome middle-aged man joined the women. He was overly chatty while gawking at Arthur and Miss Smythe and made Lavinia laugh far too much.

"What is it that interests you, Lord Petersham, if not politics?"

Ah, casual conversation. "I own a railway company." It was the easiest way to put it.

"How very modern."

"And you? I'm sure you find something entertaining other than dancing."

"I'm fascinated by archaeology."

That made him take his eyes off Lavinia. "Like Greek ruins?"

"Yes, or Roman or Egyptian or Persian."

Geoff's son was immersed in that sort of thing. "Have you traveled much?"

"You mean on your railway?"

Clever girl. He smiled. "Ah, no. I meant to study ruins."

She blushed. It was quite endearing. "No. I read books and visit museums."

She should really meet William. "Miss Smythe, one day I would like to introduce you to a young man I know. His father is a partner of mine in the railway business. The young man is also fascinated by archaeology."

"Thank you, Lord Petersham. I would like that very much."

If he had to politely disentangle himself from each one of Mother's hoped-for prospects, then so be it. At least he had a potential happy ending for Miss Smythe. He smiled before stealing a glance toward Lavinia. She still chatted with Mother, Lady Banbury, and the handsome man.

The dance ended and he escorted Miss Smythe back to Lady Banbury. Probably a bit too briskly.

"Beatrice, you look so stunning on the dance floor," the handsome man effused.

Beatrice blushed. "Thank you, Papa."

Papa? Good God. The man was his contemporary. Surely Mother could see that.

"Lord Petersham," Lavinia began, "may I introduce to you my especial good friend, the Earl of Ryburgh?" She turned to the handsome earl. "Felix, may I introduce the Earl of Petersham."

Felix? She addressed him by his Christian name?

"Petersham." Ryburgh nodded. "You were quite fine on the dance floor as well. Thank you for indulging my daughter."

"My pleasure, Ryburgh."

"Beatrice," Lady Banbury said, "we must find your next partner."

"And I'm off as well," Ryburgh said jovially. "A cigar awaits me somewhere I'm sure." He quirked a brow at Arthur. "Join me, Petersham?"

Tempting, but he hoped to get Lavinia alone. "Another time perhaps."

The earl bowed his exit and the countess and her charge bid their adieux. Lavinia was about to join them when Mother requested she stay.

"Lady Foxley-Graham, please inform my son what a wonderful girl Miss Smythe is."

Arthur rolled his eyes. "I think you just did, Mother."

"Oh, but she is, Lady Richmond, she is. Accomplished in all the feminine arts and at so young an age."

Lavinia was cruel. He wanted to be cruel as well but really should simply change the topic of conversation.

"I doubt very much she wants to be married to a man her father's age."

Mother sighed. "Arthur, I merely thought you would like Miss Smythe because of her blonde curls. Don't you think she looks like Henrietta?"

Horror sliced through his heart. No one could replace Henny. No one. "The blonde hair is the only resemblance, Mother."

Lavinia caught his eye, offering an expression of condolence. "My lord, I would be grateful for an escort to the terrace. I'm feeling a bit lightheaded in the stuffiness of the ballroom." She whipped out her fan.

He offered a weak smile for her efforts. Mother most likely had yet another child lined up on his dance card.

"Arthur," Mother said, "why don't you go along. I can fend for myself."

"Are you sure? Let me at least find you a comfortable seat."

Once Mother was deposited on a chair against the wall next to an exotic plant and a chatty matron, he offered his arm to Lavinia.

"Thank you," he said under his breath.

They walked along the fringes of the dance floor, nodding to casual acquaintances, briefly greeting others. The Earl of Thuxton approached, holding a glass of champagne carelessly, his bearing at odds with his meticulously groomed gray hair and mustache. He nodded to Arthur before turning his raw gaze to Lavinia.

"Lady Foxley-Graham, how divine to see you." He kissed her hand far too intimately.

"Lord Thuxton, the pleasure is mine." She offered him a devastating smile.

"Petersham." The greeting was polite, his attention straying only momentarily to Arthur.

"Thuxton," Arthur said, trying to maintain a veneer of civility. "How is it that you know Lady Foxley-Graham?"

"Politics." It was said curtly, never taking his eyes off Lavinia.

"Lord Thuxton and I met during debate over the amendments to the Married Women's Property Act back in '74."

Arthur quirked a brow in Thuxton's direction. "Women's rights, eh? I wouldn't have guessed that as one of your causes." Thuxton was a notorious womanizer. His striking good looks and famed bachelor status assured his success with the fairer sex.

"A confident and free woman is the best kind." He glanced at Arthur. "Of course you already know that."

"And how do you two know each other?" Lavinia asked.

"Thuxton is a major investor in *Harwell Phillips & Company*." Arthur turned to Thuxton. "Lady Foxley-Graham is a long-time friend of Joseph's new son-in-law. We're to be godparents to their first child."

"My heartfelt congratulations! Children are such a blessing." He lifted his champagne to his lips. "Especially when they are not one's own."

Lavinia snorted with amusement. "Edgar, you are terrible!"

Edgar?

Thuxton winked then perused the crowd. "Ah, I see my next conquest. Or dance partner if you prefer." He fondled Lavinia's hand too intimately once again. "I'll leave you to pursue the waltz as you wish." His mouth curled suggestively. "She's a good dance partner, isn't she, Petersham?"

The man clearly had had too much champagne. "Lady Foxley-Graham excels in most everything she does."

Thuxton nodded and made his exit.

Arthur seethed. The earl had been too familiar. "Thuxton? Really?" he said under his breath. "He's as old as my father."

"He's only in his sixties, Arthur. My husband would have been in his eighties by now. And it was years ago. No worries, my lord. It's well over."

Arthur wrapped her arm around his once again and clamped his other hand on top to secure her. "Are we going to keep meeting your lovers at these events?"

Her steps faltered. "I beg your pardon?"

"Thuxton, Ryburgh, St. Albans. I'm not so certain Joseph never tried to get you into bed."

She stopped and turned to him. "As you well know," she said under her breath. "I have a very long history with and great affection for Nicholas. I'm sure you have similar relationships."

Arthur grunted.

"I never slept with Lord Ryburgh. And while he may be handsome, the man is nothing but faithful to his wife and children. He would never betray his family. His reputation for honor and fidelity is something you should be aware of before you join Lords."

Arthur grabbed a glass of champagne from a passing footman and gulped a swig.

"As far as Joseph Phillips is concerned, if he finds me attractive and has said as much to you then I am flattered. And though I do admit he is appealing, he has a new arrangement with his wife that precludes such entanglements." Lavinia snatched the champagne from Arthur and downed the remainder before placing the glass on the returning footman's tray. "If you are feeling frustrated, my lord, I am not to blame. I cannot help it if my former lovers move in polite society and not the demi-monde."

He glared at her. "That was cutting."

"It was meant to be. I haven't slept with every man I know, my lord. It is cutting that you assume so." She glared back, her upper lip twitching, then looked away at the crowded dance floor.

She was right. Frustration was driving his bad behavior. "Christ, Lavinia, I apologize," he said softly. "I'm consumed by jealousy. I have no right to be."

"And I was jealous watching you and Miss Smythe. You looked too comfortable."

He was about to object but her expression had softened. "I feel comfortable in your arms, my lady. Shall we have a waltz before repairing to the terrace?"

"I would be delighted," she said, suppressing a grin.

And then she was in his arms and they were moving perfectly together. Too perfectly. Like long-time lovers. Or an old married couple.

He leaned in so close her perfume flared his nostrils. "Your neck, your shoulders, your bosom are so beautifully pale." His hand at her waist held her more tightly. "But I prefer to see your ivory skin suffused with the blush of desire or the afterglow of passion."

Her gaze flicked to his eyes then retreated to his shoulder. Her cheeks grew pink above her suppressed smile.

He whirled her gently, pressing his hips against her briefly. "And if I told you my cock was so hard I could take you right here in front of everyone, would more than just your cheeks flush in anticipation?"

She gasped.

"Would you like a walk in the fresh air, Lady Foxley-Graham? You look a tad over-exhilarated."

"Thank you, my lord, that would be ideal."

They walked calmly, he with the intention of not drawing too much attention to his erection.

Once out on the terrace she inhaled deeply. "It is refreshing to breathe something other than perfume and perspiration, is it not?"

He chuckled. "I thought you liked these sorts of events." He pulled off his gloves and crammed them into his pocket.

"Oh, but I do."

She led him to the ornate wrought iron balustrade. He propped himself against the railing and faced her, inching his palm down his thigh until he felt the heat of her hand at her side. He slid the pads of his fingers along the delicate kidskin of her glove to the tiny pearl buttons at her wrist.

"You can't do much better than Miss Smythe, my lord."

He threw her a sultry look. "Yes, I can." He unfastened and tugged off her glove then tickled his fingers on the back of her hand.

She glanced away but did not fight off his touch. "Regardless," she said with a slight tremor, "the Earl of Ryburgh will be a valuable associate and can introduce you to worthy members of Lords."

"Now you sound like my mother."

She met his gaze. "I thought, rather, I was sounding like a wife."

He flushed. He grasped her hand, the action concealed by the dark and the drapery of her skirts. "I think of you every single night, Lavinia." His erection nudged against his trousers.

"Arthur, don't." Her plea was barely audible.

He gently traced tiny circles with the pad of his thumb in the dip of her palm. Her expression melted from confident independence to uncontrolled arousal. She closed her eyes, her breathing slowing to the state of one in complete relaxation…or one who just had a successful romp in bed.

He stopped. She gave him a sated look and pulled her hand away. "I think I shall sleep very well tonight, my lord. That was most satisfying."

Good God. The woman was amazing.

"However, I fear you were not equally affected." She grabbed her glove then left him, descending the flagstone stairs to the garden below, tossing him a backward glance. He followed, reining in his enthusiasm.

She walked at a brisk pace, at first along a lamp-lit path, then slipping between two trimmed and shaped boxwoods to the shadows beyond. Soon they were before the high garden wall. He discerned a recessed doorway—to the mews or the neighbor's—and pulled her inside, wrapping his arms around her.

She shoved at his chest and he let go.

She unbuttoned his trousers, his drawers, and slid her hand inside, grabbing his swelling prick. With one caress he was iron-hard.

She pumped his shaft, gripping more forcefully on the upward stroke, loosening on the downward, as if it were her cunt wrapped around him. He flattened his hands against the cold, damp stone of the doorway, taking the edge off her torment. She swirled her thumb around the tip, spreading the wetness, then teased the foreskin cowled in excitement. She was languid, savoring his agitation. As her lips curved in satisfaction she increased her momentum, driving him forward to ecstasy.

There was only so much he could take before he had to be inside her.

He pushed off the wall to take her, take control. She squeezed his cock, painfully so, and propelled him back against the unyielding jamb. He relented and she resumed frigging him at an even pace, taking him to the place before oblivion once again. He sucked in air between his teeth, trying to steel himself against the inevitable.

"I, too, think of you every night, my lord, and wake every morning in frustration." She increased the rhythm of her tugs. "Something akin to what you must be feeling at this moment."

God, he needed to spend.

"I, too, want to feel that surge of desire turn to passion in your arms." She fisted determinedly. "My heart, I fear, cannot suffer another break." She slowed at the sound of his quickening breaths. "As long as the Miss Smythes of the world are clamoring for your hand in marriage, I need to stop loving you." She clutched at his cock, briskly bringing on the torturous climb to the peak once again.

He closed his eyes, damming the confusion of sensual fulfillment and emotional agony that threatened to break forth. He didn't care about the Miss Smythes of the world, he didn't.

"Lavinia," he pleaded, his voice gravelly with need.

She took him to the edge, held him there, her breaths agitated as if she were being fucked as fast as her hand worked.

His stomach tensed, he gasped for air. At any moment, he would stumble over the precipice and begin the glorious slide to paradise.

She took her hand away.

He stared at her panting, unsatisfied, disbelieving.

"I'll leave you now, Arthur." Her voice quavered. "I feel renewed vigor for joining the fray of the ballroom." She turned and walked away.

He collapsed against the cold stone, grabbing his hair and pulling at the roots, letting loose the emotion, finding relief in her admission that she loved him.

He should feel satisfied by that, but all he could think about was finishing himself off in the doorway of Viscount Roxton's garden.

Julius gazed at the landscape before him, its resplendence dreamlike.

The moon was not quite full but its light shone on the seashore like the sun on a cloudy day. The dark sky glittered with stars. Perfect for a tryst.

It was daring, it was public. They had left the cottage to walk the mile to the rocky beach, leaving her husband. The old man would be practically comatose from the laudanum. They would have all night and part of the dawn to call their own.

He carried on his back a peculiar bedroll, knowing her comfort would ease seduction, and the leather straps would promote his carnal amusement. As they walked, their hands and arms casually brushed, he sometimes catching her fingers, her giggles the melody to the rhythm of his heart pounding with love and lust.

She was so amenable. She would let him do anything.

"Do you recall the little book of verse from the bookstore today?"

"Yes," she said. "*Andromeda*. I read some of it while you were attending my husband this afternoon. Rather middling. A bit gruesome."

He chuckled. "Do you know the story?"

"The princess Andromeda is chained to the rocks for her mother's hubristic boast of her beauty. The hero Perseus saved her from being ravaged by a sea monster."

"And did you see the frontispiece?"

"Of the girl chained to the rock?"

"Yes."

She walked in silence for a spell then laughed softly. "Will you be the gallant Perseus or the ravishing sea monster?"

"A little of both."

She grabbed his hand and swung their arms to match their gait. "And shall I be garbed in a filmy gown as befits a princess?"

"No. Your beauty will be exposed to Poseidon."

She stopped and faced him. "Now you're Poseidon?"

He smiled and kissed her mouth, reveling in her luxuriant yielding. "I've mixed my metaphors. I apologize. I'm not a poet."

She gazed lovingly at him through lowered lashes. "No," she agreed. "You're a lover." She wrapped her hands behind his neck. "My lover."

The words ignited the lust smoldering in his loins. "We're almost there."

They continued on their path, she skipping at his side now, excited for her unknown defilement. He stopped at a low outcropping and looked down at the beach below, spying what he wanted immediately.

"There." He pointed to a rock, its shape perfect for what he had in mind.

Her excitement did not waver as she clambered down the embankment, allowing his assistance, then skittered to the beach. As she took off her shoes and stockings, he unfurled the bedroll and lay it on the rock, the dark-gray color perfectly mimicking the stone, the web of leather straps holding the restraints hidden on the underside. As she stood on the shore, wriggling her toes in the cold, damp sand, staring out at the inconstant sea, clutching her cloak around her, he hammered four spikes into the rock, one at each corner of the bedroll, and secured the ties to keep the restraints rigid and in place.

He went to her, slipping the cloak from her shoulders, urging her arms crossed for warmth over her bosom to her sides. He began to undress her but she stilled his hand.

"You have your own clothes to attend to, Jules."

And so he did. He stripped bare, the sea-sprayed air dampening and chilling his skin, his cock unaffected as he watched her divest herself of her attire. She had worn loose clothing, her corset forgotten in her bedroom, and was nude before him in minutes, her unbraided hair cascading down her back.

A paragon of femininity.

He enveloped her in his arms, kissing her neck, her cheeks, her mouth, she slackening sensually.

"Come," he said, taking her hand.

He led her to the rock and helped her to lie on the cushion, spreading her arms and legs. He knelt down before her and bound each of her ankles, then stood and curved over her to do the same to her right wrist, his erection rubbing against the damp curls of her motte. She stared up at him, mouth agape, breath ragged. As he restrained her left wrist, she jerked her hips with a yelp and a gasp, her submission to his will releasing her first crisis.

His cock ached to be inside her.

But he wasn't finished.

He caressed her cheeks, warm from her brief flush of ecstasy, and gazed at her, his shadow obscuring her emotion. He kissed each lid then wrapped a length of black cloth around her head, covering her eyes.

Her mouth opened as if to speak. Instead she licked her lips.

He pulled back to observe her stretched and bound, his beautiful captive awaiting her ravishment. Lust coiled in his groin. He flexed his hands, willing them to remain steady against the urge to touch.

"I'm cold."

Delicious dark beads atop her abundant breasts illustrated her plaintive words. He leaned over and breathed hot air on one then the other, watching the nipples melt before pinching and twisting each in their turn, her body arcing, thrusting out her chest as if demanding more. He sucked and licked the peaks, leaving them wet in the cool night air.

And then he wrapped a second length of cloth around her mouth.

With her face utterly shrouded, she could be any woman, any woman whose pale skin shone in the glow of the moon, any woman whose perfect form writhed voluptuously against the restraints, any woman who tilted her hips in provocation.

No. It was her. It could only be her.

The sea breeze tickled the hair between her widely splayed legs. He fell to his knees, grabbed her thighs and delved in, his tongue finding its mark instantly. She was sticky, salty, swollen, silently nudging her sex into his rapacious mouth. He feasted, digging his nails into her thighs as his cock rubbed against the mattress. He was utterly hard, painfully so, needing release, wanting hers first.

His mouth and tongue continued their assault as he bobbed and weaved to her wanton undulations. Her frenzy slowed, her hips stilled.

Then with a restricted jolt she came, flooding his mouth with her release, her muffled scream of rapture piercing his soul. He rose and slammed inside her, groaning at her clenching response. He gripped her waist, pulling her forward as he pounded, his knees pushing into the mattress for purchase, her pliant form vanquished under his control.

He came inside her, filling her, then squeezed his stones, the exquisite pain fetching another crisis, milking him of every drop to fill her further still, deep in her womb.

He extended himself over her, his sweat mingling with her sea-dewed skin, their heartbeats slowing to the same rhythm.

He untied the blindfold and gag and pulled them off.

Her countenance was not the one expected but it was still familiar. But she shouldn't be there. He stepped back and tripped on a low rock. He fell to the ground.

Between her legs the mattress grew wet, a stain growing, reaching the edge where it pooled until it dripped onto the sand. The blacks and whites and grays of midnight dulled further, highlighting the jeweled brilliance of the liquid puddling below. He stared, eyes transfixed, body frozen. She stared back helplessly. Then in one sudden burst the thick fluid gushed from the woman on the rock and surged forth to mingle with the waves.

Crimson.

Julius gulped air as his eyes flew open. He wrenched up from his awkward position on the sofa and tumbled off, falling onto carpet not sand. He was not on the beach but in his study. He shivered against the sweat dampening his clothes and the fear infecting his gut.

No. No. Never again.

CHAPTER SIXTEEN

The night after the Roxton affair, Arthur once again found himself in Lavinia's arms. This time engaged in a waltz in Lord and Lady Hawkhurst's magnificent ballroom.

Her fragrance was driving him mad, especially as her flesh heated in the overly warm space. His hand molded perfectly to her cinched waist but it took all his strength not to slide it along the satin and draw her to him.

"You look lovely tonight, Lavinia." The emerald green of her dress reminded him of the green of her odalisque costume.

"I fear you have already complimented me this evening, Arthur."

Damn. "Compliments and the frustrations of the ballroom are all I have with you anymore."

She flushed briefly and glanced sidelong. Her rhythm in his arms remained impeccable.

"Please don't say that. It's killing me as well."

Good he wanted to say out loud.

Instead he took enjoyment from whirling her around the dance floor, her body submitting to his lead, the top of her bosom perfectly in his view. As he did almost every night he would fall asleep to a fantasy of her. It didn't matter what they did. They could read to each other for God's sake and his cock would spring into action.

He was hard right now just thinking about it.

The music ended and he led her to where she had been standing before the waltz. He'd have to join his mother shortly. She probably had a whole slew of blushing beauties for him to choose from. It was a dreary thought.

"This is where I leave you, my lady."

"Thank you, my lord."

His only consolation was that she seemed flustered and kept her arm wrapped around his, her fingers weighty on his forearm.

"Petersham!"

Arthur looked up. "Peel."

Geoffrey and Anna approached, arm-in-arm, still the picture of marital bliss after almost twenty years. It gave him hope that love was not a fleeting, fickle emotion.

"Mrs. Peel," Arthur greeted Anna. She always smiled when he called her that.

"Arthur." She nodded then turned to Lavinia. "Lady Foxley-Graham, always a pleasure to see you."

"And you, Mrs. Peel. Such a stunning dress."

"Oh my, what a compliment, coming from you." The color rose in Anna's cheeks as she perused Lavinia's gown. "I think I shall never get used to these affairs. All the finery. On my own person and all around."

William Peel came rushing up from behind Anna. "Mother, I can't find her."

And then he saw Lavinia.

It was subtle but it was there. William colored then glanced at his parents and paled. He recovered quickly. It was all over in a second.

So Arthur wasn't the only one falling asleep to fantasies of Lady Foxley-Graham.

She acted first. "Mr. Peel, how lovely to see you."

"And you, my lady." He nodded to Arthur. "Uncle Ar—Lord Petersham."

"William, dear, what's wrong?" Anna asked.

"My next partner. I can't find her."

"And who would that be?" Lavinia inquired.

"Miss Penelope Hardcastle."

Arthur choked back a laugh. Miss Hardcastle was a temptress who used her skill on the dance floor to ensnare her prey. How the boy would manage her...well, he'd like to see that. Apparently so would Lavinia. She smiled broadly behind her fan.

"As the music has already started I guess you'll have to sit this one out, dear." Anna offered her son a sympathetic smile.

"What about you, my lady?"

William's entreaty surprised everyone. Especially Lavinia.

She looked up at Arthur. "If Lord Petersham is willing to let me go?"

Why the hell was she asking him? He had no hold over her. Except their arms were still entwined. "Yes, my lady. I do believe our dance is through."

She let go of him and offered her hand to a grinning William. As they strode out to the dance floor to join the other couples, Geoffrey sidled up to Arthur.

"That boy has done more growing in the last few weeks than the last few years." He smiled as he watched the pair merge onto the floor.

"How do you mean?"

"Didn't you just see what happened? Asking a viscountess, an older woman, a beautiful woman, to dance. Something's got into him."

"Darling," Anna said, "you forget he's using her library for his language studies. They've probably become good friends."

"What was that?" Arthur asked.

"Hadn't you heard?" Anna said. "Lady Foxley-Graham has graciously offered the use of her library for William to further his study of foreign languages beyond the Greek and Latin he learned at school."

Arthur hadn't heard anything of the sort. "That was generous of her."

"Especially since we certainly do not have such a library at home," Anna continued. "If William wants to read classics at Cambridge and join archaeological expeditions, he'll need a foundation in ancient tongues."

Tongues indeed.

Arthur watched the pair on the dance floor, easy to spot as William was one of the tallest men in the ballroom. They seemed very comfortable with each other. Perhaps a bit too comfortable. She smiled and chatted while he gazed at her. From his vantage he would have a wonderful view of her bosom. And weren't they a little close to each other?

Shit. He was jealous of a mere boy, an inexperienced youth who probably was grateful for the opportunity to be in the company of so fine a lady. Surely he was only interested in her library. He was very studious after all.

Arthur thinned his lips. He had to forget about his odalisque or find a way to be with her forever. He was driving himself mad.

William led Lavinia off the dance floor, keeping his eyes straight ahead and not on her magnificent endowments tightly bound in a sort of jacket-like top of emerald-green satin, a ruffle of sheer lace at the neckline only drawing attention to what lay beneath.

"Thank you, my lady. It is always such a pleasure to dance with you." *Or to simply be in your presence.*

"And you, as well, Mr. Peel." Her arm was light on his. "I'm sorry about Miss Hardcastle."

"She's a very fine dancer." And a terrific flirt. She gave him feelings not unlike those he had around Lavinia. "I hope she can fit me in tonight. If nothing is wrong, that is."

"Why look…isn't that she with Lord Norrington and Viscount Ravensburgh?"

And there she was, smiling and laughing with "Percy and Bertie", as Helena called them in private. Miss Hardcastle saw him and waved.

"Would you join me in paying my compliments, my lady?"

"Certainly."

Miss Hardcastle was all apologies and smiles. "Please forgive me, Mr. Peel. But my dear friends the Marquess of Norrington and Viscount Ravensburgh just arrived. I had no idea they would be here tonight and I always save a dance for them."

Smiles and greetings were shared all around.

"Where will you travel to next, my lords?" Lavinia asked.

"Southern France," said Norrington. "Where the Mediterranean is a heavenly shade of blue."

He flashed a grin at Ravensburgh, who grinned back.

Miss Hardcastle took William's hand. "I see you found yourself a replacement for our waltz, Mr. Peel. May I be so bold as to request the next dance?"

"I'd love to, Miss Hardcastle. What about your escorts?"

She raised a brow in their direction. "They'll keep."

"I see Lady Banbury with her new charge," said Lavinia. "I shall take my leave, Mr. Peel." She gave him a friendly nod.

He watched her bustle sway with her steps as she sashayed over to Lady Banbury.

And then he saw a vision of loveliness that almost overshadowed Lady Foxley-Graham.

The countess stood next to a young woman who could only be described as a gift from the heavens. Golden blonde curls framed a face so perfect only an artist moved by the hand of God could sculpt a likeness. Her dress was a froth of azure and pure white and clung to her feminine curves like waves and sea foam on Aphrodite rising from the ocean. His cock stirred. Luckily he had bound it tightly under his drawers.

The nymph and Lavinia conversed, obviously friends. He would request an introduction.

Miss Hardcastle sidled up to him and wrapped her arm around his. "She's lovely, isn't she?"

He flushed. His erection waned. How utterly rude of him to be staring at another woman when a decided beauty stood at his side. "Miss Hardcastle, please forgive me. That was terribly impolite."

"Not as impolite as me leaving you wanting for a partner."

"Shall we dance?"

As they glided in rhythm to the music, all William could think about was women. The expert dancer in his arms, the lover who was across the room, and the goddess he could not wait to meet.

His body grew heated again. The time had come to seek out a remedy to assuage his desires.

Despite having had only one dance with Arthur at the Hawkhursts', Lavinia could not stop thinking about him. Fatigue lulled her into a dreamlike state as she lay in bed, staring at the night-darkened ceiling, remembering the sensation of Arthur's muscular forearm under her gloved hand.

Remembering his naked arms holding her nude body.

Masturbation suddenly seemed so lonely. She closed her eyes and tried to sleep, uncertain for whose benefit feigning the act was needed.

Sims knocking lightly on her bedroom door jolted her from inevitable slumber. Wide-eyed, Lavinia glanced around at the still-dark bedroom. She couldn't have been asleep for very long. It must have been about two in the morning. And Sims' summons meant something terribly important was afoot.

She put on her dressing gown and cracked the door. "Yes, Sims?"

"Master William Peel is here to see you, my lady."

"William?" What the hell was he doing at her house? "Thank you, Sims. I'll be right down. Have him wait in the foyer. No need to rescue me. I'll be fine."

"Very good, my lady."

She shut the door and leaned against it, drawing in a deep breath. Should she scold him? No. He knew what he wanted and he wanted it now. But she should chide him for his lack of discretion at the very least. There could be no other reason for him to be on her doorstep in the middle of the night. No one would believe he needed access to her library at such an hour.

She waited a minute then went downstairs.

William ran to her the moment he spied her on the stairs and knelt at her feet. "I couldn't stand being away from you, my lady."

Lavinia had to turn away, unable to look at his urgency, the stuff of poetry and paintings. He should really be on a balcony with a young girl he truly desired. Instead he was before a matron of Society in her entryway, his heart boldly on his sleeve.

"Get up," she hissed. She grabbed his arm and dragged him to the morning room.

She closed the door and motioned for him to sit. He sat but a moment before he popped up and stared at her.

"William, what is this about?" She remained near the door, her only escape.

"I want you, Lavinia. As a man wants a woman."

He just wanted a woman and she was there.

And she just wanted a man.

She didn't want to escape.

"It was very indiscreet of you to come to my house at this hour."

"I know, I know." He sighed. "Please forgive me."

He gazed at her wide-eyed and desperate, like an ardent knight swooning before his imperial mistress. And yet, there were his hands at his sides, his long, elegant fingers so learned in how to pleasure her, quivering in anticipation.

She came toward him, steadfastly maintaining a calmness she did not really feel. She took his hands in hers, looked up at him, raised herself on her tiptoes and kissed him.

He took her in his arms and kissed her back in that wonderful way he knew how to do.

She melted in his embrace. When he kissed, he was not the boy but the man. She curved into him, tangling her fingers through his auburn locks, rubbing her mons against his groin, needing to feel his erection through her flimsy attire.

He broke away, gazing down at her with glassy eyes, a fantasy of their union probably already playing in his head.

She searched his face. "What compelled you to do this now, tonight?"

"I don't know," he said with a touch of abashment. "I think I need to experience…everything."

Restlessness. She understood. "All right, William, but I need you to have a bit more patience for a few minutes." Well, this was awkward. To have caught her unprepared. "You know where babies come from right? How women get pregnant?"

He blushed crimson. "Of course."

"Well in order to avert such a consequence, preventive measures need to be taken. You'll need to give me a moment to prepare."

"Oh." He was clearly perplexed.

"I can explain later. I wouldn't want to dampen the mood. But please wait here while I go upstairs. Give me fifteen minutes." She pointed to the clock on the mantel. "Then come join me in my bedroom. I'm sure your ardor won't have waned."

He smiled sheepishly. "Yes, my lady. Thank you."

He looked so forlorn, standing in the middle of the room as she left him. She took the stairs two at a time, deciding on a pessary over her Dutch cap.

W illiam paced the rug before the hearth, glancing at the clock far too often. He should feel guilty but he just didn't. He really did want Lavinia—she was the epitome of womanhood. But he wanted to know what the act was like…needed to know before he did it with a woman with whom he was truly in love.

A woman like his golden-haired goddess.

What was he thinking? He hadn't even met her and already he was in love with her? He was in love with her beauty, a vapid notion.

Deep in his heart he hoped she would laugh at his stupid jokes and really listen when he talked about archaeology.

God, he felt awful for using Lavinia. But it was the arrangement they had made and this culmination of their studies would have happened eventually. Just because it was happening tonight when his cock strained inside his trousers for his unnamed goddess didn't make it somehow more despicable. Besides, it was probably best he hadn't fallen in love with Lavinia, as he had feared he might. They would have sex, he would know what it was all about, then he wouldn't bother her again.

He'd have to return all her books…

All right…maybe he'd want to see her again after tonight.

He glanced at the clock. Had it been fifteen minutes? Of course it had.

He took the stairs two-by-two. The door to her bedroom stood slightly ajar. He stepped inside.

"Close the door, William, and lock it."

She was in her bed, the sheet drawn up over her breasts, her shoulders bare, the soft glow of an oil lamp on her bedside table creating a seductive mood.

He swallowed and locked the door.

"Take off your clothes and join me."

He did as she bid, laying his clothes on an overstuffed chair, embarrassed when he removed the binding fashioned from an old cravat and hunter's rifle sling to rein in his unruly cock. And when he stood naked in the middle of her bedroom, his stiffness jutting enthusiastically before him, she opened the covers in invitation and he slid beside her.

God, she was warmth and fragrance and softness. He knew what to do, had done most of it already. He pulled her to him, taking her in a deep kiss, smoothing his palms down her back, cupping her butt. She stretched one leg over his thigh, leaving herself open to him. His cock poked insistently at her quim.

She wrapped her hand around his erection. "William, it is always correct to pleasure the woman first before you proceed."

Abashment prickled the back of his neck. "Yes, of course, my lady."

He pressed her onto her back, curving over her to suck the puckered nipple of a luscious breast. The other he kneaded, letting the hardened peak slide between two fingers before closing, pinching hard. She arched under him with a moan, a delicious sight to behold.

His cock rubbed against her thigh, reminding him of his eager state. He drew his hand over her curves to the hair between her legs. He slipped a finger through her sex. She was wet. She wanted this too. That was why a man pleasured a woman first, so she would want him.

His cock twitched a complaint.

He rubbed her clit slowly, watching her face soften as a lubricious sensuality descended. He crushed harder, wanting to take her to her climax. She deserved such attention to be so gracious in accommodating him with no warning on his part.

She closed her eyes, whispering encouraging words, moaning affirmations as he took her to the edge, puffing ragged breaths as he held her at the brink, groaning a soft cry when she fell into oblivion.

He moved over her, urging her thighs apart with his knees. She held his gaze as he positioned himself, licked her lower lip when he found his mark. She nodded.

He thrust in. The shock of ultimate pleasure sparked every nerve in his body.

"Oh God, Lavinia."

He couldn't have imagined this, had no idea what to expect really, but it certainly wasn't this. Pleasure focused at the head of his cock, surrounded the shaft yet bathed his entire body. Jolts of joy spiked his toes.

"Move in and out, darling."

Her voice startled him. He stared at her, her expression pleading.

"Yes." He rocked his hips, pushing in farther, pulling out.

The pleasure was increased a hundredfold. If that were even possible.

She moved with him, undulating her hips in a devilish manner, taking him faster down the path toward euphoria. His energy coiled within, focusing around his groin. He slammed into her, needing release, sweat beading on his forehead from the exertions.

And then he was there, climbing the mountain of sensuality, reaching the peak, slamming into her one last time, jetting his come inside her in a glorious explosion.

"Oh God!"

He held himself aloft as he emptied his body of its seed, sure he spewed more than he ever had before.

He weakened and sank on top of her, his heart thudding in his throat.

She smoothed his hair. "And was it everything you imagined?"

He laughed. "It was beyond anything I could have ever imagined."

"Good." She nudged him off her then snuggled under his arm. "Get some rest. You'll have to leave before morning light."

"Thank you, my lady." He kissed the top of her head. "Thank you." His lids fluttered closed. He hadn't expected to be so exhausted.

Lavinia stared at the satiated expression on the naked eighteen-year-old dozing in bed at her side. William should have left long ago but it was such a treat to have a man sleeping next to her that she did not have the heart to send him away.

He had satisfied her and he was ready to satisfy another. For surely there was another. A young man does not visit the house of an older woman after a night of dancing unless a young lady had provoked his interest.

"William."

He opened his eyes drowsily, confusion from the unfamiliar setting dispersing quickly. "Lavinia? Is it morning?"

"It's not yet dawn. You should leave."

He livened at that. "Yes, of course." He staggered from the bed as if his legs were unaccustomed to his body weighty with satiation.

She watched as he dressed, slowly concealing his athletic body from her gaze. He did not bother binding his groin. There would be no more female temptations that morning.

She got up and wrapped her dressing robe around her. "I'll show you to the servants' door. It would be best if you left from there and not the front entrance." She stood on tiptoe and kissed him.

"This was magnificent, Lavinia."

She smiled and squeezed his hand. Whether they would ever do the act again she couldn't say. But they each got what they needed from the union.

She had imagined Arthur every moment in his arms.

Arthur stared into his brandy, its luscious golden-brown reminiscent of the color of her hair, her eyes, a dress she once wore…

He looked up. A handful of members sat scattered in pairs around the drawing room of his club, men who had gone to the theater then dinner and were not asked to continue the evening with whatever woman had accompanied them, mistress or otherwise.

So what the hell was *he* doing drinking at his club at four in the morning?

Her. It was because of her. He hated being home alone when he got this way.

This is what he'd become. A lonely curmudgeon, finding solace in liquor. Why the hell couldn't he just choose one of the lovely young girls his mother introduced him to?

Because he wanted the best. He wanted her. His heart would settle for no less.

He could stand it no longer. He downed his brandy and left the club. He walked. If he saw a cab going his direction, he'd wave. Otherwise the walk in the brisk morning air would do him good.

A cab never came. Before he knew it he was in front of her house. To do what precisely? Go up to her front door and ask to see her? No one knew about them. Her butler would simply shoo him away as another drunken admirer. Best to just go home before he got the courage to make a fool of himself.

He was about to leave when a figure appeared in the shadows of the basement service entrance. A man. A deliveryman? A servant slipping out to see his girl?

Arthur ducked into the shadows of the neighboring stairwell.

The man stood on the pavement and looked around for a moment. He was excessively tall. Probably a footman.

Except he wasn't dressed like a footman. He was dressed like a gentleman.

Shit. Lavinia had a lover.

The man decided which direction to go and headed straight for Arthur. The light from the street lamp revealed his face.

William Peel.

Shock stabbed up his spine. *Christ*. Lavinia was bedding William Fucking Peel.

He sagged against the cold concrete as the click of William's shoes faded into the distance.

It wasn't fair. It wasn't right. Not that he really cared about William. Well, he did and if anyone should relieve him of his virginity it should be Lavinia. But if anyone should be with Lavinia right now it should be him, Arthur, and not some kid who didn't have the strength and intelligence to love and understand her.

He stopped his thoughts. He should not be jealous over William Peel. Lavinia had a reputation for helping young men get established in their careers. Supposedly she was helping him with his Turkish and Hebrew. So what if the boy learned a thing or two about the pleasures of the flesh?

What young Mr. Peel really needed now was to learn about the pleasures of the heart. Arthur smirked.

Luckily he knew precisely which young lady could teach him such a lesson.

CHAPTER SEVENTEEN

London, June 1880

From his vantage point opposite the Peers' Corridor, Arthur scanned Parliament's crowded Octagon Hall looking for Thuxton and Ryburgh. The two were to introduce him around, escort him to the Strangers' Gallery. But finding two middle-aged men wearing dark frock coats and black tall hats in a sea of middle-aged men wearing dark frock coats and black tall hats was difficult to say the least. He crossed his arms and leaned against a cluster of Gothic columns, the babel of peers and members echoing against the marble and stone. As one of the few men in the central hall not wearing a frock coat, most likely the earls would eventually spot him.

And then the figure of an exquisite, statuesque woman came into view. Arthur smiled.

He rarely had the chance to observe Lavinia of late and here she was in her element. She beamed and laughed in the presence of the two earls, the three of them forming an easy association. She conveyed a confidence he'd not seen before with a casual, friendly air not tinged by the hauteur she often projected in the ballroom.

She was stunning in a reddish-brown walking costume, pleated underskirts of brick red peeking out beneath the draped and fringed edges of her dress, her tulle veil pulled back to frame her face.

Joseph and Nicholas approached from St. Stephen's Hall and Lavinia waved them over. Ryburgh gripped Nicholas' hand and Thuxton grabbed his shoulder while Nicholas shook his head and blushed. They would be inquiring about Helena who, from Nicholas' presence in the hall, clearly had not yet given birth. Lavinia smiled and let Joseph kiss her hand as he eyed her with something akin to a leer.

Arthur laughed to himself. Joseph had finally succumbed to Lavinia's charms. It was about damn time.

Then Joseph and Thuxton stepped aside to have a private conversation. Probably business. Despite the size of his investments in *Harwell Phillips*, the earl never insisted on becoming a partner in the firm. But it was in the company's best interest to keep him apprised of any news—whether good, bad, or none.

Lavinia surveyed the hall, looking for someone. Looking for him, he hoped.

She caught his eye and recognition subtly changed her demeanor. Her expression softened from amused confidence to satisfied anticipation. That she wanted to see him was thrilling. He walked over to the group, holding himself back from running to her. Upon his approach, her smile broadened.

He bowed over her extended hand. "Lady Foxley-Graham. A pleasure."

"Lord Petersham. The pleasure is all mine."

Not all of it. He tickled her palm before releasing her. She glanced away with a slight blush.

Thuxton clapped him on the back. "Petersham, welcome to the halls of power."

Ryburgh made a sweeping gesture. "One day all this will be yours."

"Not for another decade I'm sure." Arthur chuckled.

"And how is Richmond?" Ryburgh asked with genuine concern.

"He's faring quite well. His grandson-in-law made sure of that."

Nicholas appeared abashed.

"In fact," added Joseph, "I do believe Lord Richmond is having tea with the queen."

Both Arthur and Lavinia stared at him.

"The queen, Mr. Phillips?" she asked. "Queen Victoria?"

"Yes, my lady, *that* queen."

"Well then, Petersham, looks as if you won't be officially joining us for quite some time," said Ryburgh.

"God only knows what party will be in power. We Liberals have been sitting on the Government benches only since April," said Thuxton.

Ryburgh thoughtfully turned his hat by the brim. "What's the order of business for today, Thuxton?"

"Heavens," Thuxton said with feigned surprise. "I thought you would know. I just show up for appearances' sake."

Lavinia laughed. "Is there nothing shocking for Lord Petersham to look forward to?"

"Hmm." Thuxton thumped the top of his tall hat. "Perhaps there will be debate about legalizing marriage with a deceased wife's sister."

Joseph started at that. "You're joking."

"Oh no, Mr. Phillips." Ryburgh smirked. "I assure you it is up for debate this session. Very controversial you know. Incest and all that."

"Incest?" Joseph snorted in amusement. "If my wife had a sister, she'd be as beautiful as my wife. Why shouldn't I be able to marry her if I were a lonely widower? She's not *my* sister." He snorted. "My wife is lucky she only has a brother." Joseph winked at Arthur.

Arthur flushed but quickly recovered. Of course no one would suspect he and Joseph were lovers. Why would they? An affair between two men was far more damnable than pseudo-incest. Parliament would never argue such a notion.

Ryburgh waved his hat in Arthur's direction. "Aren't you going to defend the honor of your hypothetical sister, Petersham?"

"My family is rather handsome," Arthur quipped. "I believe Phillips has a point."

Lavinia pressed her gloved fingers over her lips quavering with amusement.

"It's such progressive notions that won you the revolution, eh, Phillips?" Thuxton grinned. "We should import more of your kind to help us extinguish our antiquated ways."

"Look, all I'm saying is a man should be able to marry whom he wants without an act of Parliament."

"I hope young St. Albans here is ready to defend his father-in-law's opinions." Thuxton's jaw twitched as he pursed his lips. "What say you, my boy, ready to give a speech?"

Nicholas had been gazing absently about the hall in wonder. His eyes widened. "I'm not going to give a speech." He glanced at the assembled company. "Absolutely not."

Thuxton patted him on the back. "Just a bit of humor, son."

Nicholas flushed with obvious relief.

Ryburgh gestured toward the Peers' Corridor. "Shall we?"

"I'll watch for an hour or two," Arthur said. "I'm escorting Lady Richmond to the Raeburn ball tonight."

"Oh, my dear Petersham," Thuxton began, "you'll soon get used to ruling the country and dancing in the ballroom on the same night. We never sit for very long."

"Of course Lady Richmond is not to be denied," said Ryburgh. "My daughter will be there as well—"

Arthur glanced at Lavinia. She looked away.

"Save a dance for her, won't you, my lord?" Ryburgh practically pleaded. "She'll need respite from all the overly obsequious young men."

Arthur nodded. So Ryburgh had no inkling of his being considered for his daughter. That made it a damn sight easier to steer her toward suitors her own age.

"Well, gentlemen," Lavinia said with a flick of her wrist. "I shall see some of you later this evening and others of you tonight at the Raeburnses'."

Arthur tried not to appear disappointed. "Are women not allowed?"

Thuxton chuckled. "Lady Foxley-Graham has a standing invitation from a number of peers to sit in the Ladies' Gallery in Lords."

"However," she said, "today I shall be observing the House of Commons from the Ladies' Gallery there." She held out her hand to Arthur. "I'll see you tonight. You can tell me all about your impression of Lords."

Then they would have a conversation about something other than their physical urges.

"I'll escort you, my lady." Joseph held out his arm. "I think I should like to immerse myself amongst the commoners before I join Petersham."

Lavinia smiled and wrapped her arm around Joseph's. They nodded their good-days and headed down the Commons Corridor.

Arthur watched her leave, frustration mingling with disappointment. He needed her by his side, although, of course, she'd not actually be by his side in the Strangers' Gallery, she'd be with other women in their own seats.

And as he walked the corridor toward the Lords Chamber, the growls and guffaws of men surrounded him. What a foolish thing to segregate the sexes when the female was as knowledgeable and as powerful as the male. Perhaps he should defy his father once again and take up the cause of women's rights.

The open seating of the Ladies' Gallery in the House of Lords was far preferable to the gilt cage of the Ladies' Gallery in Commons. But Lavinia did not have the stamina to sit in the same room as Arthur at the moment even if it was with a hundred other people. She sat and watched the debate on the Commons floor through the metal grille, the drone of male voices drifting up to be barely heard in the gallery. The thick, humid air and the darkness were distractions from her despondency. Or perhaps the setting only exacerbated her melancholia.

She hadn't realized how affecting it would be seeing Arthur in the Palace of Westminster. His brown and green-checked waistcoat brought out the similar colors in his eyes, his jocular banter and cool demeanor proved he was right at home with his fellow peers.

She had wanted to tear the damn waistcoat off and make love to him on the marble floor while he stared up at the ornate vaulted ceiling.

She stood and wandered to the back of the small room, removing her hat and gloves, finding momentary relief from the heat. Many of the women had already left, probably due to the horrid conditions under which they were forced to watch their government act. The debate was on ways and means with a litany of proposed levies, probably not enough to maintain a woman's undivided attention. Lavinia drew in an inhalation from whatever air there was. Upon her exhale two more women left arm-in-arm, heads together in private conversation.

She returned to the front row of the gallery. Best to have something to talk about when she saw Arthur later that night. Of course she would let him do all the talking. He'd be excited and happy and enthralled about the experience. One always was after witnessing democracy in action for the first time.

She leaned forward and rested her chin on her palms. Below the men were arguing about duties on wine and beer and she wasn't quite following the debate. The air—or lack thereof—and naughty thoughts of Arthur were making her drowsy.

"Lady Foxley-Graham?"

She stood and turned around, astonished at the familiar voice.

"Mr. Phillips. Whatever are you doing here?"

Only then did she realize that she and Joseph Phillips were very much alone.

He stood near the wood wainscoting by the closed door, his brawny shoulders and thick arms a very odd sight in a room only ever occupied by women. He stared at her with an expression so suggestive, his energy so sexually charged, it bordered on indecent.

She hadn't realized until that moment how carnally attracted to the man she was. No wonder Sophia put up with her husband's many affairs. The man was truly hers and to have this level of sexually charged physicality in the bedroom when they were together would forgive all other sins.

Lavinia flushed from fear of her own desires being exposed.

"Did the debate in the House of Lords not please you, Mr. Phillips?"

"I never did bother to attend the debates of that esteemed body."

It hadn't been that long since he escorted her to the door—had he been waiting outside all that time? "Oh?"

He walked through the small space made seemingly smaller by his masculine bulk, looping around the gallery seats facing the grille until he was at the end of the aisle where she stood. His presence was not threatening. No…if anything, it was arousing. He was an incredibly handsome man who exuded a charisma that led one toward unexpected thoughts.

"I learn my politics from reports of machinations behind closed doors, my lady. One need not attend debates except to learn formalities. Oftentimes real governance happens in conversations one-on-one with a brandy in hand."

"Very astute, Mr. Phillips." She took a few steps backward.

He grinned and took two steps toward her. "It's the accent. It always puts people off. They think me coarse and crude. Of course I am." He stepped closer.

She moved farther away, throwing a glance at the closed door. "What are you doing in the Ladies' Gallery, Mr. Phillips?"

He countered her move with another long step. "Looking for you, Viscountess."

She moved again to find the wall against her back, the *Silence is Requested* sign above her left shoulder. She spread her hands against the smooth wood paneling, her fingers dipping into the recessed curves of the ogee molding.

He met her gaze with a leer. A shiver of arousal prickled her nipples. She had nowhere to run. She averted her gaze to the carpet beyond him.

He chuckled and closed the space between them. He placed his ungloved hands against the wall on either side of her head, the metallic tap of his wedding ring resounding in the stillness. He leaned in, flagrantly sniffing the fragrance she had dabbed on her neck.

Her mind buzzed with self-conversation about what it was he was doing. Should she really be allowing him, a married man whose wife just gave birth to his son, to be so close to her, a widow notorious for her conquests? Could he be intimidating her, the former lover of his wife's most recent paramour? Or perhaps warning her from being too intimate with his daughter's husband? Or playing with the heart of his brother-in-law lover?

Was he simply going to seduce her? In a public space? The idea, while alarming, was not altogether unwelcome.

Lavinia swallowed against the increasing thrum of her heart.

He moved his face over hers as if inspecting her. "What I hope to ascertain, my lady, is what it is about you that enamors him." His lips hovered above hers. "And are you worth it?"

Shit. Joseph now understood Arthur's profound attraction to Lady Foxley-Graham. She was sex personified.

It had been a long time since Joseph had attempted a seduction but Lavinia was making the act familiar once again. Her cool confidence, unafraid of what he might do, what he might think, made the doing and thinking much easier, as if a challenge to let him do his worst. She was a woman unafraid of his control and at that moment he wanted nothing more than to control her.

She remained still, trapped between his hands, the heat of their bodies mingling in the sultry space in a pocket of charged air. He moved forward until his body touched hers.

"I'm not sure I understand, Mr. Phillips."

Her perfume was so delicately applied a man had to be this close to her to breathe it in, yet when he did, the allure of the scent shot straight to his crotch. His lips floated over the pulse point in her neck, the heat of her taunting his tongue to reach out to cool her desire.

And when he did so, the breath hitched in her throat and released in a quiet sigh.

God, she was good. Yet she was doing nothing but standing there. He tenderly pressed his lips where his tongue had been.

The sigh became a moan. She relaxed against the wall.

He dared place his hands at her waist. She said nothing. He slid up to her ribs. She did not move. He crept up further, to cup her breasts, his thumbs stroking the fabric covering her nipples.

"I wanted to know what it was about you that has my brother-in-law so enthralled. What was it about you that attracted."

"And what are you finding out?" She tilted her head to give him more access to her neck.

"I've seen your half-naked body in your lover's bed. I know of your willingness to submit to unusual carnal pleasures. You wear your desire on your sleeve, madam, but you only give that arm to some men. Men with the same measure of self-assurance and the same appetite for passion as you. Some very lucky men indeed." He trailed soft kisses to her shoulder. "Arthur is a very lucky man."

Only then did she flinch in his arms.

Joseph stopped his seduction, dropping his hands, stepping back.

"Joseph, what is this really about?"

"As I said I wanted to see if you were worth it."

"Worth what?"

"Worth making a family sacrifice for."

"Like what Arthur is doing?"

"Yes. Like what Arthur is doing." And like what he was planning to do. "Arthur cannot stop thinking about you. He's let up a little on talking about you only because he probably feels his friends are tired of hearing his lovesick laments."

"Joseph, there can be nothing between Arthur and me. He'll come to understand this presently and do his required duty for the marquessate." Her tone was desolate.

"Do you want him?"

She bit her knuckles and looked away, her face twisted in emotion.

He pulled her into his arms. "Don't cry." He held her, swaying gently, calming her.

"I hate feeling this way." Her quiet voice trembled. "I hate loving so much it hurts."

He fished out his handkerchief and she took it, flashing a glance at the door to the gallery as she gently wiped her eyes.

"There's a handsomely paid guard outside, my lady. Cry as much as you need."

She blinked up at him. "A guard?"

"I had something else in mind other than offering you a handkerchief."

Her blush was disarmingly arousing. Perhaps his seduction should continue.

But then she cupped his cheek with her bare hand and touched her lips to his.

Every nerve in his body flared with desire. *This*. He wanted this. To taste her, to wrap his arms around her and pull her against him, to arc over her in an act of possession. She submitted to his demands with a subtle play of her own.

He broke away. "You're too willing, my lady, for someone who is supposed to be in love with another man."

She tugged on his lapels. "I, too, am curious to know what it is about you Arthur finds so attractive."

A chill seared his flesh. "Ah." He searched her face for any sign of disgust but found none. "So you know about us. Did he tell you?"

"No. Arthur does not know I know. As, I am sure, he does not know you are here with me now."

"Then how?"

"I witnessed a moment at the masquerade. Another in the hallway at the Richmonds' house. And there was a trace of jealousy in your voice in Arthur's bedroom at Atherley Keep."

"Very observant." He *had* been jealous and remained more than a little protective. "You're the first threat to his heart since Henrietta."

She laughed softly as she toyed with the buttons of his waistcoat. "And he is the first threat to mine in as many years." She slid a finger down the row of buttons to land right above his fly. "I'm certain what you really mean is I am the first threat to your relationship since Lady Henrietta."

His prick swelled against his drawers. To have what Arthur wanted was far more arousing than expected. "You are remarkable, my lady." He smoothed his palm over the curve of her bosom, to the nip at her waist, along the flare at her hips. Again, she did not flinch. "I presume with you, he takes the lead." He continued his advance and ruched up her skirts. "Not so with me. When we two are together, it is I who am in control."

He tucked her skirts between her back and the wall then searched for the split in her combination underwear, the delicate fabric elusive under his thick fingers.

"Silk. How elegant." He tangled in the hair of her mons. "Shall I tell you how Arthur sucks my cock?"

Her eyes widened as she let out an almost imperceptible sigh.

He slid a finger to briefly taunt her clit. "How he gets down on his knees before me?" He probed farther. She was dripping wet.

"How he pleasures me with enthusiasm?"

He crushed his forearm against her chest, pinning her to the paneling as he teased the excited nubbin with the length of his middle finger. She squirmed but quickly relented, holding his gaze, her brow furrowed in lubricious acquiescence.

Beyond the grille, the low hum of male voices drifted into the gallery, a reminder that their privacy was tenuous.

"How I grab him by the hair—" He shoved a finger into her cunt. "Bend him over the bed—" A second finger he pressed against the tighter hole just beyond. "And fuck him in the arse?"

She gasped audibly.

There was a lull in the debate below.

Joseph clamped his hand on her gaping mouth.

"Is that what he does to you, my lady?"

Was it? The idea shot fresh arousal to his cock. He could fuck her right then and there. Or he could watch her descend into orgiastic oblivion while he maintained his composure.

The latter was preferable.

He worked his fingers against her clit, inside her clenching cunt, keeping her pinned against the wall with his hip, keeping her silent with his palm. She closed her eyes, perhaps imagining it was Arthur who was assailing her with pleasures she had never known.

"Does he fuck you furiously for his own enjoyment? Or does he take it slow for yours?"

He reached into her depths to tickle the sensitive spot women of her sort found gratifying. She opened her eyes to offer an appreciative gaze.

He smiled. She was almost there. He ground his palm against her.

"Does he spend inside you or jet hot spunk on your tits?"

She came for him, gripping his fingers, her cry silenced by his hand, squeezing her eyes shut, her utter abandon and enjoyment of the act profoundly erotic. It would be the height of happiness for Arthur to relish such sensual abandon, to wake up alongside such a beauty every morning, to know he was loved in return.

And Joseph wanted to make Arthur happy.

He released his hold on her. She shook down her skirts, abashed, then gave him his handkerchief. He wiped his hand.

"And am I worth it, Mr. Phillips?"

He pecked her cheek. "You both are."

Ever since he had seen the beauty in blue and white—his golden Aphrodite—William had been most enthusiastic to attend Society's events with his parents. Papa had spent the greater part of the day at his office wrapped up in legal documents for a very important client, some lord who knew the queen, he'd heard the servants say, so when Papa returned home, he had suggested he and William do something frivolous.

"How about a ball?" William had suggested.

Papa had beamed at that. "Any ball in particular?"

"Whatever one Lady Banbury is attending."

Papa's surprise seemed to turn to understanding. And then he grinned. "I'll find out from your mother."

And a few hours later, they were at Lord and Lady Raeburn's house on the fringes of the dance floor, William keeping his eye out for his goddess.

Papa hung behind, chatting with Uncle Arthur.

"How was Parliament today? Absolutely riveting?"

"Discussions on Armenia and Ireland I can't imagine my father being interested in." Uncle Arthur snorted. "I suppose that's why he didn't bother showing up."

"I'm sure he's not quite up to such activity with his recent illness."

"Nothing of the sort. Apparently he was having tea with the queen."

William's ears perked up.

Papa emitted a quiet chuckle. "Then I'm not sure which one of you had the better afternoon."

Which sounded as if Papa might have once taken tea with the queen.

Such a fantastical notion was quickly laid to rest when out of the corner of his eye William saw *her*. Or he thought he did. He focused on the spot in the crowd but she had moved and then he wasn't quite sure which blonde head was hers.

"Mr. Peel," came a familiar voice at his side. "Are you engaged for the next dance?"

It was Miss Hardcastle. She was very pretty but a little too old for him so he wasn't quite sure why she was interested.

"Lord Petersham, a pleasure to see you." Her emphasis of the word "pleasure" oozed with an embarrassing implication.

Which obviously was why she was there. Uncle Arthur was supposed to find a wife. Well that's what Mama had said anyway.

"Miss Hardcastle," came Uncle Arthur's voice.

He couldn't keep ignoring the company behind him. Maybe he could accept a dance with Miss Hardcastle, thereby garnering a better view of the crowd. She knew what his goddess looked like. Perhaps she would be willing to help?

"Good evening, Miss Hardcastle," he said. "What a lovely dress." That was just something to say really. He hadn't had time to inspect the garment.

If only he could take back the words. The bodice of her dress was cut rather low. Too low. And from his high vantage point, there was much to see. He hoped to God no one looked at his crotch. He tore his gaze away.

Luckily he did. For approaching them was his goddess accompanied by Lady Banbury and Lavinia.

He tried not to blush when he saw Lavinia but did so anyway once his Aphrodite laid eyes on him and smiled.

His collar grew very tight. And hot. A little trickle of sweat slithered down his back.

Introductions were said all around. Her name was Miss Beatrice Smythe. It was a perfect name.

He took a moment to consider her costume before complimenting her. Everything was shiny satin pink and frothy frilly white. Her bodice was not cut too low but it did have the appearance that she was wearing a rather pretty corset on top of her gown. Her skirts were a riot of lace and bows.

"Miss Smythe, you look lovely tonight. I dare say you compete with Lady Foxley-Graham for the evening's prize in fashion."

Miss Smythe blushed pinker than her bodice. Lady Banbury squeaked an oath. Lavinia whipped out her fan to hide a smile. Miss Hardcastle giggled.

"Thank you, Mr. Peel."

Oh God. She said his name.

Uncle Arthur turned to him. "Miss Smythe is interested in archaeology, William. Isn't that what you hope to study at Cambridge?"

It was too perfect. "Truly, Miss Smythe?"

Lord and Lady Richmond's weighty appearance at Uncle Arthur's side hampered any further conversation. The marchioness effused polite greetings all around but especially to his goddess.

"Miss Smythe, I'm sure your dance card is full this evening."

Miss Smythe offered a shy smile. "I do believe my next dance is free, Lady Richmond." Did she cast a glance his way?

He should ask her.

Except Lady Richmond asked first. "Arthur, are you engaged for the next dance?"

Uncle Arthur? And Miss Smythe? He looked at each. Neither one seemed particularly thrilled with the idea.

"I believe Lord Petersham's next dance was promised to Lady Foxley-Graham," Lady Banbury said.

"You also promised to tell me about your evening at the House of Lords," Lavinia added softly. She was gazing at Uncle Arthur with an expression he had been privy to in her bedroom.

And seconds later, Lavinia and Uncle Arthur were arm-in-arm, walking to the dance floor, chatting and smiling.

"They look happy together," William blurted to no one.

Papa cleared his throat.

"They do, don't they," Lord Richmond said. He nudged William. "Ask her."

Her? Miss Hardcastle? She was busy chatting with Lady Richmond...so, no. His collar grew hot again. Of course not. His goddess. The ball. "Miss Smythe, would you like to dance?"

Apparently she said yes because suddenly his goddess—his Beatrice—was in his arms and they were in the midst of other couples, swirling on the dance floor, his feet directed by something other than his brain.

"Are you a Cambridge man then?"

Her words almost made him lose his step. So she really was there before him, his hand really on her waist. "This autumn. I'll be reading classics and archaeology. Didn't Uncle Arthur say you had an interest in that?"

"Oh yes! I dream about digging in the ground and finding pots and such. It's all so romantic, don't you think, discovering how people lived hundreds or thousands of years ago?"

Perfection just got more perfect. "I like deciphering ancient texts to discover how people lived."

"Perhaps we can find time this autumn to discuss our discoveries. I'll be attending Girton."

"Why, we'll be neighbors!"

She giggled, a sound more melodious than the orchestra's tune.

Her laughter tempered to a heavenly smile. "Why do you call Lord Petersham 'Uncle Arthur'? Are you related?"

"No. My father and Lord Petersham are business partners. There's a Mr. Phillips in the business as well. I've just grown up calling them Uncle Arthur and Uncle Joseph."

"That's so endearing." She looked sideways as they turned. "I love my family. It would be grand to have more relations."

"I have two sisters," he blurted.

"Only two? I have four."

"There are more like you?" He cringed.

She blushed again then bit her lip to suppress a smile. The smile came anyway.

They whirled on the dance floor, gazing at each other, smiling, no longer conversing. He wanted to take her outside to the terrace, to the garden, to strip off her glove, to hold her bare hand in his, to enfold her in his arms, to kiss her in the moonlight.

No. No, he didn't. He wanted to do none of that. Not yet anyway. Miss Smythe was meant to be savored.

The music ended and he held out his arm to take her back to Lady Banbury. She obliged. They walked slowly in their retreat from the dance floor. What he had to say he didn't want to say in front of anyone else, just her. He stopped and turned to her.

"Miss Smythe, I should like to call on you. May I? I thought perhaps a visit to the British Museum if your chaperon would not be too terribly bored."

"I would love that, Mr. Peel." Her face glowed around her beaming countenance.

The promise of seeing her again thrilling his thoughts, he practically skipped back to Lady Banbury.

* * * * *

Lavinia took off her gloves in her foyer. Dancing with Arthur that evening, talking with him about his afternoon spent observing Lords, sharing a laugh or two, it all seemed so simple. Could she sustain such a fiction while he was married?

And who was he to marry anyway? Lord Richmond, from what Charlotte had told her later, had encouraged William to ask Beatrice to dance. The two apparently were besotted with each other.

Which meant Lady Richmond would have to find another candidate for her son. Which meant Lavinia had a little more time to hope.

Or a little more time to convince herself that she could be his lover and not destroy her heart.

Sims cleared his throat behind her.

She swallowed a lump of emotion. "Yes, Sims?"

"My lady, a message came while you were out. By hand delivery."

"Thank you, Sims." She took the folded paper from the silver tray, holding it against her bosom while Sims bowed then made his exit to the servants' stairs.

She opened the note. It was in a man's hand, concise and professional, writing she had not seen in years but knew all too well. She stared at the eight words before actually reading them and understanding their meaning:

Salep Hill Cottage. As soon as you can.

CHAPTER EIGHTEEN

Morning light pierced the front windows of the members' drawing room at the Merchants and Industry Club. It was far too early in the day to be drinking. Or perhaps it was just a continuation of indulgence from the night before. Joseph snorted a laugh. His fellow club members would hardly care.

"I always wondered what the inside of a businessman's club looked like," Lord Richmond murmured.

From the depths of a well-worn leather chair, Joseph took a swig of brandy and surveyed the equally well-worn room. He could only imagine an aristocrat's gentleman's club might have more gilding and more servants. And more aged peers like the Marquess of Richmond.

"And, my lord? What do you conclude?"

Richmond looked about at the readers and the snoozers. "That it's a damn sight cozier than mine." He swirled the liquor in his snifter. "I could get used to this." He shifted in his seat. "I love this chair."

"You'd have to be a businessman."

"Stranger things have happened."

"Like a dockworker marrying a marquess's daughter?"

Richmond grunted. "I hated you, you know."

"I do know, my lord."

"You took my Sophie away from me. Physically, emotionally…" Richmond's voice trailed off with relived memories.

"She needed to be protected from evil."

"I understand all that now. I may not have been the best father but I love my daughter. In my heart of hearts I know it was for the best. I did not want to believe it twenty years ago."

"As a father myself I sympathize." Joseph had been suspicious of Nicholas at first. Of course that had been utterly foolish of him.

"And Arthur. You took Arthur away from me as well."

"I'm giving him back to you, Lord Richmond."

Richmond chuckled. "In a sense I suppose you are."

Joseph gazed into his snifter before taking another sip. "Will this work?"

"Once my fellow peers knew for whom all this was to be done, they rallied to the cause."

"She really does have strong connections in Parliament, doesn't she?"

"She's a highly respected woman. And rightfully so." Richmond chortled throatily. "The only person who needed convincing was the queen. I reminded her she had been in love once and still understood the intensity of the emotion. And then I groveled. I told her the truth about Sophia's scandal, about how a peer was involved, how the man left a trail of carnage with his vicious abuse. I pleaded with her to not let another peerage be laid to waste, further dishonoring the Harwell name." He gulped a mouthful of brandy. "She eventually came around."

They sat in silence for a spell, observing the occupants of the room. It was a rather uneventful morning.

"Isn't that the Earl of Chesil?" Richmond's voice held a note of surprise.

Near the central bank of windows sat a well-built man in his thirties.

"I knew his father. He was a good man. Died too young. His son was earl at twenty-five."

The young man folded his newspaper, uncrossed his legs then checked his watch. He muttered an oath and bounded up from his club chair.

"I believe Chesil's in textiles," Joseph said.

Richmond emitted another grunt. "Do you think Henry will want to follow in your footsteps? In the railway business I mean."

Joseph drew in a long inhalation, releasing it slowly. "Of course every father wants his son to follow in his footsteps."

Richmond chuckled as he finished off his brandy.

"I had always thought if I ever had a son that once he came of age, he should make his own choices. That he should experience the fullness of life on his own. I would provide some support, of course. Now I've taken some of those choices away."

"You've given him different choices."

Joseph examined Richmond. Instead of the dour man he once knew, suddenly before him was a kindly grandfather. "Yeah, I suppose."

"And Henry can always run a railway business if he so chooses." Richmond lengthened himself in his chair as if he were about to join the dozers. "It seems these days it is acceptable for peers to be businessmen." He closed his eyes, the glass in his hand perilously close to falling to the carpet. "Did I mention I could get used to this?"

CHAPTER NINETEEN

Exeter

Lavinia sat up in the cab when the carved wooden plaque for Salep Hill Cottage came into view. Nostalgia prickled her skin to gooseflesh once the carriage pulled up the drive. It was late afternoon. Smoke puffed out of the chimney of the stone house and a dim light danced on the curtains of the front room, a homey appeal not seen since the days she and her husband sought respite there from London's chaos.

She chuckled to herself. Nowadays she thrived on the chaos of London. The refuge at Exeter was reserved for others.

She thanked and paid the driver, asking him to please just leave the bags at the front door, then waited on the entry path as he drove away. She had the key in her purse but she would not need it. The door would be unlocked and the occupant waiting for her.

She entered, closed the door quietly, left her bags in the small foyer under the man's topcoat hanging on a peg, and tiptoed into the front parlor. The couch had been moved before the hearth, the hearth had been laid with a roaring fire. The room was cozy, like it used to be.

"Good afternoon, Julius."

He peered over the edge of the sofa. "I knew you'd come." He reclined comfortably, his hands behind his head, his waistcoat and the first few buttons of his shirt unbuttoned, his shoes side-by-side on the rug.

"Did Mrs. Dinsdale let you in?"

"I still have my key but I rang first. Your housekeeper was surprised to see me."

Lavinia took off her coat and hat, placed them on a chair then went to stand before the couch, the heat of the fire at her back.

"It's been a long time since you sent a note like that. I thought I should come."

He slid his feet to the floor then rubbed the cushion next to him. "Sit."

She sat, not precisely where he indicated, more toward the opposite corner. Whatever this was all about it was best to maintain a distance.

He took her lead and shifted deeper into his corner. "Thank you for coming."

There was a melancholia to his words, a wistful distance she had never heard before. Julius was the last man to be sentimental. But here he was, suddenly expressing a hint of an emotion she had longed for over the course of twenty years.

"I thought it best to meet here. I feel—" He glanced around the room. "At home in this place."

They had both felt as such once upon a time. "I'm surprised you still had the key, Julius."

The lines of age melted around his eyes. "Of course I do, Vinny."

He hadn't called her that in years. "Perhaps I should feel flattered."

He chuckled. "It is I, rather, who should be flattered that a woman of incomparable beauty and refinement should deign respond to my plea." His voice held sincerity not seduction.

"Plea? I rather thought it was a directive."

"No," he said, elbows on his knees. "A plea." He turned his face to her, his blue eyes glinting with remorse. "For forgiveness."

Her lungs tightened. She stared at him, disbelieving yet comprehending.

He stood to pace before the fire. "Vinny, what I did to you was egregious. I wish I could apologize. But words can never be enough." He looked askance then returned her gaze, his veneer of hauteur cracked, his usual self-confidence replaced by uncharacteristic humility. "I've come before you to beg for your forgiveness. I understand if you cannot give it but I need you to at least listen to me."

A sob choked her throat. She stared into the fire until her eyes burned from the heat. Anger and curiosity froze her to her spot on the couch. "I've tried so hard to forget what you did." The tears were uncontrollable.

He was beside her in an instant. "I know." He placed his hands on her shoulders, gingerly at first, but she did not shrug him off. He wrapped his arms around her. "I was a brute. I was self-absorbed, proud, driven by greed. I foolishly thought such entanglements would hold me back in my career." He nestled his face in the hollow of her shoulder. "I realize now what a fool I was. The irony of course is that you have furthered so many in their careers since." He sucked in a tremulous breath. "But mostly I regret having lost the love of my life."

Irritation ruffled her nape. "How can you say that? You never truly loved me." But her attempt to shake him off was weak. His arms were warm and comforting. She always gave in to him too readily.

"But I did. Desperately, really, and it took quite a bit of self-control to tamp it down. Yet I failed. Instead, I turned my love for you into something horrible."

Something horrible indeed. Vicious, raw sexuality fueled by self-gratification and ambition without a thought for mutual desire.

"We've never talked about it," he said softly. "I shut you out because I did not want to feel what I was feeling. I thought if I were cruel to you I would no longer feel. I was so wrong. So utterly wrong."

He released her and retreated to his corner of the couch. Under his watchful gaze she unlaced her shoes and slipped them off. He drew her alongside, tucking her under his arm, she folding her feet under her. It was how they used to sit together all those years ago.

"I told myself I couldn't have the burden of an affair so early in my career, especially with a married woman with whom I was dangerously in love. Then in a fit of remorse I convinced myself I could not be a dedicated lover to you, that you deserved more than what I could give, that I would try to convince you of the same." He swirled intricate patterns with the tips of his fingers along her arm.

She relaxed farther against his chest.

"And then you told me you were pregnant with my child." He drew in a juddering breath, the depth of his emotion reverberating in her ear. "My God, Vinny, I don't know what got into me. I did the most brutal thing a man can do. I murdered my own child."

She wrapped her arms around him. "Jules, don't say it like that." Her tears dampened his shirt.

"But it's true. The child was a wanted child. Had you come to me and said you did not want it I would have obliged without scruples. But you were overjoyed. I was terrified. Richard and I didn't look a whit like each other. People already had suspicions about you and me, knew about Richard's infertility with his first wife. There would have been talk. I told myself all of that and more back then." He drew her to him. "I deeply regret what I did. You never became pregnant again."

"No…I was careful." And probably incapable after the incident.

"But you wanted a child."

"I did, especially after Richard died and I was alone, without purpose. I eventually found purpose in my life. I've accepted my fate and truly have grown accustomed to it. There is an immense freedom."

"It pains me, knowing Richard died only three years later. We could have been married and raised a family. I would have been content." He smoothed her hair. "But I was not ready. I was a fool. I don't want to be that man again."

Something had happened. "Julius, why are you telling me this?"

He chuckled. "Of course a man does not have a change of conscience and heart in a vacuum." He gave her shoulders a little squeeze. "I'm in love."

She looked up at him. He smiled down at her.

He chuckled again. "There I've said it out loud." He exhaled a sigh.

"Who is the lucky woman?"

"Grace Danby."

That was unexpected. "Your assistant?"

"The very same. She's remarkable. She knows me, Vinny. Really understands me. She's seen a lot of pain and brutality in her world. She's been able to see right through mine."

He grinned, a sight so rare and wonderful. It made him more handsome, as if that were possible. Julius Christopher was truly in love.

Was she jealous? No. She was happy for him. Julius loving another woman would finally sever the fatiguing hold he had over her. She could move forward with an unburdened heart.

"I would not, could not possibly understand what I am feeling is love without having had the experience of you. My body, my mind remembered the emotion." He shifted to hold her more closely. "Vinny, Grace is carrying my child. I'm utterly petrified but I want this child. I want to be a father. A good father. I want to make up for what I did in the past."

Tears wet her lashes, from joy or regret she was not sure. "I will forgive you, Julius, if you make good on that. But don't spoil the child. It won't do any good if you try to make up for your sins by overindulging."

He kissed her hair. "Ah no, of course not. I see children almost every day in my office. They behave best with a little discipline."

She laughed softly, nestling deeper into his warmth.

"I'm going to ask Grace to marry me. Twenty years ago the idea was repugnant. Now I know in my heart it is what I want. But I need your blessing. I won't go through with this unless you allow it. I owe you that much."

"You'll go through with it regardless of what I think, darling."

"No, believe me I won't. If you still hate me so much you want me to be punished by denying me any shred of happiness, I would understand."

She looked up at him. "I want you to atone for your sin with love. By being a loving husband. And by being the best damn father in the world."

He quirked a brow. "Even better than Nicholas Atherley?"

She laughed. "You should aspire to be so kind and caring."

Their eyes met, the spark of familiarity drawing their faces closer until his mouth met hers. His kiss was tender, so unlike the last time they were together when anger boiled within. Now it was heartache, sorrow, regret, and love.

He broke from the kiss, his eyes gentle. "Let me make love to you, Vinny. One last time."

"Yes, Jules." It was inevitable.

Julius held out his hand and Lavinia took it willingly, letting him lead her into the bedroom, a place that held so many memories.

She let him undress her, submitting to him like she used to, until she was naked and vulnerable before him. And still so beautiful. He trailed kisses down her neck, her breasts, her belly, kneeling to kiss the hair of her mons. He tangled his tongue in the wiry strands, seeking her surrender, finding it in the sticky wetness dripping for his delectation.

He looked up to see her smiling.

"Are you going to stay dressed and on your knees, darling?"

He rose. "No." He cupped her cheek and gazed into the depths of her amber eyes.

She gave a quick kiss to his palm before clambering onto the bed. She propped herself up with pillows, laying the covers neatly over her lap. "I'll watch."

A slight discomfiture descended as he disrobed. He had vigorously maintained an athletic physique over the years. She would think him vain without knowing he had done it for her, for the occasional moments when he would find himself in her arms. Was his future to be flabby and feeble from living a comfortable life with Grace?

It did not matter. For at that moment, Lavinia was ogling him with lascivious intent, licking her lips as her gaze dipped to his bobbing erection.

"You're looking very fine for a man almost fifty, Jules."

"Worthy of being in your arms, Vinny?"

She laughed and held out her hands for him to join her. Just the chance to hold her naked body against his would be enough.

Almost.

He scrambled under the covers, grappling her, tickling her, rollicking in her arms, until he stretched on top of her, panting. He urged her legs apart to lie between her thighs, keeping himself propped up on his elbows to see the glow of arousal on her face.

She traced a finger around his beard. "The last time we were in this position you were rather cruel. I like the changed man."

"I was angry at you. You dashed my plans." He slid his cock between her slick sex.

"You should be glad I did."

"Perhaps." He prodded her entrance.

She shifted to allow him access.

"It would be exhilarating to dominate you in such a manner again," he said.

"I always let you have your way."

He grabbed her arms, positioning them over her head, crushing them into the pillow until she squeaked in protest.

"You do." He entered her, groaning at the welcoming wet heat.

She curved against the mattress, heaving her ample bosom to him. He bent over, sucking one piqued nipple, then the other, wishing he could taunt both at the same time. He moved slowly, savoring her body.

"Do you remember Penzance?" he murmured.

"Jules, darling," she breathed. "I'll never forget." She tightened around him.

Desire pierced his core. "The rock on the beach at midnight."

Memories lit her eyes. "I would swear it was the night we conceived our child."

He would swear that too.

Her hips rocked languidly.

He increased his rhythm. "I almost told you I loved you that night, but pride held me back."

She tilted, the sign she wanted him to deepen his thrusts. He dipped his head and met her lips, melding his mouth with hers as their bodies joined more intimately below. She opened for him, as she always had, her emotions and desires exposed.

And for the first time he opened himself to her. He pulled back from the kiss. "If I could go back, relive that moment, I would change so many things."

Tears wet her lashes then dripped down the sides of her face.

He broke contact, sliding behind her, pulling her close, his cock cradled comfortably between the cheeks of her buttocks. He reached around to stroke her clit.

She moaned his name as she melted against his tender caresses.

"We watched the moon over the ocean, the waves crash on the shore." The pulse point of her neck was hot under his tongue.

She turned slightly to flatten against the mattress and gaze up at him. "You silenced my cries of pleasure." She grabbed his cock and positioned it at her sex.

He pushed in. "I won't silence you now, Vinny." He worked her clit mercilessly. "Let go."

Her expression slackened to satiation. Her cunt gripped and pulsed around him, mirroring the rise and fall of her gasping cries.

He pressed harder. "More." He kept his pace slow, caring not for his own pleasure, wanting hers alone. Wanting her to shatter in his arms, to shatter the memories of what he had done.

She closed her eyes with a sigh and a smile, purring approbations, until her breath hitched and she came, her clenching strength almost his undoing. She looked up at him, confusion clouding her expression. "Julius?"

And that's when he felt *his* presence.

Who the man was he had no idea. But she loved another. She could move forward, as well.

He curved his palm around her cheek. "It's me. I'm here." It was his moment and he would make her remember it. He clamped down on her clit, working it zealously.

She bucked up with a yelp. "It's too sensitive!" she squealed, writhing beneath him. "Jules," she pleaded, "fuck me. I just need you to fuck me."

He lifted her leg, twisting under it until he was between her thighs again. "Vinny—"

She hooked her calf over his butt, the signal she had prepared for their union.

He kissed her tenderly in gratitude and warning. And then he slammed inside her, wanting, needing to destroy the villain within, to free the new man.

"Let go, Julius."

Her countenance softened and for a fleeting moment became another, equally familiar. But this was Lavinia, the woman he owed everything to, who despised him, who loved him, who changed him. This was the last chance for gratitude.

And the last chance to command her luscious body.

He grabbed her arms, gripping her thumbs harshly in one hand, grinding them into the pillow above her head. He drove into her relentlessly, each plunge to the root of his cock, to the depths of her sex, her body yielding, flailing under his power, his rutting strength from passion and desire not vengeance and villainy.

With a barking cry, he jerked against her, emptying himself, releasing the horror of the past.

Utterly spent, he slipped to her side and held her, kissing her cheeks as he calmed from his sensual exertion. "Thank you, Vinny."

She wriggled in his arms. "It was a good last time."

He pecked her lips. "It was." He brushed a stray tendril from her face. "Who is he, darling?"

She blushed. "An earl. Our hearts want to be together. Politically it's complicated."

"Ah. If your heart knows what it wants, it will find a way."

She laughed softly. "Love has made you wiser."

He hugged her a little more tightly. "It has."

"Are you staying the night?" She nuzzled against him.

"I am." Grace knew to expect him the next day.

"Good. Then we can have one more last time in the morning."

He drifted off to sleep in her arms, for the first time in decades his dreams not disquieting.

Lavinia stretched her arm out under the covers to rouse the man at her side, finding not warm male flesh but a pocket of cool air between the sheets.

Julius had left early. There would be no morning sex.

She sighed then laughed. She should be disappointed. Instead she was happy for him.

She rose and put on her dressing robe. A cup of tea before a warm fire would help her organize her thoughts.

She poked her head into the kitchen. Mrs. Dinsdale clattered busily, humming to herself, then flushed when she saw Lavinia.

"Oh, my lady! I hope I did not wake you?"

"No, Mrs. Dinsdale. I'll take my tea in the parlor."

"Yes, my lady."

Lavinia relaxed on the sofa, the sofa where she and Julius had made love dozens of times before. She smiled. From what Nicholas had told her, he had made love to Helena on that very same sofa on their honeymoon.

Mrs. Dinsdale came in with the tea things. "My lady." She placed the tray on the end table. Lavinia watched as she poured, almost not registering the unexpected object lying on the tray.

A key with a red ribbon.

"Your Dr. Christopher left his key, my lady."

He would never need it again.

"Thank you, Mrs. Dinsdale."

Lavinia drew in a deep breath then exhaled as the weight lifted from her shoulders.

Her heart was ready for something new.

CHAPTER TWENTY

London

A sputtering pop in the parlor fire roused Grace out of her inaction. How long she had been sitting she did not know, but the waning light of day indicated it had been several hours. With the office closed while Julius visited his friend, she remained plagued by vexatious thoughts.

She rose from her chair and descended the servants' stairs to the silent and empty kitchen. With no master to serve, Mrs. Jennings had gone to her sister's. Grace laid a tray with teapot and cup and went back upstairs to Julius' examination room, closing and locking the door behind her. She placed the tray on the counter and lit a lamp then unlocked Julius' desk and retrieved his recipe book. She knew his system and found the page readily.

She went to the cupboard and pulled out the box containing the more dangerous herbs and tinctures. Grace had only partially lied when she told Julius she had not checked supplies. She had checked the supplies in the locked box after Mrs. Chadbourne had left, as they were running low on a few items. She restocked those, including the herbs to make an abortifacient.

She went through the list of ingredients one by one, taking out the bottles, checking the labels, measuring out the herbs then double checking the recipe, the bottles, and the quantities. She carefully measured out pennyroyal and artemisia, mugwort and tansy. When she was certain the proportions were right, she set the kettle on the stovetop to boil water for the infusion.

Then she sat by the stove and waited.

In the East End, women would go to a local woman, a midwife who knew about herbs, especially herbs for women's complaints. There were some stories of women who got very sick, some who even died, but most stories were from women relieved of the burden of an unwanted child. Here in the West End it was so different. Women like Mrs. Chadbourne went to doctors like Julius then took trips to the Continent.

When the water was at almost boiling, Grace placed the herbs in the teapot.

When the water boiled, she poured it in the teapot. She stared at the teacup.

She knew in her heart she did not want to do what she was about to do. She wanted Julius' child, but he didn't. She would do anything for Julius. She had already proved that to him again and again.

She swirled the concoction, the motion jiggling the lid of the teapot. She just needed to wait about fifteen minutes.

She would do this one last thing for him.

The sound of a key scratching in the lock sent a shiver up her spine. *Julius?* Back so soon? She'd have to look as if she was working. Checking supplies is what she would say. And she had decided to make tea while she worked.

But the bottles and the recipe book were right on the counter.

The doorknob turned and Julius walked in.

"Grace?"

"Julius! You're here!"

He smiled his usual gentle smile. "I've just returned." He strode forward. "I saw the light—" He caught sight of the recipe book still open to the damning page, then the teapot, a few drops of water on the counter next to it.

The smile faded to panic.

"*No.*"

In one swift movement he swept the teapot off the counter, sending it crashing to the floor, hot water and herbs exploding beneath shards of stoneware. He scooped her up into his arms, out the door, into the hall. He fell to his knees, taking her with him, his arms wrapped tightly around her.

His body shook against hers until he heaved a breath.

"Julius?"

He was crying.

"Grace, love, what were you thinking? What were you planning to do?" He placed his hands on her belly then bowed before her, his face pressed into her stomach, kissing her there, his tears wetting her dress.

"I just thought…I thought you wouldn't want it."

He stared at her, wide-eyed and pale. "Wouldn't want it?"

"I…I…" She'd have to tell him. "I read the letter you left on your desk. The one from Lady Foxley-Graham. About your child. About how you didn't want to have a child."

He paled. "Oh God, Grace. No…it's not true. I mean that was a long time ago. I was young and foolish. I didn't know what I wanted. I was cruel." He pulled her into his arms once again, stroking her back, kissing her hair. "Darling, I want what we have made together. I want our child."

Her tears fell uncontrollably. She weakened in his arms, letting him hold her, letting him offer soothing words. He pulled her against him as he sat on the floor and leaned against the wall.

"I know I've never said it. I've felt it and didn't know what it was. Only recently did I understand." He gently rubbed her belly. "Then I had doubts that I could truly feel such an emotion. Now, seeing what you were about to do, I realize what I feel is true." He tilted her chin up, then leaned in and kissed her tenderly on the lips. "I love you, Grace. I do not want to live without you."

"Oh, Julius."

Fresh tears poured forth from both of them.

"Grace, will you marry me?"

Emotion welled in the pit of her stomach, surging forth to constrict her lungs. "Marry you?"

He beamed through his tears. "I'll post the banns as soon as you say yes."

She sucked in a mouthful of air and let out a stammering sob. "Oh, Julius," she cried into his chest. "I dared not dream of such a possibility. Yes, oh, yes."

"Then it's settled." He kissed her hair.

She looked up at him. "When did you know…about the baby?"

The corner of his mouth twitched upward before he laughed. "Darling, I'm a doctor. A women's doctor. I suspect I knew before you did." He spread his hand on her belly, warm and protecting. "August, I should think. We'll be married in a month."

"We'll be a family." She smiled and nestled against the comfort of his chest.

CHAPTER TWENTY-ONE

The peace of Salep Hill Cottage was so restorative Lavinia stayed on in Exeter for almost a week. Upon her return to London, she headed straight for the bath. To wash off the dirt from traveling is what she told Marie. Really she was washing Dr. Julius Christopher from every pore, every wrinkle, every crevice of her body. And from her soul.

And in doing so, she would open her heart to Arthur.

The heat of the bath was already doing its part, relaxing her muscles, calming her mind, opening her to possibilities of what could lie ahead.

She and Arthur belonged together, that was a certainty. And if they could not be married, then she would settle for an affair. For all she knew her husband had been in love with another woman. Perhaps it was his yearning for another and not his age that had kept him from her bed. She most definitely had not been in love with Richard. If he had loved another, she would not have cared one whit.

Which meant she would have to find Arthur a wife who would not mind his devotion to a mistress.

"My lady?" Marie's gentle entreaty prodded her to the present. "Shall I wash your hair?"

"Yes, Marie. Thank you."

Lavinia settled her head against the rolled edge of the tub while Marie placed a stool behind her. She began pulling pins when a tentative rap sounded on the bathroom door.

"I'll go see, my lady."

When Marie returned her smile was hidden behind an enormous bouquet of lavender roses in a plum-colored vase adorned with swirling gilt arabesques. The maid breathed in the scent. "Flowers for you, my lady."

Lavinia's pulse quickened. "Roses." She dared not hope who the giver might be. "Was there a card?"

Marie handed her a small envelope. Inside was a calling card, the printed name centered in a blocky and thick authoritative script:

Arthur Harwell, the Earl of Petersham

Lavinia kissed the card before returning it to her maid. "Please put the roses where I may see them."

Marie placed the vase on a side table next to the green-tiled fireplace and arranged the roses, releasing their fragrance. Lavinia melted into the curve of the tub, breathing in the steam, the scent of roses mingling with the lavender and rosemary soap, teasing her senses. *Arthur*. She would face whatever future awaited the two of them. She leaned her head back against the rim and closed her eyes, restraining her hand from drifting to the thatch of hair between her legs.

She would dismiss her maid after she had washed her hair and would dream of Arthur then.

Marie resumed her position on the stool to pull pins from Lavinia's hair. The maid seemed as pleased as Lavinia with the gift. It wasn't as if Lavinia rarely received roses. She did, rather frequently. But both women were satisfied with the sender. Marie had been a good accomplice during the visit to Atherley Keep.

"Lord Petersham knows your tastes, my lady."

"He does, Marie."

"It is good when a man remembers—"

The door swung open.

"*Mon Dieu!*" Marie's oath was dampened by the clatter of the stool against the tiled floor.

Arthur strode in. "I see you received the roses."

Lavinia straightened. "How on earth did you get past Sims?"

He chuckled, his brown eyes twinkling above his smile. "I told him to send up the footman in the event you should scream from my unwanted advances."

Lavinia dismissed Marie with a wave. "Tell Sims and Archie that I shall be quite safe."

Left alone, Arthur turned the lock and leaned against the bathroom door, his leer the only window to the lewd fantasy playing in his mind. "You've not been at home for several days."

"Ah. So you've been pestering poor Sims all week."

"I have. I tried to wrench out of him where you were." He walked slowly toward her. "But then I realized it was none of my business." He drew a finger along the lip of the tub. "I don't care who you were with. I don't care about your past, about any of your lovers. I only want to be part of your future."

He righted the stool and sat alongside, surveying her nudity longingly before resting his elbows on his knees, linking his fingers together and staring at the floor. "I've thought and thought about us, about almost nothing but us for the last few weeks. I tried, believe me I tried, but I cannot find a way out of this marriage business or my duty to provide an heir." He lifted his head, his gaze deep. "Lavinia, I cannot live without you, I must have you in my life beyond mere friendship." He sucked in a breath and exhaled slowly. "I could only think of one resolution to our dilemma." Anguish furrowed his forehead.

So he had come to the same conclusion as she.

"I know." She reached out a hand and he took it, letting the water drip on his trousers. "But you do not need to pay for my house or buy me jewels. I'll be the least troublesome mistress you've ever had."

He kissed her hand. "That's not quite what I meant."

"Oh?"

"I thought I might purposely seek out a particular type of wife. I thought I might find a wife who wouldn't mind if I lived with you."

That was definitely not what she had expected. "So a wife who is kept like a mistress and a mistress who lives with you like a wife?"

He nodded. "I would perform my marital duty until I had a son. An arrangement something like what Joseph and Sophia have."

"Joseph and Sophia are each married to their true love. They have affairs with others."

"I meant on a philosophical level. A woman who would not require fidelity." He cleared his throat. "A woman such as Penelope Hardcastle."

"And you know this how?"

He grinned. "Darling, a man can tell what type a woman is from her salacious propositions. And her perfume."

Lavinia laughed. "She might possibly be perfect."

"Or, I could find a wife who for some reason needs a husband but does not need him to be the man she is in love with. Perhaps she herself is in love with the wrong man. A married man."

"And do you have another candidate in mind, Arthur?"

"Unfortunately no. And how to find such a woman would be difficult."

"Charlotte and I might be able to sift through gossip."

He brightened. "So you're game?"

"I think I would seethe with jealousy during your nuptials to Penelope Hardcastle."

"You could conveniently be traveling abroad." He got up and took off his jacket, hanging it on the back of a chair. "Lavinia, I know it's not what either of us want but it's all we can have." He unbuttoned his waistcoat.

Lavinia rubbed her thighs under the water. "You would live here with me?"

He worked on his collar and tie. "While my wife and children lived at my house in Belgravia."

"The Richmonds will never put up with such an arrangement."

"They will have to." He lay his waistcoat over his jacket and placed his collar and tie on the dressing table.

"It's not just your wife I will have to share you with."

He unfastened the top buttons of his shirt. "I *will* have to play the part of father upon occasion."

She scowled. "I will settle for nothing less than you being the most adoring and devoted father, my lord." She glanced down at her very feminine nudity. "I didn't mean children."

He stilled.

"I meant Joseph."

"Oh." He rolled up his left sleeve, then his right. "I suspected you knew. The night he saw you in my bed at Atherley Keep." He sat on the stool. "Darling, I don't need to continue the affair." He snorted grimly. "I'll be far too busy with women and children."

"A man can give a sort of comfort a woman cannot. I would not expect you to give him up. However you will need to keep the secret from your wife."

"I know. I hate keeping secrets." He stood and bent over to kiss her cheek. "You will not be a secret." He moved the stool to the head of the tub and began removing her hairpins.

"What are you doing?"

"I believe Marie was about to wash your hair. I'll do it instead."

"Do you do this with all your mistresses?"

He laughed as he finished. He grabbed her silver-backed hairbrush from the dressing table and brushed out her tresses.

"You've done this before."

He chuckled. "Perhaps." He leaned over. "Let me take care of you," he said in a seductive drawl.

She gazed up at him, his expression softened with supplication. He knew the risks to her heart. He would have to endure the same. She nodded, finally ready to take the plunge into the waters of love.

He said nothing of import while he urged and prodded her into position to wet her hair in the warm water then hunched her over while he massaged soap into her scalp. The gentle pressure of the pads of his fingers eased her anxieties before clean water rinsed away lingering apprehensions.

He lay her back against the porcelain to hold her arm while he glided the soapy sponge up and down, carefully avoiding touching her breast. He lifted a leg and squeezed the sponge from knee to foot, she flinching when he tickled her arch, his smile under knowing eyes revealing he would remember that particular weakness. He moved to the other side and repeated his ministrations, first with her leg then with her arm, not touching her intimate areas, the room silent but for the slosh and trickle of water and the crackle of the fire.

He gently bent her forward to attend to her back, dredging the sponge over the ridges of her spine, the fragrance of lavender and rosemary imbuing the rising steam with their soothing essence. He encircled her waist to draw the sponge over her stomach, from the hair between her legs to her rib cage, once again avoiding erogenous areas.

He slid a hand over her face in a request to close her eyes. Her sight obscured, other senses heightened, the aroma of herbs and flowers, the heat of the bath, the sound of him fussing too long with something behind her.

And then he touched her. His hands curved around her sides to each cup a breast, weighing them before kneading the buoyant flesh under the water. He pinched a nipple, her flinch much like when he tickled her foot, sending water to slosh over the rim. He moved slightly to slide a hand across her belly to tangle in the hair of her mons.

He slipped a finger inside her sex. She opened her eyes in surprise.

"Do you always become aroused when having a bath, my lady?"

He slid a finger then two in and out, his face stoic as she descended to the depths of sensuality.

Only then did she notice he was utterly nude.

She reached up to his chest, gripping his hair as he shifted his erotic torment to her clit, taking her to the moment just before climax, holding her there as his gaze locked with hers.

"Please," she begged.

He picked her up and out of the water, his hands gripping her slippery skin, then bent her over the rolled porcelain rim, giving her backside a little swat. He straddled the edge of the tub, one foot between her calves, and wrapped a strong arm around her. His cock nudged her sex until he found his aim.

He slammed inside her, jerking her forward, splashing water onto the floor. She slapped her hands against the wet tiles, seeking purchase. He held her securely, one hand digging into her waist, his other grabbing the tub's edge, his fingers curling to the iron underneath. His thrusts were determined, his rhythm frenzied. He had cared for her, had pleasured her and now was taking possession of her.

And she gave herself to him willingly.

"Touch yourself," he commanded with a low growl. "Come for me."

He squeezed her waist, the sign that he held her fast. Awkwardly she maneuvered her hand between her body and the porcelain, between her legs, as determined for satisfaction as he. She found the unrequited nub and pressed down, shooting a pang of pleasure to pulse around him. He groaned in appreciation. She rubbed to his rhythm, closer to the cusp of rapture than she had thought.

She came with a jolt, clamping around him, taking him to the brink. He spent inside her with a guttural cry, his hold determined while he emptied himself.

He pulled her up to standing, helped her out of the tub then wrapped a warm towel around her back and pulled her to him. She sobbed against his shoulder, relieved they had found a way to be together, an imperfect solution but a solution nonetheless.

He draped another towel on her wet hair and scrubbed vigorously, his indelicacy sending her into giggles.

"Ah, that's better. My mistress should always laugh with delight."

She kissed his lips. "There will be loads of scandalous gossip."

"And it will all be true." He smiled. "Your cook can begin providing dinner for two this evening. And your housemaid can learn to expect a man in your bed, starting tonight." He hugged her to him. "I love you, Lavinia. I want the world to know."

Arthur could have sworn it was the middle of the night, but that didn't seem to stop Sims from knocking on Lavinia's bedroom door.

She stirred at his side in bed. "Yes, Sims?"

The butler remained behind the closed door. "My lady, I apologize. There are callers."

At this hour?

"The Marquess of Richmond and Mr. Joseph Phillips are here to see you and Lord Petersham—"

Their arrangement had just begun and already they were entertaining callers? At three in the morning?

"The marquess assures me it is urgent."

Arthur jumped out of bed. "It bloody well better be urgent."

He pulled on his trousers and threw on a robe, his chest bare but for his braces, while Lavinia dressed in a nightgown and robe then hastily tied back her hair.

They held hands as they went downstairs to the morning room. They would certainly have to brave a hearty berating from Father.

Sims led them inside the morning room and waited by the door. Joseph leaned against the opposite wall, peering through a lifted curtain to the dark street. Father stood by the hearth, watching the housemaid light the fire, the yawning girl slightly disheveled. Sims snapped his fingers. The girl looked up then blushed deeply. She scurried out. Sims followed and closed the door behind them.

The fire crackled in the silence. Arthur led Lavinia to the sofa and sat her down then took his place, standing at her side.

"What is this about, Father?" He tried to keep the annoyance out of his voice.

"And good morning to you, Arthur." Father nodded to Lavinia. "My lady." He remained by the fire, holding his hands over the warmth. "I do apologize for the intrusion, Lady Foxley-Graham. Phillips and I went to Arthur's first but we found him not at home." Father lifted a brow at Arthur. "Your valet did not seem to think it a secret where you were."

Upon his note that afternoon Owens had arrived at Lavinia's with a small trunk, had attended Arthur in dressing for dinner then had left, preferring his own bed in Belgravia. "I did not instruct him otherwise. I refuse to keep my relationship with Lady Foxley-Graham a secret any longer."

"Good."

An unusual response, especially from Father.

"We are here at this hour because Parliament has just ended for the night."

And politics couldn't wait until after breakfast?

Father paced before the hearth. "Arthur, remember when you suggested little Henry be named heir to the Marquessate of Richmond?"

Lavinia looked at Arthur in shock. He had never told her. There had been no reason to. Father had dismissed the idea categorically.

"Yes, Father."

"When the letters patent creating a peerage are affixed with the Great Seal, the succession detailed therein becomes immutable. Well…practically." Father stopped his pacing. "There is only one way in which the authority of the Great Seal can be circumvented." He smiled at Lavinia. "I think you know the answer to this, my lady? Unless it is too early in the morning." He chuckled.

Lavinia's forehead crinkled in lines of surprise or worry. She glanced up at Arthur before returning her attention to Father. "By Act of Parliament."

"Yes. To change the terms of the original letters patent, including the rules of succession, a peer can submit a Private Bill. This is rarely done and the circumstances must be extreme." Once again Father smiled at Lavinia. "Apparently members of both Houses thought this situation extreme. They acted swiftly."

Her eyes widened as if comprehending. "I'm not sure I follow," she said warily.

"Earlier this morning, Parliament passed an act effectively naming Henry Abraham Phillips as the heir to the Richmond marquessate."

Stunned, Arthur dropped onto the sofa next to Lavinia. She gaped. Her hand covered her mouth as her face twisted in emotion.

"The queen and I discussed the possibility of the extinction of the peerage given the recalcitrance of my son." Father scowled at Arthur. "She thought such a situation would be a shame. She drew up the letters patent to create a new peerage, a new marquessate with the same title but with a remainder clause creating a different line of succession. There will be two Marquessates of Richmond held by me concurrently. Upon my death, the original marquessate will descend to you, and Henry will become effectively the heir apparent, worthy of the title Earl of Petersham. When you die, Arthur, the first marquessate will die, the second will take effect and be held by Henry."

Arthur gasped. He had been holding his breath at the unbelievable news. He eyed Joseph. "Your son? A British peer?"

Joseph grinned. "Remember our conversation in the House of Commons, my lady?" He quirked a brow at Lavinia. "When I mentioned sacrifice?"

Lavinia blushed with a sidelong glimpse at Arthur. He bristled. Knowing Joseph, they probably engaged in more than mere conversation.

"You asked if I was worth making a family sacrifice for," she said softly.

Joseph turned to Arthur. "Twenty years ago, I was a poor dock worker in New York City. I fell in love with the daughter of a British peer but she was promised to a blackguard, the very same scoundrel who had destroyed your future." He walked toward the sofa. "You sacrificed everything to save Sophia, sacrificed your family's heritage and history, sacrificed your own beliefs in such a system. And most astonishingly, you sacrificed your own heart by not allowing yourself to ever fall in love again." He stopped before Arthur. "But a heart is a disobedient thing, isn't it?"

"Joseph—"

"Besides enabling my marriage to your sister, you've made me a very wealthy man, Lord Petersham. After our quibble, Richmond and I swallowed our respective pride and discussed what we could do, both of us realizing you deserve to be with the woman you love."

Lavinia croaked a sob. Joseph gave her hand a little squeeze.

"It took an Act of Parliament to allow you to be married, my lady," he said.

The floodgate holding her tears burst. Arthur wrapped her in his arms, his brain mired in a fog of incredulity.

Father cleared his throat. "I realized your marrying Lavinia would be for the benefit of the marquessate, son. Her political connections run deep." He handed Arthur a small box. "However I suggest we hold the wedding after the Royal Assent for the act, just to be sure."

Arthur opened the box. Nestled within the pale-pink satin lining was Mother's betrothal ring, a golden topaz set between two diamonds. The same ring worn by all the future Marchionesses of Richmond. Henrietta had once worn it. Now there was to be another.

Lavinia sucked in a tremulous breath. He slid to the rug to kneel before her, holding her face to look at him. She smiled through her tears, like sunshine spearing the clouds on a rainy day.

"Darling, oh my darling." He tried to stop his own tears but could not. "Will you marry me? Be my countess, be my marchioness, be my wife? Please, please say yes."

Her choking sobs prevented speech until she closed her eyes and strained to steady her breath. Recovered, she gazed at him. "Yes, Arthur, yes. It is my utmost desire to be your wife." She wiped an errant tear from her cheek. "I love you with all my heart."

He took her left hand in his, trembling with giddy joy, and slipped the ring on her fourth finger. He raised her hand to his lips and kissed the precious setting. "You have made me the happiest man alive." He glanced up at Father and Joseph. "Thank you."

Father lay a hand on his shoulder. "Come to dinner tonight and we'll celebrate."

"Yes, Papa." It was all still seeming like a dream.

"Phillips, let's go wake up my secretary. Billings will have to be prepared to fend off press inquiries as soon as the papers come out."

Father and Joseph nodded their farewells.

Arthur barely saw them leave. He was too busy kissing his fiancée.

CHAPTER TWENTY-TWO

London, November 1880

Arthur's invitation to Countess Winthrop's annual masquerade had been rather exceptional that year. Under the usual scroll-work and feminine typeface enumerating the vague details of the event was a note engraved in a somewhat more lavish script:

> *Lady Petersham has prepared an exclusive gift for the Sultan in celebration of your marriage.*

Lady Petersham. Lavinia Harwell, the Countess of Petersham. His *wife*.

Three months since their wedding day and he was still giddy.

He stood on the landing of Countess Winthrop's dramatic entryway overlooking the grand lobby and surveyed the guests. A waft of floral perfume announced the presence of a masked odalisque at his side, her bounty barely shielded. She extended a slender and bejeweled arm and escorted him down stairs, through corridors, and beyond double doors to a lavishly decorated room. The dim glow of hanging braziers revealed an excess of velvet and embroidered pillows strewn on top of Persian carpets, and lengths of silken textiles draped tent-like from the ceiling. Two divans framed a darkened central space. A shadowy figure reclined on the divan on the right.

The odalisque bowed and departed, closing the door behind her.

The figure on the divan lit a lamp, then another, revealing himself to be dressed as a sultan as well, black bearded and masked, his bulk obscuring the slender sofa, his robe a deep blue to Arthur's rich red.

A third lamp revealed a figure in the space between the divans.

A boy—or a youth rather, as he was too tall for boyhood—knelt on a pillow with his back to Arthur. He wore a crimson waistcoat and striped trousers, loose and baggy in the Eastern style, embroidered slippers, and a fez cap over his cloth mask. The blue sultan extended his arm in a gesture of presentation.

His wedding gift was an obeisant youth.

Arthur had never been the dominant with another man and he had only ever been with Joseph. Now he would play the aggressor.

The idea was far more arousing than he had ever thought it would be. His wife knew him too well.

He approached and the youth bowed his head, the act of submission sparking lust in his loins. On a low table sat a small lusterware jug, the sheen of the liquid therein proclaiming it to be oil. Arthur unfastened the frog closure of his robe then knelt down behind the boy.

He lay a palm on the youth's shoulder and caressed his arm, the hairless flesh soft under his touch. Would his gift bear the sculpted muscles of an athlete? Or the supple form of one on the cusp of manhood? He preferred neither and wanted both. He would leave the vest to cover the boy's torso until his passions needed the excitement of the unexplored.

Arthur reached for the jug and poured out a measure of oil. He smoothed the liquid over his erection, coating it, increasing his desire, breathing lewdly against the neck of the boy. The blue sultan shifted on the divan. Under his robe, he too was stroking himself.

It was a harem of a different sort. A night at a caravansary. Two sultans and their *ferrash,* a camp servant ready to do more than pitch their tent.

He snaked his arm around the youth to find the tie at his waist. He yanked the bow then slid the striped linen over the slender hips, revealing the temptation of rounded buttocks.

Arthur lay his hands on either side of the pale bottom before him, smoothing his thumbs over the orbs of his arse. "And now, my innocent, we shall slake our hunger in a forbidden way," he murmured. "Bend over, my ferrash."

The youth obeyed. Arthur stripped off his robe as he gazed at the glorious sight.

He stretched the cheeks to reveal the puckered hole shadowed in the crevice, the hair indicating the youth had reached the age of manhood. He poured oil on the delicate ridge of the coccyx, letting it flow into the dark split, then massaged it into the crinkled aperture. The youth gasped, a light, yearning sound that inspired his cock to full-stand. Was his ferrash as aroused as he?

He prodded the hole until the tightness abated. He eased in the head of his cock, the youth's wanton sigh encouraging him to proceed.

The blue sultan came up behind to wait his turn with the youth.

Arthur delved farther. The youth yelped.

"Shh, shh, my ferrash. Let me allay your pain." He reached around to grab the youth's cock.

But he had none.

Shock faded to understanding when he discovered a feminine slit instead, slick with want. He growled a chuckle. He would thank his wife later. Until then it was much more fun to play the fantasy.

"A eunuch. Then you comprehend the unrequited and proscribed desires of men."

He teased her clit as he pushed in slowly, increasing his ministrations until he was buried to the hilt.

He exhaled at the glorious constriction before commencing his carnal rhythm, savoring every beat.

Without warning, the blue sultan grappled him from behind. Arthur jerked to no avail against the muscular arm encircling his waist. One hand dug cruelly into his side as oily fingers probed his anus, thick and insistent, familiar in their path. His cock, slackened from astonishment, hardened anew.

And then the blue sultan pressed his prick against his unyielding passage, ramming in relentlessly, Arthur's groaned complaints futile in the face of the sultan's fervor.

Once sheathed, both men began a syncopated sensual rhythm and pain dissolved into a most exquisite double pleasure.

Arthur's hand slipped away from the ferrash, his mind seeking his own bliss, pounding the arse before him as he was slammed into from behind. The sultan's balls, heavy with seed, slapped against his, sparking pangs of tortuous delight through his groin. The cock inside him rubbed the root of his sex, inciting his ascension to a new rapture. Grunted oaths filled the air around them, prayers for reprieve from the sensual torment.

The blue sultan increased his momentum, ignoring Arthur's cries as he strove for his own climax, his pistoning prick delving to unexplored depths. Pleasure and pain merged into one euphoric sensation to which Arthur was slave and not master. He let it overtake him, push him forward to oblivion, his howl of release a split-second before the blue sultan's.

Arthur's heart pounded, sending blood to rush dizzyingly to his head. His lungs burned from want of air.

His ferrash slumped to her stomach, freeing him from their union. The blue sultan's cock slackened and fell out.

"Shit."

Joseph's relieved curse set Arthur laughing. Which made Lavinia giggle.

She rolled over and untied her mask, letting it and the fez fall to the floor. She gazed up at him then glanced at Joseph sitting splay-legged on the floor, tugging off his beard, panting his own exhaustion.

Her breasts were bound under her cropped waistcoat, her hair covered by a boyish wig. She smiled.

"And was the present to your liking, Lord Petersham?"

"To quote the *Rubaiyat*, Lady Petersham, 'All begins and ends in Yes'."

EPILOGUE

London, May 1881

Lavinia breathed in the spring air of Kensington Gardens as she strolled arm-in-arm with her husband along the path toward the fountains of the Italian Garden. Behind them, sauntering at a slower pace were the nursemaids and fretting parents of her godson and nephew. Still new to parenthood, Nicholas and Helena unabashedly cooed over their little Robert Louis Atherley, already almost a year old. The older and more subdued Sophia and Joseph tried not to let worry overtake reason with their Henry. Neither Robert nor Henry, of course, had any idea of the responsibilities that lay ahead.

Lavinia gave Arthur's arm a squeeze. "Did you hear the news yet?"

"News? What news?"

"Helena. She's expecting."

"Hmm. I suspect St. Albans would like to keep his wife in such a state until she protests. He adores children."

"And you adore that others have them."

He chuckled. "I do, Mrs. Harwell."

Lavinia flushed under her smile. Arthur liked to remind her of the fact that she was his wife whenever he could. The sobriquet would be hers whether she was the Countess of Petersham or the Marchioness of Richmond.

Passersby were numerous given the good weather, and polite nods were quick and too frequent at times to be able to clearly register the recipient. Some faces were quickly recognized—members from Arthur's club or subjects of recent gossip. The Earl of Ryburgh tipped his hat with a beleaguered smile as his wife and eldest daughter chattered next to him.

An older man with a young woman—perhaps his daughter?—pushing a perambulator, came toward them. The man grinned as he spoke, his face crinkled in happiness, his blue eyes shining like jewels in the morning sun. The woman giggled and rested her blushing cheek against his shoulder, gazing up at him with shared joy. Somehow they were a striking couple, he with his graying imperial-style beard and top hat, she with her unassuming demeanor and simple gown under which she was obviously pregnant. They were the picture of blissfulness, not of father and daughter, but husband and wife, perhaps newlyweds still very much in love.

The breath hitched in Lavinia's throat.

They were very much Julius Christopher and his assistant Grace.

Julius caught her astonished gaze, a twinkle in his eyes as he recognized her. He said something to Grace and they stopped as Lavinia and Arthur approached.

Arthur had never met Julius. He smiled politely, unaware that the jovial man before them was the horrible Dr. Christopher from her past.

"Julius," she blurted. "You look happy." To say such a thing was simply not done but she was utterly taken aback by the change in him.

"Good day, Countess," he said with a touch of his hat. Clearly he had followed the society columns to keep apprised of her life.

"Oh, where are my manners?" she said. "Julius Christopher, may I present my husband, the Earl of Petersham. Arthur, Dr. Christopher, a long-time friend."

A memory flickered behind Julius' blue eyes. Perhaps a memory of his affair with the insatiable Sophia Phillips, and knowledge that the brother might be much like the sister in that regard. "My lord, a pleasure to meet you."

Luckily Arthur kept his composure. He knew damn well who Julius was. "Dr. Christopher. A pleasure to finally meet you."

"Countess, Lord Petersham," Julius smiled courteously. "My wife, Grace Christopher."

Lavinia extended her hand to the woman who had softened and tamed Julius' heart. "Lady Christopher, felicitations on your marriage."

Grace blushed with a glance at Julius. Probably not many called her by her proper title. That Julius was a baronet was something he did not flaunt. "My lady." She quickly clasped her hand.

Lavinia indicated the perambulator. "And who is this?"

Grace pulled back the blanket to show off the sleeping babe. "Hope, my lady. Our daughter."

Lavinia had to choke back emotion. *Hope.* "What a poignant name."

"We've another on the way," Grace added excitedly.

"Congratulations." It was sincere. Seeing Grace's sheer joy and its reflection in Julius' face was heartwarming.

The others approached. Silence seemed to descend despite the bustling crowd. Julius was subdued before those he had wronged in the past. He greeted them one by one, his comportment, his soft voice, his clear devotion to Grace thoroughly disarming to each in their turn. Then suddenly, Sophia, Helena, and Grace were engrossed in conversation about babies and mothering, and Nicholas and Julius were discussing attending their respective wives during the births of their children. Joseph stood at Nicholas' side, his interaction with the two spare but cordial.

Arthur sidled up to her. "A penny for your thoughts."

Lavinia turned a smile to him. "I was just thinking how each of these couples owes their inception to either you or me."

Arthur chuckled.

"And their children." Lavinia wrapped her arm around her husband's. "Really we are parents to them all."

"'A lamp to guide the little children stumbling in the dark'." Arthur slid his hand around her waist.

"Guiding them to their own homes so we can do a little stumbling in the dark of our own."

He laughed. "I would have it no other way, Mrs. Harwell."

About the Author

Regina Kammer is a librarian, an art historian, and an award-winning, international best-selling, multi-published writer of provocative historical romance and contemporary romance with a touch of history. Her short stories and novels make history sexier, whether the era is Roman, Byzantine, Viking, American Revolution, or Victorian. She's even sexed up contemporary settings, Steampunk, and Greco-Roman mythology. She has been published by Cleis Press, Go Deeper Press, Ellora's Cave, House of Erotica, Story Ink, Loose Id, The Naughty Literati, and her own imprint, Viridium Press. She began writing historical fiction with romantic elements during National Novel Writing Month 2006, switching to erotica when all her characters suddenly demanded to have sex.

Keep up with Regina

Check out her website: https://reginakammer.com/
Never miss a new release! Subscribe to *Kammerotica News*:
https://reginakammer.com/newsletter/

Historical erotic romance by Regina

Victorian

The Pleasure Device (Harwell Heirs Book 1)
Disobedience By Design (Harwell Heirs Book 2)
Where Destiny Plays (Harwell Heirs Book 3)
The Westerman Affair (Art & Discipline Book 1)
The Demonstration
The Invitation
Disputed Boundaries (Stories from the San Juan Islands)

American Revolution

The General's Wife: An American Revolutionary Tale
Winter Interlude: An American Revolutionary Novelette
On the Eighteenth of January, '78; or, A Night At Valley Forge

Ancient World

Hadrian and Sabina: A Love Story
Ancient Shorts: An Ancient World Romance Collection

Steampunk

One Cheek Or Two? (Ockham Steam-Works Laboratory Chronicles 1)
Delia's Heartthrob (Ockham Steam-Works Laboratory Chronicles 2)
Swing Follies (Ockham Steam-Works Laboratory Chronicles 3)